ARTHUR C. CLARKE'S
VENUS PRIME™

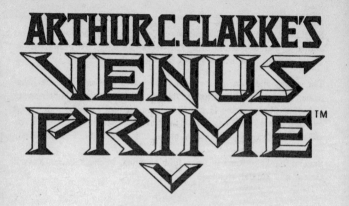

ARTHUR C. CLARKE'S VENUS PRIME™

VOLUME 2
MAELSTROM

PAUL PREUSS

A BYRON PREISS BOOK

AVON BOOKS NEW YORK

ARTHUR C. CLARKE'S VENUS PRIME, VOLUME 2: MAEL-STROM is an original publication of Avon Books. This work has never before appeared in book form. This work is a novel. Any similarity to actual persons or events is purely coincidental.

The setting and some of the events of Blake's initiation into the Athanasian Society were inspired by the watercolor entitled "Subterranean Labyrinth for a Gothic House," by Jean-Jacques Lequeu, reproduced on page 186 of the catalogue of the traveling exhibition *Visionary Architects*, by Dominique de Ménil, et al., University of St. Thomas, 1968.

Special thanks to Rena Wolner, John Douglas, Michael Kazan, Russell Galen, and Randall Reich.

AVON BOOKS
A division of
The Hearst Corporation
105 Madison Avenue
New York, New York 10016

Text and artwork copyright © 1988 by Byron Preiss Visual Publications, Inc.
Arthur C. Clarke's Venus Prime is a trademark of Byron Preiss Visual Publications, Inc.
Published by arrangement with Byron Preiss Visual Publications, Inc.
Cover design, book design, and logo by Alex Jay/Studio J
Front cover painting by Jim Burns
Library of Congress Catalog Card Number: 88-91525
ISBN: 0-380-75345-6

First Avon Books Printing: September 1988

AVON TRADEMARK REG. U.S. PAT. OFF. AND IN OTHER COUNTRIES, MARCA REGISTRADA, HECHO IN U.S.A.

Printed in the U.S.A.

K-R 10 9 8 7 6 5 4 3 2

PROLOGUE

The thin wind whistled shrilly along the knife-edged ice. Needles of ice and scallops of ice thrust out of the compacted sand into the wind-borne grit. Gargoyles of ice hung from cliffs a kilometer high, brooding over the polar plain.

The wind was too thin to sustain a living thing but not too thin to carry the abrasive grit. The grit etched the rock and heaped the sand and carved the ice and the hard stone into arches and buttresses and buttes. The thin wind was a digger.

The hole it was digging now, in the sand beneath the ice, had a piece of metal in it. The metal was shiny and hard, not so hard that it had not been shattered—who knows when or how—but so hard the wind-borne grit could not mar its mirror surface.

Something else had etched the metal and dug channels in it. The channels were different from each other but all the same height and width and depth. They ran in straight lines. There were three dozen different kinds of them, but they repeated themselves in various sequences until the total number of them, etched in the metal, was a thousand and more.

A Martian year after the wind dug the etched

mirror out of the sand beneath the ice, a man in a pressure suit came along and found it lying exposed there and carried it away.

"You're crazy, Johnny, you can't keep a thing like that secret. How you gonna make money on somethin' looks like nothin' nobody's ever seen before?"

"Are you sayin' it's not valuable, Liam?"

"I'm sayin' it's too valuable. It's one of a kind. You won't get no money fer it, under the table or over."

This was about as private as you could get around here, in the poker nest under the pipe rack in the drill rig dome, where the booze and the dope were cached. The crew boss knew all about it; he didn't give a squeak, as long as nobody showed up high on any company monitors. But you had to whisper in here. These damn domes carried sound from one side to the other just as good as a phone-link, and you never knew who was standing over there listening in.

"Huh. Never thought I'd be accused of bein' in possession of somethin' *too* valuable."

"Quit poor-mouthin'. You been takin' plenty off us."

"Yeah, and I'm plannin' to do it again tonight. You got one more chance before the others show up. Front me to these pals of yours in Lab City, you can keep a third."

"Forget it. Best turn it straight in. That way at least you're a hero. Every day you keep it you're askin' fer a ticket to jail."

Passage doors popped, away on the other side of the dome. Somebody's belch echoed off the stacks of pipe.

"What if I said there's more out there, Liam? Other stuff with this funny writing. And stuff I can't tell what it is."

"You tryin' to con me, Johnny?"

"Hell, no."

"A lot of stuff?"

"Make up your mind first."

"I'll mull it over."

"Boo, you guys." A laugh sounded right behind them, slung over the arch of the dome. "It's game time."

"I want no tales circulatin', Liam"—hardly even a whisper now—"You're the only soul on Mars knows what I got."

"You can trust me, John."

"Good. We'll both stay healthy."

A week later, already four days behind schedule, the crew finally got the rig up and started to sink pipe. The sun went down in the red Martian sky, taking a pack of sundogs with it. Liam and Johnny were working the drillhead. They'd been hard at it for four hours and they were already down to permafrost when the pipe kicked—nobody ever did figure out how it happened, but it was no surprise, this was not a tight ship—but then Johnny really screwed up and it got away from him and the business end of the pipe blew a hole in the ice. Which normally would have resulted in maybe some people getting a quick ride back to the unemployment line in Labyrinth City, except right underneath them there was a big pocket of pressurized gas in the permafrost and it blew too, and the whole pipe rack went way, way up like a bundle of straws, and then all the straws came back down on Liam and John.

A man's fine blond hair fell to within millimeters of the etched metal where it rested on the green baize desktop. "How did he come to be in possession of this exquisite thing?" The man was big-boned and tall, but his movements were precise and delicate. As he bent to inspect the plaque, he was careful not to let a hair touch it; he was reluctant even to let his breath cloud its shining surface.

"He must have picked it out of the sand, sometime within the past two months. Certainly he hadn't the slightest idea of its worth." The other man was older, pinstriped and crewcut. He flicked a holomap of the North Pole onto the mapscreen. "Our crew has hit these four sites since they went out in the spring. Spent roughly two weeks in each." His blunt index finger pushed at four glowing dots that formed a ragged curve around the terraced ice. "The discipline was appalling, Albers. People took rovers and went joy-riding whenever they liked. Just where to is anyone's guess. I've sacked the foreman and the district manager. Not in time to do us any good, I'm sorry to say."

The tall man, an arachaeologist, straightened and pushed his hair back. The sadness of his wide, down-turned mouth was offset by eager gray eyes, exuberantly bushy eyebrows, and a forehead that climbed to the high latitudes of his skull before disappearing under his blond hair. "This couldn't possibly have been an isolated artifact. Surely there's an incomparable treasure out there."

"And we'll do our best to find it," said the executive. "Can't hold out much hope, though. At least this piece is in your good hands now."

Together they studied it in silence. The drilling man's reverence was as profound as the archaeologist's.

The blond archaeologist had spent ten years following the drilling crews, searching the frosted sands, tracing Martian watercourses that had dried to powder a billion years ago. He and his colleagues who specialized in paleontology had found fossils in abundance, simple forms highly adapted to a climate that had swung between frightening extremes of wet and dry, cyclone and calm, cold and colder.

But what drew archaeologists to this sparse

ground were the scattered remnants of a different order of life—not fossils, not scraps of shell or bone, but the remains of what might have been implements made of novel alloys, and here and there tantalizing hints of what might have been structures. All these creatures—the abundant life that had crept across Mars and wallowed in the wet sands beside the desert-scouring flash floods, and the beings, whatever they were, who had left only hints of their advanced development—all these had flourished and vanished before life on Earth had evolved to anything more complex than blue-green algae.

Now the metal mirror on the desk, incised with a thousand characters, gave testimony that a billion years ago Mars had been host to a high culture.

"I suppose Forster knows of this already."

"Yes, I regret to say," the driller replied. "The word spread fast on the grapevine. Forster's on his way from Earth now."

A smile flirted with the archaeologist's mournful mouth. "It will be amusing to see what he makes of it."

"He's already held a media conference, you know. Already given the makers of this a name."

"Oh? What name?"

"He calls them Culture X."

The sad archaeologist allowed himself an amused grunt. "Dear Professor Forster. Always energetic. Not always very original."

"That at least is to our advantage."

No efforts of drilling teams or scientists ever found any trace of a treasure hoard on Mars. But ten years after the discovery of the Martian plaque, a mining robot on the surface of Venus—a planet as different from Mars as hell from limbo—was prospecting in a narrow canyon near an ancient beach, a beach a billion years old. The robot's diamond-edged proboscis cut through a wall of rock and came upon strange things. Within hours news went out across the solar system that Culture X had been, without doubt, a spacefaring species.

PART
1

CONCERNING
RESEARCH
INTO LOST TIME

1

Sparta closed her eyes, stretched in the tub, and let her chin bob at the water line. At the threshold of sound, the water fizzed. Droplets condensed on her eyelashes; invisible bubbles tickled her nose. The odor of sulfur hung lightly over the baths.

The precise chemical formulation of the minerals in the water appeared unbidden in her mind's eye; they changed every day, and today the water cocktail mimicked the baths of Cambo-les-Bains in the Pays Basque. Sparta analyzed her environment wherever she went, without thinking about it. It was a reflex.

She floated easily; she weighed less, and the water weighed less, than they would have on Earth. She was a long way from Earth. Minutes went by and the warm water rocked her into relaxed drowsiness as she savored the news she had long awaited and only today received, her orders from Space Board headquarters: her assignment here was ended, and she was recalled to Earth Central.

"Are you Ellen?" The voice was quiet, tentative but warm.

Sparta opened her eyes and saw a young woman standing shadowed in the mist, naked but for the towel wrapped around her waist. Her straight black hair was tied in a bun.

"Where is Keiko?"

"Keiko was unable to come today. I'm Masumi. If it is all right with you, I will give you your massage."

"I hope Keiko isn't ill."

"A minor legal matter. She asked me to apologize for her, most sincerely."

Sparta listened to the woman's soft voice. She heard nothing but the simple truth. She rose from the tub. Her slick skin, rosy with heat, gleamed in the filtered light from the terrace. The diffuse light played over her dancer's small taut figure, over her slight breasts, over her flat stomach and abdomen ridged with muscle and her slim hard thighs.

Her disheveled blond hair, soaking wet in back where it had been submerged, fell straight to her jaw line; she kept it chopped off straight, with little regard for fashion. Her full lips were perpetually parted, tasting the air.

"Here's a towel for you," Masumi said. "Would you like to go on the upper terrace? We still have an hour of Venus-light."

"Certainly." Sparta followed the woman along the row of steaming tubs and up the steps to the open roof deck, brushing the water from her shoulders and breasts as she walked.

"Excuse me a moment, please. They forgot to take the tables in before the last rain." Masumi spilled the film of water from the waist-high massage table and rubbed it dry while Sparta stood at the low rail, swiping at the last drops of moisture on her flanks and calves.

She looked down over the houses and gardens of Port Hesperus. The flat roofs descended below her in steps, like the roofs of a Greek village on a steep hillside, each house with its enclosed courtyard of citrus trees and flowering plants. At the bottom of the hill were the parallel main streets of the village, and between them, gardens of exotic shrubs and towering trees, redwoods and firs, tall poplars and yellow ginkgoes. These famous gardens, landscaped by Senō Sato, were what made Port Hesperus a destination worth a wealthy tourist's visit.

The streets and the gardens curved sharply up to the left and right and met high above Sparta's head. Behind her and to both sides a huge concavity of glass slats swept up to embrace the houses and trees in a single globe. Half a kilometer away in the enclosed sky, a metal spindle threaded this sphere of glass and metal and plants and people; around the shining spindle the whole populous globe turned twice a minute.

To Sparta's right, sunlight poured into the sphere. To her left, an arc of Venus blazed like a polished shield; the planet's white clouds showed no detail, seemed not to move, although they were driven by supersonic winds. Over Sparta's head the whirling sun was rivaled by the reflection of Venus—a million reflections, one in each louvered pane, rolling around the axis of Port Hesperus.

The high-orbiting station would take another hour to pass over the planet's sunlit hemisphere and into the night. By natural sunlight, the days on Port Hesperus were only a few hours long, but people here made their own time.

"Is there anything you particularly wanted to work on?" Masumi asked. "Keiko mentioned recurring headaches?"

"I seem to have a lot of tension at the base of my skull."

"If you would just lie down—"

Sparta climbed onto the table and lay with her cheek pressed into the padding. She closed her eyes. She heard the woman moving about, arranging her things—the oil, the towels, the footstool she would stand on when she needed to reach Sparta's lower back from above. With her acute hearing, Sparta heard the almost inaudible sound of fragrant oil flowing onto Masumi's hands, heard the louder sound of Masumi's palms briskly stroking each other and warming the oil. . . .

The heat of Masumi's palms hovered an inch above Sparta's shoulders, then descended strongly, moving the flesh. . . . As the minutes passed, her strong fingers and the heels of her hands plowed the muscles of Sparta's back down the whole length of her trunk, from shoulders to buttocks and back again, and down her arms to her upturned, lightly curled fingers.

There Masumi hesitated. To pause at this moment in a massage, just after a strong beginning, was not characteristic of an alert, trained masseuse—but Sparta was used to it, and anticipated the question.

"You were injured?"

"A traffic accident," Sparta mumbled, her cheek pressed hard into the fabric. "When I was sixteen. Almost ten years ago." It was a lie, repeated so often she sometimes forgot it was a lie.

"Bone grafts?"

"Something like that. Artificial reinforcements."

"Any sensitivity?"

"Please don't worry," Sparta said. "Keiko usually goes deep. I like that."

"Very well."

The woman resumed her work. The repetitive long strokes of Masumi's hands on Sparta's bare skin warmed her; she felt herself sinking warmly into the padded table, under the warm sun and the reflected warmth of Venus and the circulating warmth of the space station's great garden sphere. Before long she had been kneaded and stretched into complete and rubbery relaxation.

Sparta's eyelid opened at the hot bite of pain, as Masumi's fingers pressed into a knot in her right shoulder. Under the insistent pressure of the masseuse's fingers, Sparta's spasmed muscles slowly began to unclench—not without her willed cooperation. And when the knot finally unraveled, she felt an unaccustomed rush of emotion. . . .

She could be the greatest of us
She resists our authority
William, she's a child
To resist us is to resist the Knowledge

A groan escaped Sparta's parted lips. Masumi went on with her work, making no comment. Under deep tissue massage, people often found themselves involuntarily reliving moments of past anguish; letting those memories resurface was part of the process.

Sparta had learned that lesson early, shortly after her first visit to the spa—one reason she had taken to Keiko's style of massage. Keiko's expert hands had not only soothed her aching body, they had allowed and encouraged Sparta to reach deeper into her own buried memories, as Masumi's hands were doing now.

Memories and lies. Lying memories.

The voices she heard were the voices of the people who had tried to erase all her memories. They had tried to cut them out with a knife. They had not wanted her to remember what they had done to her. They had not wanted her to remember her parents, or ever to question what had become of them. And in the end, they had not wanted her to live. They had done their best to kill her; they had tried again and again.

A compassionate doctor had made what repairs he could, but years had gone by before he acted.

Her somatic skills had survived. She could do things she did not remember learning how to do. Her body had been interfered with in ways she only partially understood. In her memory many facts survived from before the intervention, but only a few fragments of fact survived from afterward; things came up at odd moments, in odd contexts. Yet she knew she did not want to be what she had been.

Sparta took a new name, a new identity, a new face.

Then they had learned who she was and where she was.

She did not know who they were, except for one of them who was now permanently disabled and out of the way, and one other, the one she feared and hated most. She did not know whether she would recognize him, when it mattered.

Masumi's hands dug into her shoulders again. Sparta floated into the pain and through it and found herself becoming very drowsy. Her eyes closed. A cheerful babble of voices—English, Arabic, Japanese, Russian, some of them children's voices—floated in from far away, from the busy streets that flanked Sato's gardens.

Another memory came to her, this one less than a half a year old. The first time she had laid eyes on Sato's beautiful gardens, she had been hiding in a transformer room up inside the central spindle, peering through a grille. She had not been alone. With her was another man who had pursued her and found her, whom she had not spoken to since her former life, whom she did not trust but wanted to. His name was Blake Redfield; he was almost her age, and like her he had been chosen for the experiments, although they had never done to him what they had done to her. As the two of them hid in the transformer room from enemies still unknown, Blake had told her what he'd learned about her past, about the SPARTA project which had brought them together and from which she took her secret name. That time they had escaped their pursuers, but they were far from free of danger.

Almost half an hour passed in thoughts of Blake, thoughts that alternately pleased and frightened Sparta. Four months ago he had left her to return to Earth, warning her that she would not hear from him for a while, but refusing to tell her why. She had not received any word from him or about him since. . . .

Masumi lifted her hands and said, "Take a moment now. When you feel comfortable, roll over, onto your back."

After a long, deep breath Sparta did so, rolling onto her back, settling onto her buttocks, letting her heels snub into the fabric. For a moment, as always, she felt terribly exposed.

Masumi stood behind her head and cradled it in both hands, rolling it gently from side to side, stretching the neck muscles, slowly working down to her shoulders.

When her hands moved to Sparta's chest and ribs, Sparta's eyes opened in involuntary fright. There were structures under her diaphragm, artificial structures that were sensitive to touch. Sparta willed herself to relax, to allow Masumi's hands to travel over the oblique muscles of her abdomen, trying not to betray her invisible, internal strangeness.

Masumi's knowing hands sensed her tension and brushed lightly over the surface of Sparta's belly, working on down to her thighs. Sparta allowed a soundless sigh to escape her lips and closed her eyes on the view of whirling planets and suns, the trees of the gardens growing upside down and sideways.

Many minutes later Masumi's hands left her body. Masumi flipped the end of the sheet gently over Sparta's closed eyes and said, "Relax a while before you get up. Sleep if you like."

Sparta listened to Masumi gather her things and walk quietly away. She lay peacefully, feeling a current of cool air flow down from the windows as the sun fell gradually away to the side and the disk of Venus became a crescent. Port Hesperus was approaching the terminator.

She saw the spinning universe in her imagination. The stars became bits of colored glass, whirling, jerking into new patterns as they wheeled and fell, as regular and as infinitely variable as snow-flakes or the patterns of a kaleidoscope. The colors became brighter and brighter, whirled faster and faster. . . .

Sparta slept. The whirling colors faded, and the spinning shards of glass became dancing leaves, an autumn cyclone, sucking her deeper into the vortex. She clung dizzily to the falling raft. The swirling tunnel walls were streaks of green light and black shadow, not watery and slick but infinitely open, a million blackbirds coursing against the apple-green sky of a winter dawn.

She peered down, was forced to peer down into the funnel by the leaning of the raft to which she clung. The eye of the vortex was vanishing as fast as she fell toward it; there was a blackness at infinity into which the infinitely numerous blackbirds were descending, accompanying themselves with an echoing chorus of shrill screams, their blackness blending to black and their cries echoing among their own soft bodies.

The blackness warmed, and the cries rounded. *"Rrrr, rrrr, rrrr, rrra, rraa, raaa, rrre, rree . . ."*

The swirling blackbirds began to disintegrate, their bits to coalesce. The blackness below was purple, throbbing like a heart. An infinity of bits of black curve flew past, bits of black slash, bits of black spot, sliding down the nautilus spiral into the heart, which now began to glow like a hot brick.

And the boom of the hieratic choir: "RRRREH, RRRREH . . ."

And the swirling signs, forming strings of black light, and beading themselves. The infinite heart below shifted upward through the color scale as the throats of the choir swelled: "UHHHHH, SSSSSS, EEEEEE, YUHHHH, MMMMMM, JUHHHH, THEHHH. . . ."

The swirling signs *were* signs, and the beaded strings gave off sounds, as they were swallowed and made ash by the heart that had become a fiery eye the color of the sun, an eye into whose mouth she was streaking like a meteor.

The choir of signs was everywhere, each sign falling to be consumed like a spring snowflake on the swelling white field of the beating sun, giving off its essence in vibration as it expired: "AAUWWW, BBBEEE. . . ."

She plunged into the fire. It was icy cold. From the groans and meaningless plosive bellows, meaning suddenly spurted: "HOW BEAUTIFUL ART THOU." A mass of voices sang the hymn. "HOW BEAUTIFUL ART THOU, UPON THE EASTERN HORIZON. . . ." A pounding drumbeat roared and drowned the chorus.

Sparta woke up startled, her heart racing.

A galaxy of colored lights surrounded her in the arching darkness; Port Hesperus was soaring across the dark hemisphere of Venus. A darker mass loomed out of the twilight in silhouette, moving toward her, hand outstretched—

—then Sparta, seized with fear, was off the table, crouching naked on the planks behind it, poised to fight.

"Oh, miss, I'm terribly sorry." It was Masumi, in a dark blue cotton wrap. "I told them you could not be disturbed, but they say it is an emergency."

Sparta straightened; her heart continued to pound. She took her commlink from Masumi, which she had left in the dressing room, and slipped it into her ear. "This is Troy."

"Board dispatch—we've got a problem on the surface. Mount Maxwell is erupting. Get over to Azure Dragon, ASAP."

Ten minutes later she stood in the control room of the Azure Dragon Mutual Prosperity Mining Endeavor, peering at videoplate screens that should have been displaying views of the surface of Venus, but were filled with electronic snow instead.

"What's your reading?" she asked the man at the console.

"We had just reestablished contact when everything cut out on us. At first we thought lightning from the eruption—but it's more than just atmospherics. We can't rouse them on any channel."

"The HDVM?"

"Ditto. We get nothing."

"How long have you been in LOS?"

"Loss-of-signal occurred thirteen minutes ago."

"What have you done about it?"

"Additional HDVMs have been scrambled from Dragon Base."

"That'll take too long." Sparta's answer was instantaneous. The HDVMs—Heavy Duty Venus Miner robots, self-propelled and remotely directed from Port Hesperus—were huge metal beetles that even at their considerable top speed over the rough surface of the planet would take hours to cover the distance. "We've got to go down."

"I can't make that decision," said the controller.

"You don't have to," Sparta said. "Load Rover Two into the manned shuttle and tell launch control to stand by."

The controller turned to protest. "The CEO has given explicit orders. . . ."

"Tell your CEO I'll meet him at the shuttle launch bay. I want a rover pilot standing by and I want the pre-launch sequence to be underway by the time I get to the ready room, is that understood?"

"As you say, Inspector Troy. But even the Space Board can't order a rover pilot to go down involuntarily."

"There will be a volunteer," she said.

As she swam through the weightless central corridor of Port Hesperus toward the space station's shuttle docking complex, her commlink chimed softly. "Troy here."

"Board dispatch, Inspector. We have just received a faxgram addressed to you. Do you want it now?''

"Go ahead.''

"After the code block the text reads, 'Let's play hide-and-seek again, if you're in the mood and promise to play fair.' That's all. No signature. The originating block is encrypted.''

"Okay, thanks.'' Sparta did not need to know where the faxgram had originated. With his usual lousy timing, Blake Redfield had chosen this moment to resurface. He wanted to play. Just now she had no time for hide-and-seek.

2

"Let's play hide-and-seek again, if you're in the mood and promise to play fair. . . ."

Blake Redfield and the woman who called herself Sparta, though others knew her as Ellen Troy, had been playing hide-and-seek a long time. She'd done most of the hiding, like the time more than two years ago that she'd led him into the Grand Central Conservatory in Manhattan and vanished into a tame tropical forest. That was the first time he had seen her since both of them were teenagers, and he'd recognized her immediately even though she had thoroughly disguised herself. It was also the moment when he'd begun seeking her in earnest.

Trying to retrace her hidden past, he began at the beginning, with the program known as SPARTA. The SPecified Aptitude Resource Training and Assessment project had been the dream of two psychologists, Sparta's mother and father—Sparta's name was Linda then—who believed that every person possessed a wide range of innate "intelligences," or talents, which could be developed to a degree that many people would consider evidence of genius. But to Linda's parents there was nothing magical about genius or the processes that led to it; it was a matter of trained supervision and a carefully controlled learning environment. For a long time the SPARTA project had only Linda herself to demonstrate its goals and methods. So spectacular were the little girl's achievements that her parents attracted funding and more applicants. Blake, while still a small child, had been among the first of the new students.

But the SPARTA project was dissolved a few years later when its founders were reportedly killed in a helicopter crash. By then Blake and most of the others were teenagers, and they went their separate ways to colleges and universities around the world. Linda, however, had vanished, leaving behind only vague rumors of a crippling mental disorder.

Blake grew up to be a handsome young man, inheriting from his father the strong jaw and wide mouth of the Black Irish, and from his Chinese mother the high cheekbones and liquid brown eyes of a Mandarin. A sprinkle of freckles across his nose and a glint of auburn in his straight black hair saved him from too-devilish good looks.

His interests were varied, but even as a youth he had gained a reputation for his knowledge of old books and manuscripts. So valued was his expertise that he was often retained as a consultant by libraries, auction houses, and dealers. While still in his early twenties, he accepted an offer from the London office of Sotheby's.

Blake's avocation gave him an excellent base from which to research any number of topics, not just old books, so when he unexpectedly encountered Linda in Manhattan—and saw that she had no wish to be recognized—he decided to find out more about the origins of the SPARTA project he had taken for granted. He found himself faced with too many interesting coincidences to ignore. . . .

On Blake's last night in Manhattan before moving to London, his parents threw a party in his honor. That was the excuse, anyway; Blake didn't know any of the people who came although he recognized them from the society strips and viddie propaganda spots. It was perhaps his parents' not-too-subtle way of saying they'd expected more of him than a passion for old books.

Blake rarely drank alcohol, but as a gesture to his parents he carried a full glass of the very expensive Chardonnay they'd broken out in his honor. He spent much of the evening standing at the windows staring out at the night, while the party guests cooed and chattered behind him. The Redfields owned an eighty-ninth-floor penthouse condo-apt in the Battery, with a wall of glass looking south over Old New York Harbor. Far below, the dark harbor was spotted by clusters of lights on the giant harvesters that floated on a swelling carpet of algae that stretched to the Jersey shore; the matte surface of the algae was scored by ruler-straight lanes of black water.

"You are Mr. Redfield. The younger?"

Blake turned and said pleasantly, "The name is Blake." He carefully shifted the wine glass to his left hand and offered his right.

"I'm John Noble. Call me Jack." The square-built man had a sandy crewcut and wore a pin-striped suit. As they shook hands he said, "I've looked forward to meeting you, Blake."

"Why's that?"

"SPARTA. Your mother and father were certainly proud when you were admitted. I used to hear a lot about your spectacular progress." Noble's black eyes were hard bright buttons above the ledges of his cheekbones. "Frankly, I wanted to see how you turned out."

"*Ecce*"—Blake spread his arms—"Hope I'm not too much of a disappointment."

"So you're in the book business."

"So to speak."

"Plan to make a lot of money that way?"

"Hardly."

"Did the SPARTA program turn out other scholars like yourself?"

"I haven't kept in touch with the others." Blake studied Noble a moment and decided to take a risk; he interrupted before Noble could speak. "But why don't you tell me, Jack? You're a Tapper."

Noble grimaced reflexively. "You've heard of our little organization." The Tappers were a philanthropic group that met once a month for dinner at private clubs in both Washington and Manhattan. They never admitted guests and never publicized their activities.

"You sponsored several of us SPARTA kids, didn't you?"

"I didn't realize that was general knowledge."

"You sponsored Khalid, for example," Blake said. Blake's parents and their friends belonged to some of the same clubs—only the first of the coincidences Blake had uncovered—so he knew that the Tappers' aim was ostensibly to discover and encourage young talent in the arts and sciences. Encouragement took the form of scholarships and other, unspecified support. No aspiring youth could apply for Tapper aid, however. Discovery was a Tapper prerogative. "What's Khalid up to these days?"

"In fact he's a rising young ecologist with the Mars Terraforming Project, of which I'm one of the directors."

"Good for Khalid. Why do I get the sense you're needling me, Jack? Don't you approve of book collecting?"

"You are a blunt young fellow," said Noble. "I'll be just as blunt. SPARTA was a noble undertaking, but it seems to have produced few like Khalid, people with an interest in public service. I wondered about your perspective on that."

"SPARTA was intended to help people live up to

their potential—so they could make choices for themselves.''

''A recipe for selfishness, it would seem.''

''We also serve who only sit and read,'' Blake said flippantly. ''Let's face it, Jack, you and I don't have to worry about the roofs over our heads. You made your fortune selling water on Mars; short of some disaster, I'll inherit mine. Books are my hobby. Do-gooding with the Tappers is yours.''

Noble shook his head once, sharply. ''Our purpose is a bit more serious. We believe the world, all the worlds, will soon be confronted with an unprecedented challenge. We do what we can to prepare for that event, to search out the man or woman . . .''

Blake leaned imperceptibly closer, his expression relaxing into frank interest. It was one of those tricks known to the socially adept, one of the tricks one had been apt to pick up at SPARTA.

And it almost worked, before Noble recovered himself. ''Well, I was about to bore you,'' he said. ''Please excuse me, I really do wish you the best of luck. I'm afraid I must run.''

Blake watched the man walk hastily away. From the corner of the room his father raised an eyebrow in a silent question; Blake smiled back cheerily.

Interesting exchange, that. Jack Noble had certainly confirmed Blake's suspicion that the Tappers were not what they seemed. Through discrete inquiries of his parents and their friends, Blake had already compiled a list of the dozen men and women currently on the Tappers' rolls and looked into their backgrounds. Their circumstances and occupations were quite varied—an educator, a nanoware tycoon, a well-known symphony orchestra conductor, a cognitive psychologist, a medical doctor, a neuroscientist, a free-booter like Noble— but they had more in common than just their interest in encouraging youth, and this too seemed an odd coincidence: all the Tappers had had ancestors who had left England in the 17th century, after having been arrested as "Ranters."

Blake continued his researches when he moved to London. In the reading room where Karl Marx had written *Das Kapital*, Blake came across tantalizing information about the Ranters.

Under the rule of Cromwell, according to one distraught observer, "heresies come thronging upon us in swarms, as the Caterpillers of Aegypt." Especially noxious were the Ranters, concentrated in London, infamous for their rioting, carousing, and shouting of obscenities—as well as of slogans that seemed innocent but had some special meaning to initiates, such as "all is well." Ranters disdained traditional forms of religion and professed loudly and ecstatically that God was in every creature and that every creature was God. Like their contemporaries the Diggers, the Ranters believed that all people had an equal claim to land and property, and that there ought to be a "community of goods." Not only goods and real estate were shared. "We are pure, say they, and so all things are pure to us, adultery, fornication, etc. . . ."

The authorities cracked down. Some Ranters died in prison. Some Ranters repented; many converted and became gentle Quakers. Some, driven into hiding, adopted secret languages and clandestinely continued to propagandize and recruit. Some, evidently, had made their way to the New World.

Theirs was the legacy of a savagely suppressed heresy which had persisted in Europe since the first millennium, known at its height as the Brotherhood of the Free Spirit, whose adepts called themselves *prophetae*. The great themes of this hopeful heresy were love, freedom, the power of humanity; explicit expressions of their dreams could be found in the prophetic books of the Bible, written eight centuries before Christ, and repeated in the Book of Daniel, in the Book of Revelation, and in many other more obscure texts. These apocalyptic visions foretold the coming of a superhuman savior who would elevate human beings to the power and freedom of God and establish Paradise on Earth.

But the Free Spirit were impatient with visions; they wanted Paradise now. In northern Europe they repeatedly rose in armed revolt against their feudal masters and the authorities of the church. The movement was crushed in 1580 but not eradicated. Later scholars could trace its connections— by influence, if not as a living cult—to Nietzsche, to Lenin, to Hitler.

From what he knew of the Tappers, Blake suspected that the Free Spirit was still alive, not only as an idea but as an organization, perhaps many organizations. The Tappers were in touch with others like themselves on other continents of Earth, on other planets, on the space stations and moons and asteroids.

To what purpose?

SPARTA had had something to do with that purpose. The woman who called herself Ellen Troy had had something to do with that purpose. But Blake's attempts to learn more through ordinary methods of research had encountered a blank wall.

In Paris there was a philanthropic society known as the Athanasians, whose business was to feed the hungry, or at least a select few of them. The same Paris address housed a small publishing company that specialized in archaeology books, everything from scholarly works to coffee-table tomes full of color holos of ruins, a list running heavily to the glories of ancient Egypt. One of the Tappers was on the board of the company, known as Editions Lequeu.

Blake sniffed a further connection: the name Athanasius meant ''immortal'' in Greek, but it had also been the first name of a famous early scholar of hieroglyphs, the Jesuit priest Athanasius Kircher. When business for Sotheby's took Blake to the Bibliothèque Nationale in Paris, he used the excellent cover of the occasion for a bit of on-the-spot private investigation. . . .

Blake strolled the broad sidewalks of the Boul Mich. The broad green leaves of the chestnuts spread out like five-fingered hands over his head; bright sunlight filtered into the deep shadows beneath the trees. The light had a greenish cast. As he walked, he pondered his options.

Urban universities are great attractors of the homeless, and the university of Paris had never been an exception. A woman approached him, dressed in genteel tatters, perhaps thirty years old, wrinkled as an apple doll but pretty not long ago. "Do you speak English?" she asked in English, and then, still in English, "Do you speak Dutch?" Blake shoved some colored paper bills into her hand and she thrust it crumpled into the waist of her skirt. *"Merci, monsieur, merci beaucoup,"* and in English again, "but guard your wallet, sir, the Africans will pick your pockets. The streets are swarming with Africans, so black they are, so big, you must guard yourself. . . ."

He strolled past a sidewalk cafe where another woman, her baby face smudged and her hair wildly awry, was entertaining the patrons with a Shirley Temple imitation, tap-dancing *The Good Ship Lollipop* with demonic energy. They tossed money at her, but she wouldn't go away until she finished her wretched performance.

A big black African approached and offered to sell him a wind-up plastic ornithopter.

A row of men in their twenties, bearded, their brown faces splotched with broken red blisters, sat on the sidewalk and rested against the fence of the Luxembourg gardens. They didn't offer him anything or ask him for anything.

Blake reached Montparnasse. On the horizon, above the centuries-old roofs of the city, rose a ring of high-rises which enclosed central Paris like a palisade. The wall of cement and glass cut off what breeze there was, trapping fetid summer air in the basin of the Seine. Around him the eternal traffic of Paris swirled, quieter and less smoky now that all the scooters and cars were electric, but as breakneck and aggressive as ever; there was a constant hiss of tires, accompanied by the jackass whinny and neigh of horns as drivers tried to shove each other out of the way and cut each other off by sound and fury alone. Paris, City of Light.

Blake turned back along the same route. This time the African didn't try to sell him an ornithopter. Shirley Temple was opening a new show, farther down the boulevard. The apple-doll woman came at him again, her memory a blank. "Do you speak English? Do you speak Dutch?"

Blake knew what he had to do next—he had to find a way to join the Free Spirit. Although the Tappers knew Blake Redfield all too well, other arms of the international cult fished in other waters; the homeless youth of Europe were a deep reservoir of malleable souls. After three days in Paris he had no doubt that Editions Lequeu and the Athanasian Society were the same organization. The Athanasians might find a derelict with a fascination for things Egyptian an especially attractive catch.

Before Blake could act on his plan, though, he had to return to London on unfinished business. . . .

Almost two years had past since Blake saw Ellen Troy in the Grand Central Conservatory. At a Sotheby's auction, Blake had agreed to represent a Port Hesperus buyer in what turned out to be a successful bid to acquire a valuable first edition of *The Seven Pillars of Wisdom*, by T. E. Lawrence. Then, while transporting the book to Port Hesperus, the freighter *Star Queen* had had a fatal mishap.*

When Blake learned who had been assigned to

*The *Star Queen* incident is related in *Arthur C. Clarke's Venus Prime, Volume 1: Breaking Strain*.

investigate the incident, he immediately booked passage on a liner to Venus—ostensibly to see to the safety of his client's property, but actually to confront the Space Board inspector who was handling the *Star Queen* case, Ellen Troy herself. This time Blake made it impossible for her avoid him.

Thus it was on Port Hesperus, in that transformer room in the central spindle of the garden sphere, that Blake for the first time was able to share with his old schoolmate Linda the startling knowledge he'd gained. "The more I study this subject, the more connections I find, and the farther back they reach," Blake told her. "In the 13th century they were known as adepts of the Free Spirit, the *prophetae*—but whatever name they've used, they've never been eradicated. Their goal has always been godhood. Perfection in this life. Superman."

But when Sparta asked him why they'd tried to kill her, Blake could only surmise that she had learned more than she was supposed to. "I think you learned that SPARTA was more than your father and mother claimed. . . ."

"My parents were psychologists, scientists," she'd protested.

"There has always been a dark side and a light side, a black side and a white side," he'd replied.

When Blake was forced to leave Sparta on Port Hesperus to return to Earth, he went with renewed determination to infiltrate the "dark side" of the Free Spirit as soon as possible . . .

That was four months ago. Sparta had not heard from him since—until she received that brief, enigmatic message at a moment when she was much too busy to deal with it.

3

The shell that contained her split open. She stumbled forward on six shaky legs, into a wall of stone.

Her hind legs supported her while she stretched her barbed forelegs to grasp the top of the ledge. The soft stone crumbled in her pincer grip. Momentarily scrabbling for purchase, she hefted herself upward, her wobbly joints creaking. She paused to spread her wings, to peer around and taste the air with waving antennas. It carried a tang of rotten eggs. Bracing.

The atmosphere was like thick glass, clear, suffused with red light. She swung her armored head from side to side, but she couldn't see far; the horizon vanished in the scattered light. Her antennas dipped, and she picked up sensations of the terrain in front of her. Somewhere ahead, these other senses informed her, great cliffs rose into the glowing sky.

Her titanium claws rested lightly on the crusted ground, its baked surface cool to her touch. Liquid lithium pulsed through her vitals and flowed through the veins of her delicate molybdenum-doped stainless-steel wings, carrying away her body heat as gently as mild perspiration in an April breeze. She had stepped dewily from her chrysalis into the morning of a long Venusian day.

Spindly legs, antennas, and radiant wings notwithstanding, she was not a sixteen-tonne metal insect, she was a woman.

"Azure Dragon, do you read me?"

There was a half-second delay in the link while the signal was relayed to Port Hesperus and back. "Go ahead, Inspector."

"I'm moving toward the site now."

"We have you," said the voice of Azure Dragon's shuttle controller. "Your shuttle came down ninety meters west of the targeted landing site. Sorry about that. Bear four degrees right of your present heading and continue for approximately three point five kilometers until you reach the base of the cliffs."

"All right. Any change in their situation?"

"Nothing since the oh-five-hundred signal—from either the rover or the HDVM. We have additional HDVMs on the way from Dragon Base, ETA about forty minutes."

"I'll check in when I make contact. Over for now."

It had been almost two hours since the last signal from the grounded expedition. Twenty-four hours ago they had landed at Dragon Base and made their way to their goal in a rover like Sparta's. Soon they had made the first of what promised to be many triumphant discoveries. Now triumph was forgotten. The challenge was to bring them out alive.

Sparta picked her way carefully along a shallow channel. Long ago this plain had glistened with a film of water; over it, almost imperceptible tides had gently advanced and receded. Now it was a sheet of orange sandstone, its surface furry with corrosion. She thought it a curious sensation to put her feet through the rotted rind of the rock, kicking up lazy clouds of dust as she moved ahead.

Nothing apparent came between Sparta's natural

senses and the world through which she moved. The eyes of the seven-meter-long rover were her eyes—or might as well have been—peering directly into the dense Venusian atmosphere through diamond lenses that took in a 360-degree field of view. Its six jointed legs and claws were hers—even the two that grew out of her midsection—and its stainless steel skin and titanium skeleton were hers. The nuclear reactor—quite realistically palpable in Sparta's abdomen—generated the warmth of a good turkey dinner.

The real woman, small and thin-boned, her muscles those of a dancer, sat forward in the vehicle inside a double sphere of titanium aluminide, a sort of diving bell with one overhead hatch and no windows. But the computer-generated Artificial Reality in which she was immersed persuaded her that she was a naked creature, to this planet born. To move, she willed herself to move. Inside her opaque helmet, laser beams tracked her eye movements. Microscopic strain gauges embedded in the skintight control suit monitored and magnified her body's motions. Surround-sound, retinal projection, and the suit's orthotactic fabric—200 pressure transducers, a hundred heat-exchange elements, a thousand chemical synapses per square centimeter—fed back a vivid sense of the world outside.

Inevitably, something was lost in the translation. For the fragile human female inside the bell, the outside temperature—almost 750 degrees Kelvin, sufficient to soften type metal—was scaled down to that of a balmy morning. The air outside was almost pure carbon dioxide, laced with a few rare gases, but inside the bell she breathed a familiar oxygen-nitrogen mix. The outside pressure—ninety Earth atmospheres, enough to crush a submarine—was rendered neutral. Even the light-bending distortion of the thick atmosphere had been corrected, so that her human visual cortex registered a familiar flat world instead of a bowl-shaped one. But its horizon was only a few hundred meters away; if it had not been for her vehicle's radar and sonar, Sparta would have been traveling blind.

In twenty minutes she would reach her destination, where the billion-year-old beach ended against the cliffs, and the mouth of an ancient canyon debouched upon the vanished sea. Inside the canyon she would learn if the men in Rover One were dead or alive. . . .

Venus is an astonishingly round and rocky planet. A sphere almost the size of Earth, its retrograde rotation is a slow 240 Earth days; it shows no noticeable bulge at its equator. Unlike Earth, with its half-dozen floating continents, its cloud-piercing Andes and Himalayas, its mid-ocean ridges and abyssal trenches, most of Venus is as hard and smooth as a billiard ball—

—with a few prominent exceptions. Ishtar Terra is one. One of the planet's two "continents," Ishtar Terra is anchored on its eastern flank by Mount Maxwell, a vast shield volcano higher than Everest. The whole raised mass of land is roughly twice the size of Alaska, and is situated at about the corresponding latitude; its northern and western curves are also belted by mountains, far less spectacular than Maxwell, while most of the continent is taken up by the flat Lakshmi Plateau.

It was toward the steep southern flanks of the Lakshmi Plateau that Sparta now drove her six-legged rover. The farther and faster Sparta moved, the more confident she felt. Her path took her across a series of shallow impact craters, their steep rims long since melted like putty in the heat. The slope continued to rise, punctuated by traces of wave-cut terraces, remnants of the beach that had continually widened as the planet's shallow ocean had dried under the heat of a runaway atmospheric greenhouse. As Sparta moved up the beach and crawled over the terraces she moved backward in time, to that era when the ocean had been at its greatest extent, covering all of Venus but for the two small continents and a few scattered islands.

A volley of immense explosion rattled the pressure bell, and moments later the ground shook violently, throwing the machine to its knees. Around Sparta the landscape heaved and groaned; rhythmic waves of soil raced past and slowly died away, leaving floating red dust in their wake.

The explosions were thunder arriving swiftly in the highly conductive atmosphere from a corona of lightning bolts that had bloomed about the head of Mount Maxwell, 300 kilometers away and eleven kilometers up in the sky. The simultaneous earthquake came from the bowels of the mountain, continuing the violent eruption which had begun three hours earlier.

"Rover Two, this is Azure Dragon. We show you at the cliffs. The canyon mouth is one-half-kilometer to your right."

A reddish-black volcanic scarp emerged with startling suddenness out of the bright glow at horizon's edge. Sparta veered right—

—and felt the first sign of trouble, a dragging reluctance in the second joint of her right front leg. There was no point in stopping. She could keep going on five legs, if she had to. Or on three.

She favored the troubled limb, holding it off the ground, but by the time she reached the canyon mouth five minutes later she knew it was useless— a seal had failed, and the lubrication in the joint had fried. She jettisoned it, leaving it behind like a cast-off stick. She held her surviving foreleg aloft and scurried into the canyon mouth on the remaining four.

Twisting, turning between narrowing walls of rock patinaed with a dark metallic sheen, once a rushing watercourse . . . milleniums of recurring flash floods had carved cinctures into these desert walls, but that was a billion years ago, and the heated rock had sagged like belly fat, obscuring the thin soft layers of chalk and coal that would have shouted "life" to the cameras of any passing probe.

Evidence of past life had eventually emerged anyway, when remote-controlled prospecting robots grazed over the surface of Venus. In the scattered calcium carbonates and shales and coal beds, a dozen fragments, no more, of macroscopic fossils emerged from the stone—a dozen fragments in twenty years of exploration, but those were more than enough to fuel the human imagination. Those bits of intaglio had been reconstructed a hundred ways by sober experts, a thousand ways by less inhibited dreamers. No one really knew what the organisms had looked like or how they had lived, and the prospect of ever finding out seemed dim.

Then, only months ago, a prospecting robot had broken into a cave in the cliffside of this canyon. . . .

Sparta rounded a rocky shoulder and came to a halt, blocked by a fresh fall of boulders from high up the cliff. The pale exposed facets of rock were shockingly bright and crisp against the blackened and corroded cliff.

"Azure Dragon, this is Troy."

"Come in, Inspector." Port Hesperus was closer now; the radio delay was hardly more than a hesitant pause.

"The site's buried by a landslide. Meter-length radar shows the rover and an HDVM underneath. Weak infrared, low reactor flux, they must be in auto-shutdown. Probably crushed their cooling fins. There's movement in the bell. I'm going to dig them out."

"Stand by, Inspector."

With her one good foreleg she began clawing at the rockpile.

"Inspector Troy, our instruments show you have lost the use of your right forelimb. LS controller advises against risking the remaining forelimb. Do you read?"

Another lightning bolt crackled the aether. Moments later the thunderclap shook the rover.

"Rover Two, please acknowledge."

She heard them loud and clear, as well as they heard her effortless breathing and read her steady biostats. "Let's both save our breath," she said.

Her remaining foreleg was efficient at yanking the blocks of basalt and solidified tuff from where they had fallen. Her multiple joint-motors whined ceaselessly, loud in the dense atmosphere. Dust rose in that thick air like swirls of mud. She dug into the slide a couple of meters and then had to back out, taking time to rearrange the debris. The deeper into the mound she went the more she risked being buried herself. On Mercury, on Mars, on Earth's Moon, on any of the asteroids or outer moons, it would have been different, but Venus was Earth's sister. A block of basalt on Venus weighed nearly what it would have weighed on Earth.

"Troy, this is Azure Dragon. Dragon Base HDVMs are no more than twenty minutes from your position." Dragon Base was Azure Dragon's robotic ore-processing complex and shuttle station on the heights of the Lakshmi Plateau. "Back off, will you? Let the robots do the heavy work."

"Good thought," she said. "I'll just keep at it until they get here."

"Inspector Troy . . ." the controller began. He gave up.

Sparta began to sweat. It seemed natural that with all this effort she would work up a sweat. Except that she was only providing the will, she wasn't doing the work. Why was the air getting hot? Was something wrong with the AR suit's heat exchangers? She flicked the helmet to internal display . . . no evident problem. Unless there was something wrong with the internal cooling system of the rover itself.

This machine, along with its twin, had been built for the first manned exploration of Venus a quarter of a century ago. Both of the giant steel bugs had landed successfully on the planet in tubby shuttles, and both had been retrieved. But when they were opened the occupants of one of them—this one—had been found baked alive.

That lesson sank in: remote-controlled robots had taken over the exploration and exploitation of Venus. This was the first mission in two decades that had warranted a human presence on the surface. Most of the past three months had been spent overhauling and refurbishing the two rovers and outfitting a shuttle to accommodate humans.

All known problems had been corrected. Which left only Murphy's Law.

Her titanium arm pulled loose another boulder and on the next stroke hooked into Rover One's aft port strut. The rock fall had crushed the bug's hind legs as well as its wings. The men inside were alive by courtesy of a superconducting refrigerating system that kept liquid metal coursing through the white-hot coils belting the pressure sphere.

Cautiously, as quickly as she could, she removed the overlying rubble from the front of the rover, exposing one side of the pressure bell's shining sphere. The refrigerator coils were still functioning, but the rover's antennas had been sheered by falling rock. Sparta fixed acoustic couplers to the outside of the bell to establish communication.

The visual scene changed as sharply as a cut in a holo viddie. Rover One's pressure bell was suddenly sheared open, as if she were peering directly into it from where she sat. There were three men inside the bell: the pilot, hunched forward and completely sheathed in a shiny black AR suit and helmet like her own, and two men in overalls behind him. They were obviously cramped, but they all appeared healthy.

"Ohayo gozaimas', Yoshi. *Dewa ojama itashimasu."*

The pilot chuckled. "Don't mention it, Ellen. Drop in any old time." Because he was wearing the

AR helmet he was the only one of the three who could see her, but all of them could hear her through the acoustic links.

"You're here at last," said the shorter of the two passengers, peering peevishly in Sparta's direction. He was a tiny bright-eyed fellow in his mid-fifties, a banty rooster caught in a crowded cage—Professor J.Q.R. Forster. A believer in natural authority, he did not hesitate to speak for the three of them. "It's vital we communicate our records to Port Hesperus without further delay."

Sorry I'm late, Sparta thought, but she said, "Sorry your work was interrupted, Professor." To the pilot Sparta said, "Your frame is crushed aft of the bell, Yoshi. To get you out of there we're going to have to drag you back to the shuttle. We'd better sit tight and wait for the HDVMs."

"I think we have a coolant leak. The temperature in here has gone up a couple of degrees in the last ten minutes." Only Yoshimitsu's husky voice indicated his appreciation of their fix.

It reminded her of her own discomfort. "Give me a moment." She opened her helmet and sniffed the air inside the pressure bell. Ozone. If she hadn't been wearing the sealed suit she would have smelled it earlier.

"I'm going to reset the couples." Sparta deliberately disengaged the acoustic couplers, breaking the sound and video links. From her point of view and Yoshimitsu's, both pressure spheres became opaque again.

Ozone accounted for her extra body heat, but what accounted for the ozone? She peeled the orthotactic glove from her right hand. From beneath her close-trimmed fingernails, chitinous polymer-insert spines emerged. She slid them into the auxiliary I/O port of her rover's master computer.

PIN spines were not standard among Space Board inspectors. Hers were another of her secrets, like the name she called herself that no one else knew.

Her data search of the rover's internal sensor net took a fraction of a second, much less than the rover's own outdated diagnostics. She pulled her spines from the console and retracted them, then replaced her orthotactic glove. With her rover's good titanium foreleg she refastened the acoustic links: Rover Two's bell became transparent again.

"I can see you better now," she said; it was a white lie. "Seems I've got a problem too—sparking in a compressor, and for some reason the scrubbers aren't handling the ozone. At this rate I'm going to poison myself in twenty minutes. I think I'd better pull you out of there and make a run for it."

"Rover Two, please hear this." The shuttle controller's voice sounded urgently in both rovers. Port Hesperus was now directly overhead to the south, passing through the same longitude as the Lakshmi Plateau. "Your vehicle is handicapped. We urge you to leave the scene immediately and get back to the shuttle. HDVMs will arrive in an estimated ten minutes to assist Rover One."

"Your passengers are dripping sweat," Sparta said to Yoshimitsu.

"Right," he said. "HDVMs are good for eating rocks, and that's about all."

"We'd better start now," she said.

"You would make life easier on everybody if you'd play by the rules," Azure Dragon's radio voice said petulantly.

"Lend me a hand, Yoshi," Sparta said.

"How about a whole arm?"

Rover One's second passenger, the tall man with the fine blond hair and bushy brows, had listened patiently to the exchange without comment until now. "Perhaps this is not a good time," he suggested diffidently, "but if someone could kindly—"

"Don't interfere, Merck," Forster snapped at him. "They're replacing her rover's handicapped limb with one of our own."

Forster's guess was accurate. Sparta and Yoshimitsu were inserting the good right foreleg from his crushed Rover into her empty socket. It was a dry socket incorporating only control connections and requiring no lubrication, designed for just such emergency limb transplants as this, in dessicating temperatures and the driest imaginable atmosphere.

The two pilots had an excellent view of each other, as clear as if they had been a couple of surgeons standing across an operating table. But an outside observer would have seen the two rovers squatting head to head like a pair of blind mantises. One glowing bug was half crushed, nervously offering the other a jointed foreleg, perhaps hoping its vital parts would be spared—

"Okay, the leg's in and working. Pull your locking pin and I'll lift you out."

"Pin's clear."

—but the sacrifice was in vain, for the mantis that now had two good forelegs suddenly reached out and grasped the head of the other bug and tugged upward. The second bug's round head came entirely away.

"I've got you," Sparta said.

When the locking pin in the floor of the bell was pulled, all connections to Rover One's motive power, external sensors, and long-term life-support systems were severed and sealed. Yoshimitsu was blind now, his AR suit rendered useless. With the aid of recirculating filters the three inhabitants of the bell would normally have six hours to live, maybe a little more.

Sparta backed cautiously out of the trench she had dug in the mound, holding the sphere aloft until they were clear of the landslide. Then, as fast as she could, she turned and scuttled back the way she had come, holding the survivors egglike in front of her.

Sparta's decision not to wait was proven sound when a few seconds later the ground began to shake, and a thousand tonnes of fresh rock poured down the cliff to dam the canyon behind them. Sparta didn't bother to radio an I-told-you-so to Port Hesperus.

Her burden did not obscure her view. Artificial Reality is more easily adjusted than the other kind, so Sparta merely tuned her sensors to peer through and around the pressure sphere in front of her, leaving only a kind of double exposure, or ghost presence, to reassure her of the health of the bell's inhabitants.

Cannon-fire crashes of distant lightning pursued her as she scurried down the twisting channel between walls of slickrock. When the ground waves arrived seconds later stones plunged through the thick atmosphere all around her, but she reached the canyon mouth safely. The final dash across the plain should have been easy.

Halfway to the shuttle, a massive tremor set the ground to flapping like a sheet in the wind. The sudden upward movement of rock against the crush of atmosphere flattened the rover. Sparta's midlegs took most of the force; one bent beneath her. An instant later the trough of the wave passed, and atmospheric suction yanked the pressure sphere out of Sparta's grasp.

She jettisoned the useless midleg and ran forward over the heaving ground. The bell bounced ahead of her, bounding over a ledge, over a broad shelf, down another ledge. Leaping, she caught it. She rolled the sphere upright and steadied it. As she was reattaching the communication couples, she noted the spurt of molten lithium from a rupture in the refrigerating coils—

She discovered that her left hindleg was also useless. She dropped it where she stood.

The bell's passengers were piled on the floor behind the pilot's chair. Merck's blond hair was stained with bright blood from a cut across the top of his high forehead. Forster looked seriously perturbed, though not visibly damaged; he was massaging his chin. Yoshimitsu had been strapped in; he seemed unaffected.

"Your coils are ruptured," she said. "We've got maybe ten minutes left before your coolant's gone. Tie yourselves down. I'm going to drag you to the shuttle."

Merck looked up, befuddled, holding his bleeding scalp. "Is this really essen . . . ?"

"Do it, Albers, if you want to save yourself!" Forster snapped at him. Forster had stripped the belt from his coveralls and was using it to tie himself to the back of the pilot's chair.

Merck, after a moment of confused indecision, did likewise. The two passengers huddled against the floor as Sparta circled the bell, gripped it with her forearms, and started dragging it backwards across the eroded landscape.

She radioed a terse message to Azure Dragon. The space station was already sliding over the curve of the planet; when the delayed reply came back it was a simple acknowledgment.

Sparta's progress was slow. She was short two legs and had to keep the sphere from rolling over, further crushing its refrigerating coils. The egg left a bloody track as it was pulled along—a thin bright stream of metal jetting from the ruptured coil, emerging red hot, then quickly cooling to splashes of liquid silver on the rock.

Watching the rate of loss, Sparta could estimate with great precision when the volume of lithium in the coils would drop too low to carry off the heat of the atmosphere. When that moment came, the bell's internal temperature would rise catastrophically, baking the inhabitants black in minutes.

"We're doing fine. We'll be inside the shuttle in five minutes," she told the quiet men inside the sphere.

She had less than two minutes left when the squat shuttle became visible over the short horizon behind her. She knew she wasn't going to make it, not at this dragging pace. She had to maneuver the bell over the ledge that partially blocked the shuttle's hangar doors, close and seal the doors behind them, refrigerate and depressurize the hangar . . .

Sparta fell into a trance, but it passed so quickly no observer would have noticed. Within a millisecond her brain proposed and analyzed half a dozen possibilities and chose the least unlikely. She came out of her trance and acted upon her decision without hesitation—and without warning.

She spun violently, wrenching the sphere into position in front of her. Bracing herself on a tripod of her remaining legs, she used her fourth leg to shove the bell away from her. It rolled toward the open hangar like a massive soccer ball—

—but with a slowness that was exaggerated by Sparta's slowed time-sense. She knew how little time they all had, but within that brief span there was leisure to do whatever could be done. She directed a tight beam of radio waves toward the waiting shuttle, instructing it to close the hangar doors and initiate emergency refrigeration and depressurization. She saw the bounding sphere's own refrigeration coils burst and spew glowing lithium over the ground just as it sailed over the lip of the low ledge and smashed into the shuttle's still-open maw. The doors were already beginning to close, slamming shut as an explosion of steam spewed out of the hangar—the reaction product of emergency coolant cascading from the shuttle's tanks into the hot, dry atmosphere.

The shuttle continued to vent high-pressure steam for half a minute after the hangar doors sealed themselves. Sparta studied the scene with the senses remaining to her. Sight could tell her little, and radar bounced off the curved metal skin of the blunt cone; while she had radio contact with the shuttle's robot systems, she had none with the men inside the bell. Sonar was her only good source of information, and she listened carefully to the bangings and hissings, the whistles and pump-throbbings that would tell her whether any of the shuttle's vital systems had been ruptured, whether the men inside the bell were alive and conscious and able to release themselves from their cramped prison. . . .

Finally she heard the unmistakable sound of the pressure bell's hatch opening.

"Shuttle, this is Rover Two. Put me on comm-link, please."

"Done," the shuttle's robot voice replied.

"Yoshi, can you hear me?"

"Mr. Yoshimitsu is momentarily indisposed," replied a gruff voice, unmistakable by its British accent; Professor Forster was still firmly in charge—of himself, if not of events. "You may be interested to learn that all of us have survived without serious injury."

"Glad to hear it, Professor. Now would you and your companions clear the hangar so that I can come aboard—before another earthquake does me in?"

"We'll see to it."

When the hatch of her rover opened into the steaming, repressurized hold of the shuttle, Sparta found the kindly-sad face of Albers Merck peering down at her. "Are you all right?"

"I'm fine," she said, hoisting herself through the narrow hatchway with the aid of his helping hand. Standing next to him on the catwalk, she studied his mournful face and noted the dried blood in his hair and the purple bruise along one cheekbone. "Is there more?"

"Besides this?" He touched long fingers to his scalp and cheek. "Some very sore ribs, but nothing broken, I think. Mr. Yoshimitsu had the worst of it. His wrist is badly sprained. I'm afraid I kicked him. Or perhaps fell on him."

Sparta looked around the hangar. The remains of the Rover One pressure sphere, scorched and dented, rested against the leg of the overhead crane. Rover Two, its reactor powered down, sagged crookedly on four off-center legs. Pumps were sucking puddles of emergency coolant back into the tanks.

"Quite a mess. It's a shame we couldn't salvage anything from your dig."

"No material artifacts, of course, and that is unfortunate," Merck said. "But we have chemical analyses and holographic records stored in the rover's computers. Enough to keep us quite busy."

"Would you give me a hand locking this machinery down? I'll feel safer when we're back in orbit."

Minutes later they climbed onto the shuttle's makeshift flight deck. Yoshimitsu lay in his acceleration couch with his left arm in a sling. Forster was bent over the disabled pilot, expertly taping the arm tightly across the man's chest.

"You okay, Yoshi?"

"Slightly bent," he said, grinning. His long black hair hung down across his dark eyes. "I scoffed at those stories they tell about your luck, Ellen. Not anymore."

Forster straightened and studied her. "The Inspector does not seem the sort to depend on luck."

"Only when all else fails," Sparta answered. "I'd say we're *all* lucky."

"Why did they send you instead of one of the regular pilots?" Forster asked.

"Because I insisted," she said. "Your expedition is going to owe Azure Dragon a pile of money for this manned-shuttle trip. They figure you can't pay. They thought it would cost them less to dig you out with HDVMs and bring you up in a robot shuttle."

"I'll have to speak to them sternly. Our expenses are underwritten by the Cultural Heritage Committee, not to mention the trustees of the Hesperian Museum. . . ."

"I didn't argue with them," Sparta said. "I invoked interplanetary law."

"I see. But why are *you* here, Inspector? That is, your job is detection, is it not?"

"In addition to the many other courtesies Azure Dragon has extended to your expedition, they have donated the services of Mr. Yoshimitsu, one of their best shuttle pilots. Neither of the two other persons trained in the use of these old rovers were available for this trip.''

''I think you mean that neither of them volunteered,'' Yoshimitsu said quietly. ''And the bosses wouldn't order them.''

''Gomen nasai, Yoshimitsu-san.'' She inclined her head sharply in a respectful bow. Strapped into his couch, he tucked his chin to his collar bone, trying to reciprocate.

''I see.'' Forster was quiet, ruminating. ''And when did you receive your training in the use of these specialized vehicles?''

''For God's sake, Forster, stop interrogating the woman,'' Merck said, his face pink with embarrassment. ''She's just saved our lives.''

''I'm well aware of that,'' Forster shot back. ''And indeed I am grateful. I simply want to understand what's going on here, that's all.''

''I have a . . . talent for this kind of thing,'' Sparta said.

''We ought to discuss it later,'' Yoshimitsu suggested. ''Our next launch window is coming up fast.''

Half an hour later the bullet-nosed shuttle blasted away from the surface of Venus, climbing swiftly into the clouds, forcing its way through hurricane gales of sulfuric-acid rain, sparking vicious lightning bolts by its passage, driving steadily upward through thinning layers of sulfur-dioxide smog, until at last it won free into clear space and closed on the shining rings and green-gleaming garden sphere of Port Hesperus.

4

It came swirling out of the darkness, a catherine wheel of shadow, not fire, and with it the voices:

She could be the greatest of us
She resists our authority
William, she's a child
To resist us is to resist the Knowledge

As the wheel spun, the voices reverberated upon themselves, increasing to a howl. Sparta's heart thudded violently, shaking her ribs and the mattress beneath her.

Her face was crushed into the pillow; she opened an eye. A peculiar stench filled her nostrils, a bold vegetable smell turning sour, becoming the odor of a cat.

Bits of black curve, bits of black slash, bits of black spot, moving and changing . . . a tiger moving through the tall grass

She sat up, terrified, and opened her mouth to call out, then choked back the unvoiced cry. Her skin was slick with sweat. Her heart chugged like a dry pump.

She got control of her breathing; her pulse rate slowed. The vision in her right eye stopped zooming dizzily in and out, and the spinning catherine wheel collapsed in on itself. Then the imaginary stench vanished, and she was left with the familiar odors of her cabin. Overlaying the ubiquitous space-station stink of rustcoat, lubricating oil, and human sweat was the perfume of hoya flowers.

The hoya flower, a pompon of pink velvet stars, emitted its odor only at night. Night was arbitrary here, but for Sparta, now was the middle of the night. The hoya vine clung to the ceiling above her in intricate whorls, a product of the weightless topiary for which Port Hesperus was famous; the vine had been grown in microgravity under a constantly moving, programmed light source.

In her A-ring cabin the vine's weight, and Sparta's, was Earth normal. If the heart of Port Hesperus was a fantastic garden, the rest of the space station had about as much charm as a battleship. Main ring A, starside of the garden sphere, housed most of the station's maintenance workers, dock hands, interplanetary traffic controllers, and other service personnel. Sparta's temporary quarters were in the Visiting Officer's Quarters of the patrol barracks. Barring another emergency like the one that had drawn her to the surface of Venus, this would be her last night in the cheerless room of plastic and steel.

With that realization came another, unbidden, one that had come often in the past months. She missed Blake Redfield, missed him with something bordering on obsession, missed even more because she had not heard from him for so long. And then a trivial, teasing message, unsigned and enclosing no hint of deep affection. ''Let's play hide-and-seek again. . . .''

Exhausted, but with no hope of sleeping, she threw back the tangled sheet and walked to the center of the windowless room. Something had happened; the nightmare had not come out of nowhere. For a moment she stood and *listened*. . . .

The vibration of the steel walls brought her the electric hum, the metallic screech, the hydraulic plunge and suck of the endlessly turning station;

her inner ear easily filtered these to retrieve the human coughs and moans and chuckles, the voices raised in complaint or enthusiasm. The life of Port Hesperus was stumbling along normally. Most of the workers who bunked in Sparta's sector were sound asleep; their day shifts did not begin for three more hours. The rest were working as efficiently as they ever did.

Close overhead, the spacecraft controllers in the traffic control dome kept track of the hundreds of small craft and robot satellites that crowded surrounding space. Only one interplanetary vessel was nearby, a Space Board cutter due to reach the radiation perimeter in six hours. Sparta's replacement was aboard it, and she herself would be on it when it burned for Earth.

At the other end of the station, two kilometers away—the end that always pointed straight down toward the center of Venus—the Ishtar Mining Corporation and the Azure Dragon Mutual Prosperity Mineral Endeavor were busily conducting business as usual. The rival companies were the station's economic base, its reason for existence. Twenty-four hours each station day they dispatched and received the big ore shuttles and directed the hives of metal beetles that scoured the surface of Venus for precious metals.

Still Sparta *listened*. . . .

She heard no one in the corridor near her cabin. Tuning her visual cortex to infrared, she scanned the darkness of the low apartment. She saw nothing but the glowing wall circuits—no living thing had passed this way in the last hour.

Her chemical senses reported nothing out of the ordinary.

She willed herself to relax. She was in no danger. Nothing external had awakened her, nothing external had triggered the falling dream. Another fragment of her wrecked and submerged memory had broken off and floated to the surface.

The *signs* . . . the stripes of the dream-tiger were made of signs. Sometime not long ago she had dreamed of signs, but she couldn't remember where, or what she had dreamed.

She went to the room's single big window. The heavy steel shutter was the old-fashioned kind, operated by a handcrank. Slowly she cranked it back. As the shutter folded upon itself, Venus light flooded her cabin, and the starside bulge of the green garden sphere swelled before her, ending in an artificial horizon a kilometer away.

As she gazed upon the tiny world of glass and steel, she felt the headache that had been plaguing her in recent weeks coming on again. She set her thumbs into the corners of her jaw and reached behind her neck, massaging the back of her skull with her fingertips. It helped a little. She went to the closet and began to dress.

She pulled on sleek black pants that hugged her legs and gave them the look of machined plastic; she sealed their ankle seams over ribbed black boots. Her top was tight and high, of banded black vinyl. She wore her clothes like armor.

She looked toward her wall screen, fixing it with her dark blue gaze. The screen's remote-control unit lay on her bedside table, two meters away. She stretched her arms and curved her hands in an ancient symbol of benediction, but this was no blessing: under her heart, the structures built into her diaphragm sparked into life. The odd web of doped ceramic "wires" that looped around her bones coursed with electric current. Her belly burned—

—and the wall screen brightened with an image.

Good trick, making things work at a distance—she was learning to do it more easily. With her arms still raised, she aimed another silent burst of intention at the screen; the image skipped forward, then steadied. Sparta lowered her arms to her sides. The recorded image was one of those Forster and

Merck had brought back from the surface, one of the best.

The picture that unscrolled on the wallscreen looked like an aerial reconnaisance film from a low-flying aircraft, an aircraft that was buzzing columns of tanks or maybe rows of factory buildings—intricate structures at a uniform height above the plain. Sparta heard the voice and watched the picture out of the corner of her eye and imagined it playing to an audience of bomber pilots in a Quonset hut, receiving their final mission briefing. It was the lighting of the recorded image—a single strong light from below—that tricked the brain into switching depth for height and misreading the scale. The columns and rows were inscriptions, scanned by a wide-angle lens, lines upon lines of characters deeply incised in metal plate.

These were the signs painted on the dream-tiger's hide.

From the screen a voice boomed in the shadows, Professor Forster's voice, hearty with menace, reciting facts that had to be faced. "It will be conceded by my colleague Professor Merck, I think, that in every example found at this locus we have now firmly established the run of the writing—not strictly left to right, as Birbor has insisted on the basis of the Martian fragment, nor strictly right to left, as Suali has surmised on grounds known only to himself—nor even, for those of you who have just jumped to the conclusion, boustrophedon, as the ox plows, back and forth. It is none of those. Anyone care to venture a guess as to what it is?"

Offscreen there was nervous rustling; the unseen audience, not of bomber pilots but of media-hounds, had gathered to watch the pictures on wallscreens in the comfort of a Port Hesperus lounge. Sparta had been there, as interested as the others in seeing what she'd helped to salvage. Someone said, "Up and down?"

Forster's reply was mocking. "If you can find

any three marks in either these texts or the Martian plaque which are vertically aligned, young man, you will confound a generation of scholars." A nervous laugh started, but Forster squelched it. "No other suggestions? Look again, people."

Sparta glanced at her own screen as she reached for her jacket. The image had been recorded by a remote-control lens operated from inside the archaeologist's rover; the low-flying camera was wheeling and diving, strafing the columns of signs. Sparta had seen it instantly, the first time she'd watched the recording: the script alternated by column. . . .

"The run of the writing in all these inscriptions alternates by column—the left column invariably reads left to right, the right column invariably reads right to left," Forster said. "What's more interesting, the opposing columns bear virtually identical texts. Some of you may see this as unfortunate, in that it cuts in half the amount of unique text we have to work with, but let's look on the bright side. Redundancy is a hedge against error and will help us fill lacunae."

Sparta closed the flap of her shiny white jacket, broad in the shoulders and tight at the waist; its high collar protected the back of her neck. She pulled open a drawer and started to push the rest of her clothes into the duffel bag. It would be eight hours until the cutter pulled into the starside docking bay, another few hours of debriefing before she could say goodbye to Venus. She'd be ready and waiting.

Packing should have been easy, but her anxious nature made it hard. She traveled light, carrying only a small polycanvas duffle which made it difficult to fold her clothes. And—because she had eidetic memory of each earlier failure of topological perfection, of each resulting ugly wrinkle—where another finicky person would have spent a minute refolding each garment, she spent five.

Behind her, the scene switched to Forster at the podium of the lecture hall, his bewhiskered face rendered fierce by the yellow light of the lectern's dim bulb. "Now I should like to outline what statistical analysis of the recent finds has revealed about the sign system of Culture X."

Sparta concentrated on her packing; she remembered Forster's speech perfectly. Statistical analysis of undeciphered texts—how many characters and combinations of characters appear how often, and in what context—had been an exact but laborious science since the 19th century. Since the invention of electronic computers in the middle of the 20th century it had become ever more exact and ever less laborious, and now, in that late 21st century, the machinery was so compact, the algorithms so precise and quick, that statistical analysis could be performed even as the texts were unearthed from the rock and sand in which they had lain hidden for millenniums.

"Whoever inscribed these tablets wrote with forty-two distinct signs—three more than were previously known from the Martian fragment. In a moment Professor Merck will present his interpretation of the data. For now, I will say that I am convinced that twenty-four of these signs are alphabetical letters—representing sounds. Of the remaining eighteen, at least thirteen are simple numerals. Of course it is impossible to know whether any of the alphabetical signs correspond to 'vowels' or 'consonants,' as we understand these terms, because no one can responsibly guess at the speech-producing anatomy of the beings who made this writing."

An alphabet? A system of numerals? Statistical analysis could reveal a few things, but it could not by itself reveal the existence of an alphabet. Forster was operating on faith.

"In conclusion, let me note that the nature of the site remains an enigma. We had only a few hours there, enough to see that the cave complex was extensive and artificial. The beings who built it packed it with hundreds of objects. Many were reconstructions—or possibly perfectly preserved specimens, mummies—of animals utterly alien to us, as you have seen. But the collectors left us no representations of themselves—no paintings, no sculptures, no recordings. Certainly none that we have recognized as such." Forster fussed with his notes, then abruptly turned away. "My distinguished colleague, Professor Merck, will now present his views."

On the screen Merck's pleasant face, with its slightly distracted expression, replaced Forster's in the podium light. Sparta liked Merck; he seemed much less the raging egotist than feisty little Forster. A man as tall as Merck might find it easier to be polite, never having strained to assert himself.

As diffident and even as indecisive as his manner suggested he was, Merck's ideas about the so-called Culture X texts were fixed: the signs were not alphabetic, they were ideographic, although some probably doubled as syllables. Merck had written extensively on the probable meaning of the signs and had even attempted a partial content analysis—the media had instantly dubbed it a "translation"—of the Martian plaque, which had been the subject of much controversy. But no matter how vociferously the small community of xeno-archaeologists might dispute the merits of Merck's content analysis, most of them sided with him on the question of the nature of the signs: they were ideographs.

None of these matters were of urgent interest to Sparta. Why had she dreamed of the signs? Because she'd risked her life to recover them, probably. It didn't have to be more complicated than that.

She frowned at the wallscreen, lifted her arms, and signalled it to go dark, blanking Merck's image.

She concentrated on her packing for another ten minutes. When she'd convinced herself that she would not get it any better, she sealed the duffle's fabric seals. Her right eye zoomed in on the micromechanical links of the seal, a miniaturized zipper made of microbe-generated polymer chains.

Each hook and eye was a black squiggle: linked, they produced closure, hid meaning. Unlinked, they opened on . . . what? Laundry archaeology. The evidence of her lifestyle. In this dig the evidence was meager, the lifestyle sparse.

An odd thought came to her then. She believed—she couldn't be sure—that she had dreamed of the alien signs before she had seen them. Odder yet was the irrational conviction that she knew how to pronounce the letters of that unearthly alphabet, if only she could bring its sounds to consciousness.

Eight hours later the warning siren for launch was hooting as Sparta arrived at the security lock. The cutter's gleaming prow dominated the view outside the lock's wide black-glass port.

A mere dozen graceful white ships, bearing the blue band and gold star of the Board of Space Control, were the fragile links in the slim chains of authority from Earth to the isolated settlements of the planets, moons, asteroids, and space stations. Powered by fusion torches, cutters went when and where they had to go, at whatever acceleration they had to pour on to get there. Every Space Board outpost hoarded torch fuel in massive tanks of frozen lithium and deuterium, and a cutter could turn around in the time it took to replenish its own propellant tanks.

The cutter that had brought replacements to Port Hesperus was needed back on Earth. Four hours after it slid gently into the high-security side of Port Hesperus's docking bay it had loaded the consumables it needed for the return trip.

Sparta had a few minutes more to say goodbye to the one friend she'd made during her assignment. They floated in the lock, weightless in microgravity. "I'm going to miss you, Vik."

"That's what you said the last time," the tall

blond Slav said sourly. "Before the commlink caught you."

"I took out my commlink, in case somebody tried that again. This time I'm really getting out of here."

"If you should get to Leningrad. . ."

"I'll beam you a holo. More likely they'll send me back to the Newark docks."

"Save the false modesty."

"You're a tough cop, Proboda.'

He thrust out his square hand and she offered her fine strong fingers to his grip. "If you don't keep in touch, I'll know you for the running dog lackey of the capitalist-imperialists I always suspected you were," he grumbled.

Still holding his hand, she pulled him to her and squeezed him gingerly. "I *will* miss you"—affection and caution balanced neatly—"you atheistic totalitarian commie." Abruptly, she let go and floated away. "Don't let Kitamuki get your goat."

"She's going to be a real pain in the *zhopa*. She certainly thought she was going to make captain."

"The new guy looks competent. He'll keep her in line." Sparta saw him shrug and said, "Sorry. Talking shop."

The launch siren wailed again.

"Get out of here," Proboda said.

She nodded, then turned and dived toward the airlock's tube.

Just before she disappeared into the long passage, Proboda called after her, "And give my very best wishes to our friend Blake."

She cast a quizzical glance over her shoulder. Were her feelings for Blake really that transparent?

PART
2

SECRETS OF
THE ANCIENTS

5

Paris, four months earlier: behind the beveled plate glass of a brass-framed window, warm light caressed yellowing fragments of papyrus. The Egyptian scroll unrolled upon the brown velvet was much deteriorated, with shredded edges and jagged lacunae, but hieratic script painted in glossy black and wine-red ink flowed across it with calligraphic grace. Its borders were painted with miniatures of musicians and naked dancing girls, at once stylized and animated.

A hand-written card pinned to the velvet identified the scroll as a XIIth-Dynasty variant of the *Song of the Harper*: ''Life is brief, O beautiful Nefer. Do not resist, but let us seize the fleeting hour. . . .'' The papyrus was not rare as such things go, not sufficiently unusual for a museum, but certainly special enough to be worth the steep price the dealer was asking.

Odd, then, that the man who studied it so intently through the glass was not one of the richly dressed tourists or silk-suited businessmen strolling this street of galleries and decorators' salons in the blue summer evening. He was not one of the leaner, hungrier-looking students from the nearby technical schools and outlying classrooms of the Sorbonne; he was hungrier even than these.

His cheeks were hollow below the high bones of what must once have been a handsome Eurasian face. His jaw was darkly fuzzed and his auburn-tinged black hair was greasy-bright, of an odd length, not quite long enough for the pigtail that sprouted from the back of his dirty neck. His shirt was in shreds and his plastic pants were too tight and too short, more badly glued patches than original fabric, with holes in the wrong places. His antic figure—teetering on high-heeled, high-topped shoes, its gaunt waist cinched in by a strip of yellow neoprene tubing—was that of a dilapidated jester.

The proprietor of the Librairie de l'Egypte did not seem amused. Several times he had looked up from his bits of stone and scroll, his cases of scarabs and amulets, to find the eyes of the starving fellow staring at him, while well-dressed men and women, quite possibly potential customers, looked askance and walked too quickly past the shop's open door. And this had been going on every night at this time for the past three days. The proprietor decided enough was enough.

"Get along," he said. "Go, go."

The bum looked ostentatiously around. "This your sidewalk, *mon cher?*"

"Want to sit on it? Come on, move. Quick, quick."

"*Trou de balle, toi.*" He resumed his calm inspection of the papyrus.

The proprietor's beefy face reddened; his fists clenched. He had no doubt he could have knocked the fellow off his ridiculous high heels with a swift backhanded slap, but the mockery on the bum's face gave him pause. Why risk a lawsuit? In five minutes the *flics* would hustle this *type* off to work-shelter without wasting breath on him.

He turned abruptly and walked into his shop, closing the door behind him. He put his hand to the commlink in his ear.

The bum watched and grinned; then his dark-eyed glance darted sidelong to the woman who had been watching the show from the corner of the rue Bonaparte. She'd been watching his show for two days now, she and her friend. He was a long-haired guy in a black plastic jacket who looked like he'd be at home in a prize ring.

The evening promenade filled the narrow rue Jacob from sidewalk to sidewalk, a tide of stylish humanity. Aside from the occasional bleat of a superped's horn no vehicular noise interrupted the soft babble, so it was easy to hear the burp of the police van's oscillator while it was still around the corner a block away, clearing a path for itself. Inside the Librairie de l'Egypte the proprietor took his hand from his ear and sneered at the bum.

A hand touched his sleeve; he jerked it away and stumbled back, his face twisting in a snarl. "Don't touch."

"Don't be frightened. All is well." It was the woman. Up close, her height was impressive. Her face was tan and round, with high Slavic cheekbones and gray almond-shaped eyes under invisibly fine brows. White-blond hair, straight and unfettered, fell to the waist of her white cotton dress. She was muscular, leggy, with a predatory beauty emphasized by lips that seemed swollen from sucking at her slightly protruding incisors. "We can help you."

"I don't need your . . ."

"They're almost here." She pointed her round chin at the blue light bouncing off the street's stucco walls and shuttered windows; the police oscillator burped again, closer, impatient with the crowds. "We can help you better than they can."

"So? How?"

"All is ours to give," she said. Her voice was pitched low; she spoke urgently and intimately, only to him. "Food, a place to live, friends if you want them—other things. Don't be afraid."

She touched his sleeve, grasped the soiled fabric with her colorless fingertips. She tugged gently, and he took an awkward step forward.

"Don't let them take you," she said. "You were meant to be free."

"Where are we going?"

Her companion had watched expressionlessly until now. He said, "With me. Stay close."

They turned and pushed into the crowded street. The man opened the way and the woman followed, holding the bum's arm in a tighter grip, her fingers surprisingly strong around his elbow as she steered him.

As the police van halted in front of the Librairie de l'Egypte it was immediately surrounded by curious onlookers. Meanwhile, half a block away, the fugitive and his rescuers ducked into a courtyard off the rue Bonaparte and hurried across the cobbles to a black-enameled door. A brass plaque identified the offices of Editions Lequeu. The man pushed it open and they went quickly in.

The narrow hall was paved with gray marble. To the right were tall double doors, firmly closed; on one, an engraved card in a small brass frame bore the words "Societé des Athanasians." To the left, a warped staircase wound around the shaft of a caged elevator, which stood open. They got in, pulled the grille closed, and waited silently as the two-hundred-year-old car ascended; it sang softly as it passed each floor, its squeaking electrical contacts sounding like the call of a dove.

"Where's this?" the bum demanded edgily.

"We're going to the registrar," said the woman. "Then we'll get you something to eat."

"Rather have something to drink," he said.

"We don't mind that. Let us feed you first."

They stopped at the top floor. The black-jacketed man pulled back the grille and let the other two off, then closed it and rode the elevator down, his chores apparently complete.

The woman led her charge to the end of the hall, where a doorway stood open. They entered a high-ceilinged office lined with bookshelves. Tall windows opened onto a balcony; the tower of Saint Germain des Pres was prettily framed by lace curtains.

"Ah, here is our scholar." The man lounged comfortably against the corner of an Empire desk, swinging a polished slipper at the end of a corduroy-clad leg. He was fifty-ish, sun-tanned, elegant in a white knit shirt. "And what would his name be?"

The woman said, "I'm afraid we didn't have time to become acquainted."

The bum stared at the man. "You call me a scholar?"

"You are a student of Egyptian antiquities, are you not? You have been studying the poor objects in our friend Monsieur Bovinet's window with such passion these several evenings now."

The bum blinked. A perplexed look crossed his face, wiping off the belligerence. "There's something about them," he mumbled.

"They speak to you, perhaps?"

"I don't read that writing."

"But you would like to," the older man said, confirming what had been left unspoken. "Because you believe some secret is hidden there, some secret that might save your life, set you free."

The bum's expression hardened. "What do you know? You don't know me."

"Well . . ." The man's smile was very alluring and very cool. "You are right, of course"—he leaned back across the desk and tapped the keys of a filescreen—"I don't know your name. And if we are to enroll you we will need that, won't we?"

The bum stared at him suspiciously. The woman, whose hand had never left his arm, leaned close, encouraging him. "I'm Catherine. This is Monsieur Lequeu. What is your name?"

He blurted it out: "My name is Guy."

"Don't worry, Guy," said Lequeu. "All will be well."

Unlike the purse-seining tactics that other fishers of men have employed since antiquity, Lequeu and the Athanasians were highly selective. They were uninterested in anyone over thirty, anyone badly sick, anyone with an apparent physical or mental disability, or anyone so far gone into drugs or drink that organic damage was likely. They cared nothing for repentance, and hardly more for need. The Athanasians proselytized not so much as a fisherman fishes but as a rancher buys calves. Had Blake's derelict disguise been too persuasive, they might have passed him over completely, and Monsieur Bovinet of the Librairie de l'Egypte might not have bothered to alert Lequeu before calling in the police—a move that had the desired effect of forcing Blake into a quick choice, or so the Athanasians thought.

The first thing "Guy's" saviors did for him, after they fed him and gave him a glass of rather good red wine and showed him to a room in the limestone-walled basement with a bed, a locker, and a change of clothes, was to escort him to a nearby clinic for a thorough physical examination. The technicians treated him with that special Parisian hauteur Blake had to get reaccustomed to every time he visited Paris, but they quickly declared him grade-A beef.

Then came long days as a pampered guest of the Athanasians, spent getting to know the staff and his fellow inmates, who were also referred to as "guests." There were five other guests in the basement dormitory, two women and three men. One had been there for six weeks, one for only a few days. Blake gathered that the basement was a staging area; after a period of time one passed on to greater things—or went back to the streets.

Each guest had a separate cubicle in the low-ceilinged basement. There was a shower and water closet at one end of the narrow hall, and at the other end, a kitchen and laundry. Guests were invited to volunteer to help with the work. Blake refused at first; he wanted to see what would happen if he didn't try to ingratiate himself. No one seemed bothered. Starting the second week, he began doing his share in the laundry. This too was apparently normal, and the only remarks were simple thank-you's.

Meals were served in the big room on the ground floor, whose windows overlooked the courtyard. The food was good and simple: vegetables, breads, fish, eggs, occasionally meat. People with business in the other buildings that fronted the court were thus assured by a glance inside that the Athanasians were going about their meritorious work of feeding the hungry.

In the same room each morning and afternoon, after the dishes were cleared away, there were "discussions" led by members of the staff—discussions very like group therapy sessions, except that their only stated purpose was to let the guests get to know each other. Blake was not pressed to tell more about himself than he wanted to.

Catherine was never far from Blake's side in the first days, although the suave Lequeu had vanished from sight. Blake counted three other staff members, the big man who had effected his rescue from the police, whose name was Pierre, and two other men, Jacques and Jean, who along with Catherine led the discussions or sat in to keep one or more of the guests company. All were in their late twenties. Blake had no doubt that all were using assumed names.

Perhaps the guests were, too. Certainly "Guy" was.

Vincent had been there the longest; he was an Austrian, a self-styled troubador who scraped along by playing classical guitar and nine-stringed karroo at various restaurants in the Quarter, singing whatever he thought the patrons were hoping to hear but specializing in the folk songs of the workers who had built the great space stations. "My dream someday is to go into space," Vincent said, "but the corporations will not take me."

"Have you applied for the programs?" someone asked.

"As I have explained, I do not dare. Because of things, you know, in my past. . . ."

"We don't know, Vincent, you haven't explained."

Blake listened to Vincent speak about his dreams and realized that he was a seducer, so well armored behind his charm that no amount of mere talk would reach him. Which is probably why he was still in the anteroom of the program. Blake wondered how much more time the Athanasians were willing to give him.

Salome came from a farm near Verdun. She was a dark, tough girl who had borne her first child at fourteen, married at sixteen, and had three more children but never found enough time for an education. Her mama had the children now; Salome, twenty-one, was making her way in the streets of Paris.

"How?"

"Doing what I have to do."

"Stealing?"

"When I have to."

"Sleeping with men?"

"Only if it feels like the right thing to do."

And dreaming of joining the theater. Salome was writing a play; she had a manuscript of ragged pages she offered to read. Her aggressive, intelligent style in conversation did not transfer to the page. No one criticized her work, but as the days passed, Salome described a change in her goals, from playwriting (she admitted that her writing was hampered because she did not read that well) to helping spread the good work of the Athanasians.

Salome had arrived in the program only a few days before Blake. He was not surprised when, two weeks after he arrived, she was gone; he knew she'd already been promoted.

"I admit that when you approached me, I hadn't eaten for four days. I was beginning to hallucinate." The speaker was Leo, a thin, quick Dane, a wanderer and diarist who sent long letters by radioing to his friends around the world whenever he could scrape up the tolls, and who had washed ashore in Paris after crossing North Africa on foot. "I should worry that I'm not worried, but what can I do?" He gave everyone a sunny smile.

Blake saw that Leo had an ego problem—his ego wasn't as big as he pretended it was, and he depended absolutely on constantly being rescued. Leo would probably respond quickly to the processes of the group, but whether he was the sort of material the Athanasians were looking for was yet to be seen. Of all the guests, Leo was the only one who did not profess a goal beyond the present. He maintained that he was happy with his life the way it was.

Lokele was muscular and tall, a West African black who'd been brought to the Paris suburbs as an infant. His parents had died in the influenza epidemic of 2075—"And then I met many, many nice people, but never did they stay long enough to let me get to know them," he said, smiling, "so I began to hit them to keep them from running away"—until at last he ended in a rehabilitation camp after being convicted of robbery and assault. The Athanasians had picked him up a week after his release, after a week of fruitless job hunting, just as his hunger and despair and determination to stay out of work-shelter were tempting him to rob again.

Of wit and deftness Lokele had plenty. He needed

education. He needed socialization. His family and his culture had been destroyed; the bureaucracy had failed him. Blake wondered if and how the Athanasians would pick up the pieces.

Bruni was German, broad-shouldered and blond. She'd been living in Amsterdam for the past two years because work-shelter there involved little or no work, but she'd become bored and moved to Paris.

"Would you like to tell the other guests how we met you, Bruni?"

"That pimp tried to force me to work for him, but I refused.

"You said, 'No thank you' ?"

"I broke his arm."

"And when his big friends tried to help him?"

"I broke their knees." She said it without humor, her arms crossed, staring at the floor.

In fact the Athanasians had whisked her out of the way of the police, who thought they were responding to a riot.

Bruni's anger was held on a spring catch, and in discussion it sometimes exploded into insults and obscenities. But it was clear enough what Bruni wanted; she wanted simple love. Blake wondered how the Athanasians were going to give her that.

And when it was Guy's turn. . . .

"I am from Bayonne, the Pays Basque. My parents speak the ancient tongue, but I did not learn it. I was not home much because I was with the circus." The circus, as subsequent confession revealed, was a cheap carnival that worked northern Spain, and while with it, Guy had learned a great many ways to cheat. "I was very good at telling fortunes, but they arrested me for that in Pamplona and I had to spend a week in their filthy jail before they sent me back." His post-deportation adventures, getting from the border to Paris, were intricate but not interesting, he claimed, but he expressed a confused desire, inspired by the pseudo-Egyptian hocus-pocus of his fortune-telling act, "to learn the true language of the ancient Egyptians. For I have heard that the Basques are the descendants of a colony of Egyptians. . . ."

At which earnest pronouncement, everyone nodded politely.

In the few days Blake had spent in the Basque country before coming back to Paris, he had prepared this cover story as carefully as he could. If the Athanasians bothered to check, they'd find that there really was a disreputable little carnival with a clandestine "Egyptian" fortune-teller—Blake had encountered it on a previous trip to the continent—presently in Catalonia, if it had kept to its flexible itinerary. Blake hoped that denials of Guy's existence on the part of the carnies would be taken by any interrogator as convenient lapses of memory.

Blake sat through two weeks of these discussions, playing his role with as much skill as he could muster, watching the others play theirs, observing the techniques of Jean and Jacques and Catherine. Group leaders have their agendas, and Blake was impressed by the united purpose of these three, their skill in shaping the eclectic talents and temperaments of the guests toward acknowledgment of a common goal—the goal Jack Noble had expressed to Blake a year ago as "service."

Each night after supper there were classes. Three nights a week these involved the entire group, and one of the leaders would talk about the aims and methods of the Athanasians. The language was mild, the message as radical as it had been for centuries: humans were perfectible, sin did not exist, the just society—"or Utopia, or Paradise as we sometimes call it"—was a matter of inspiration and will. Hunger would be eradicated, war was a fading nightmare. What was needed was Inspiration. Will. Service. The reward was Freedom, Ecstasy, Unity. Light. These principles were embodied in the ancient wisdom of many cultures, but one source was most ancient. . . .

Other nights of the week there were private instructions, held in the guests' own cubicles or in one of the empty offices of Editions Lequeu upstairs. During Blake's second week, Lequeu himself reappeared and casually offered to teach Blake to read hieroglyphics. An offer that may have been made out of idle curiosity quickly turned serious when Lequeu discovered a ready and gifted pupil.

They worked in a small conference room, spreading out the beautiful hand-colored codexes and the holo reproductions of wall carvings on a well-worn table. Lequeu not only knew the sounds, the syllables, the idiograms—he spoke the language. But he cautioned Blake that no one knew how it really sounded. "The last native speakers of ancient Egyptian were the Copts, the Christians of Egypt," he told Blake. "I am very much afraid that by the end of the 19th century they all had died. Who can say what transformations their language had already undergone?"

Under Lequeu's tutelage Blake quickly learned to sound out texts in hieroglyphs, in the corresponding hieratic script, and in the later, bastard-Greek demotic. "Guy, you have a gift," he said, smiling, "and perhaps you will soon find in the texts the secrets you have mystically divined must be there."

Lequeu disappointed him in only one matter: "I regret that there is no connection whatever between the Egyptians and the Basques—your ancestors were living in the Pyrenees ten thousand years, maybe more, before the first pyramid rose beside the Nile."

Thus the Athanasians tangled Guy and the others in a net of dependencies: food, clothing, shelter, friendship, cooperative labor, the gentle stripping away of ego defenses, the subtle substitution of a common goal. They neglected nothing. Before Lequeu began his lessons in hieroglyphics, Blake's evenings had been administered by Catherine; he'd been there only a week when she announced that the night's lesson would be held in his cubicle. She brought no books.

The yellow reading lamp beside the bunk emphasized the pitted blocks of raw limestone that were the basement's outer wall. Catherine's hair was liquid in the light; her clinging dress molded her bold figure, until she began to pull the dress away.

Blake could not pretend aversion or even surprise. But as Catherine's gray eyes and swollen lips descended toward him, as her cool and expert body joined his, Blake felt a passing shiver of anger, dissolving into sadness. There was another woman he loved, who cared deeply for him, but who had never allowed him more than a child's kiss.

After Guy had spent three weeks as a guest of the Athanasians, Catherine told him he had been chosen to learn the deeper mysteries.

6

Suddenly "Guy" was on the street again. They'd fixed him up with an ID sliver and enough credit to buy clothes and rent a room of his own. They'd even arranged a job for him, as a superped messenger. He was expected to show up at weekly discussion groups, held in the same room on the courtyard, but beyond that he was free.

It was a test, of course. What would he do with his freedom? How thoroughly had they managed to bind him to them?

Blake made Guy into a model apprentice. He aped Pierre's style and wore a high-collared black jacket and tight black pants. He lived in a tiny *chambre de bonne* in Issy and went to work conscientiously every day, moving swiftly through the crowded streets on his electric bike like a black shadow, silent except for frequent horn-bleats. He spent his spare time in bookstores and museums, pursuing a new hobby. He was always early to the weekly discussions. He avoided contact with anyone outside the Athanasians, in person or by phonelink.

At the first weekly meeting, Salome's face was familiar, and Lokele's, but the rest were strangers.

He didn't know what had become of his other fellow guests, and he thought it better not to ask.

"Hello, Guy," Catherine murmured that first night, but she did not look at him. She waited until he sat down, and then she sat far away. When she repeated this behavior at the next meeting, he asked her why she was avoiding him.

"Be patient," she said. "Soon you will be called to a great undertaking"—she smiled thinly—"and if you succeed, I promise we will be united forever. . . ."

One evening two months after he'd arrived in Paris, Blake delivered a package of drugs to a pharmacy in the Sixteenth. The stern pharmacist told him to wait, went into his office a moment, then emerged with an envelope. "For you."

Blake took the envelope without comment and waited to open it until he'd ridden his superped a few blocks. The note inside said, "*500 hrs. demain matin, La Menagerie, Jardins des Plantes. Seul.*"

In late summer the light creeps into Paris long before sunrise, and the sky to the east was a clear, pale apple-green behind Sacre Coeur's ugly goat's-udder dome. In the west, the edge of the full moon was creeping down behind the dark foliage of the Jardin des Plantes' huge old trees.

The gates of the Menagerie were closed, but as Blake was chaining his superped to the iron fence he saw a man emerge from the tiny gate-house; judging by his size and walk, it was Pierre. The gates swung open with a screech and Blake went inside.

The zoo was old and small, built by kings in a romanticizing past; the cages were of fanciful wrought iron and the animal houses were built of imitation rubble and mud piled up between unshaped tree branches. The effect was supposed to be primitive, exotic. Low brick buildings with tile roofs squatted in the shadows of huge chestnuts and planes.

Blake followed his shadowy guide past a bronze statue of a leaping black youth, dressed like an Indian, playing the panpipes to charm a snake. The statue was inscribed "Age de Pierre." The Stone Age. Perhaps taciturn Pierre had been inspired by it—certainly the name suited him. Pierre stopped beside the statue and handed Blake what looked like a velvet bag. "Put this on."

It was a hood. Blake dragged it awkwardly over his head and Pierre pulled it straight down over his shoulders. In the pitch darkness Blake was instantly sensitized to the sounds and smells of the zoo. Nearby, birds were screaming in an awesome cacophony of barnyard and jungle. Growling cats stalked in their cages, impatient for their morning meal.

Blake thought of Rilke's panther, its will benumbed behind a thousand bars—and beyond the bars, no world.

Pierre took Blake by the arm and urged him forward. Blake stepped out as boldly as he dared. They walked a long time, silently. The asphalt path gently sloped, down and up and down again. The temperature of the air dropped as they walked among groves of trees. Blake felt a slight breeze. The path turned to gravel underfoot, and he could picture crumbled yellow limestone. The animal smells drifted away. There was a scent of herbs—he recognized sage and thyme, but the rest was a fragrant sachet—and a little later the heavy perfume of Mediterranean pines.

"Get in."

An electric car, parked somewhere on the grounds . . . Blake slid in, and it started with a quiet hum and drove off slowly. The ride lasted perhaps twenty minutes. Blake didn't know if Pierre was still with him or not.

The car stopped. "Get out." Pierre was still with him. "Step down. Steep stairs. Keep walking down until I tell you."

The steps were of brick or possibly stone, something smooth and cool. Pierre let go of Blake's arm, but his footsteps stayed close behind. Two sets of shuffling footsteps echoed from the walls of a tunnel, as if they were descending into an old Metro station.

At first the air was cool, but after a hundred or so treads on this seemingly endless stair, Blake felt the air stirring and growing warmer. Somewhere far away, a heavy door closed.

The heat was dry; the air got hotter. A distant whisper became a steady sigh, and then a fluttering roar. Blake kept walking down at a steady pace, but he suddenly stumbled as he tried to drop his weight onto a flat floor. Pierre had failed to warn him that the stairs were ending.

Blake waited a moment, expecting to feel Pierre's hand on his arm, but there was nothing. The oppressive heat and the blast-furnace roar had covered Pierre's silent departure.

Blake tugged off the hood and dropped it at his feet.

He stood in blue light at the base of a round cement tower, as big as a silo. Its upper reaches were invisible in the darkness far above. Behind him were the stairs down which he'd come, a dark passage now barred by an iron gate.

The silo was an air shaft. Warm wind, sucked down from above, blew toward the massive stone portal in front of him; through it, orange light flickered in a hypostyle hall of columns shaped like bundles of papyrus reeds. On either side of the opening stood massive seated statues. They were in the Egyptian manner, but each had three jackal heads—an 18th century conflation of Anubis and Cerberus, fanciful, anachronistic, yet imposing.

By the dim blue light that seeped into the shaft he could make out hieroglyphs carved in the stone lintel. With his new skill at reading Egyptian he recognized that they were meaningless, or at best arcane. Centered below the hieroglyphs, however, was a short inscription in French: *Ne regardez pas en arrière.* Don't look back.

He walked slowly forward. As he approached the threshold, flame belched from the jaws of the jackals, and a booming bass voice made the air tremble: *"He who follows this route alone and without looking back will be purified by fire, by water, and by air; and if he can master the fear of death, he will leave the Earth's bosom, will again see light, and will be worthy of admission to the society of the wisest and bravest."*

Blake heard this solemn invocation with a mixture of apprehension and amusement—apprehension because he wondered just how far the Athanasians were prepared to go to "purify" him, amusement that they had the humor to mock themselves. The sentiments and flowery phrases, like the architecture, were straight out of the Age of Enlightenment.

Ostentatiously he marched forward into the hall of columns. His steps were bold, but his nerves were jangling.

The heat and the roar increased. At the far end of the hall was a double-doored gate of wrought iron, the decorative work so thick with spikes and curlicues that little could be seen in the interstices except a bright, wavering gleam of orange. The hot gates smelled of the forge; as Blake approached he could make out a word, shaped in the voids of the iron strapwork, radiant with an orange light he realized was a distant wall of flame: *Tartarus.*

Another step. The gates groaned and swung open and Blake, forgetting his pose, gasped at what he saw. He was looking into an enormous domed pit, filled with flames. Its floor was a circular lake of fire, twenty meters in diameter; in the center of the lake stood a bronze statue, the figure of a bearded man caught in mid-stride with legs apart, left arm forward, right arm upraised. In each fist he held a forked thunderbolt. Fire jetted in spurts from his eyes and mouth; his face was stretched in a horrid grimace. This, surely, was the god Baal.

The immense chamber was filled with smoke and flames. Flames licked up the brick walls, incurving like the walls of a kiln, which rose fifteen meters to a wide circular balcony. Billows of black smoke poured upward, past a ring of fire on the balcony rim; at the apex of the higher dome above, a chimney sucked out the smoke and kept the flames leaping.

Blake stood watching the scene for a long minute. Then the gates of Tartarus screeched again, and began to close. Hastily, he stepped through them.

The heat was withering. From the smell, Blake judged that the flames were fed by highly volatile kerosene. The hot wind at his back constantly fed oxygen to the bottom of the furnace, and most of the heat was carried to the upper chamber and out the chimney, but he knew he could not stay here for long before dropping of heatstroke.

There was no path around the walls, which were a wall of fire right down to the edge of the fiery lake. There was no bridge across the lake. There were only the six wide brick steps before him, leading down into the floating flames.

The plastic fabric of Blake's clothes was already softening in the heat. He stripped them off.

Naked, he walked down the first two steps. The heat was punishing. He knew he could go no further. He backed away, ran forward and jumped—

—as high and as far as he could, wrapping his arms around his pulled-up knees, ducking his head. He cannon-balled into the flames.

The pool was deep, and the splash scattered the flames; immediately he swam up for air. Using the technique that, of necessity, had long been practiced by wrecked sailors and ditched fliers, he swam through the fire—taking a breath, diving, swimming underwater, pushing the floating, burning liquid aside as he came up for air. He knew he could get across the fiery lake. He could only assume there was a way out.

The light below the surface was a weird dance of rippling orange shadows, barely bright enough to see the underwater brick walls. Blake made a circuit of the pool as quickly as he could without exhausting himself and found himself back where he'd entered; he hadn't seen a hint of an opening in the wall, not even a drain.

There remained the island in the center, the pedestal of the fire god's statue. Blake moved toward it, his body writhing in the flickering submarine light, gasping harder for air each time he resurfaced. As he neared the towering statue, he felt a light current pushing outward at the surface and a stronger current running toward it a meter below. He surfaced again. Pipes at the rim of the brick pedestal poured fresh water into the lake, creating a zone of clear water. He could wait here and catch his breath, although burning drops of fuel fell from the statue's flame-spurting mouth, singeing his hair and blistering his shoulders.

He gulped and dove. A meter down, there were grilled drains in the brickwork, wide enough to admit his shoulders. He tried two of them, but they were set fast in mortar. The third gate swung open at his touch.

He surfaced behind the statue, avoiding the rain of fire. He breathed long and deep, considering what he had to do.

At the very best, it was a ten-meter swim under water before he reached the edge of the pool. He wondered if the drain was big enough to swim in for the entire distance, if it was blocked or barred inside. If he swam all the way to the edge and ran into a barrier there, would he have enough strength to return?

Blake took a long look around the fiery furnace, soot-blackened with the smoke of centuries. His gaze traveled up past the bronze statue, up to the cathedral-high dome filled with oily smoke and flame. All this had *not* been built to drown would-be initiates miserably, invisibly. If he was to be sacrificed, some more spectacular end must await him. With that line of reasoning, he made up his mind.

When his head was ringing from hyperventilation and his lungs were filled with air, he dived.

The current pulled him into the drain. He bashed his head painfully where the drain took a sharp turn and leveled off. He grabbed at the sides but found them slick with algae. He couldn't even use his arms, for the brick tube was too narrow. He thrashed his feet like fins and kept his hands to the sides, streamlining himself as much as he could. In moments he was in utter blackness. His lungs were aching unbearably, but he knew he had long minutes remaining before he really began to get short of oxygen. He put his fingers out to trail along the wall of the drain, hoping to measure his progress.

To his surprise, he was darting through the drain like a dolphin through the sea. He had been unable to feel the swift current that sucked him forward, faster and faster. The water became cooler—

—then cold, then painfully cold, almost freezing. His ankles and wrists throbbed with pain. His teeth were so many frozen stones in his aching jaw.

His shoulder slammed into the wall as he encountered another turn in the pipe. A rush of bubbles overtook him. Blue light speared down from above.

He was expelled into air, only to fall flailing back into cold water.

He was in another pool, this one icy blue. Slick irregular blue-white walls surrounded him, their tops lost in bright clouds of thickly condensing vapor. The opening of the fountain that had spewed him out was in the form of a great bronze jar, held in the arms of another colossal statue, a naiad carved of marble—enough bigger than the god of fire to drench him thoroughly: *La Source.*

Blake was so cold he could not keep still. He sidestroked swiftly around the base of the statue, examining his new prison. There seemed no way out except, possibly, to climb the walls, and the tops of those were invisible. But he knew he must get out of the water before the last of his strength ebbed away.

He swam to the side and hauled himself out. The walls were wet concrete, shaped and painted to look like the face of a glacier, hardly warmer than the ice they mimicked. But there were ledges and crevices in the concrete, enough to let him climb into the clouds.

As he started up the cliff he heard a trembling groan and the sound of great engines rhythmically throbbing, slowly at first, then with an increasing tempo. The sound was reminiscent of something, but Blake couldn't place it. Then he realized that the sound was of an old-fashioned steam engine. The technology of this chamber, the chamber of waters, was a century more advanced than that of the chamber of fire.

At the same moment he recalled that the steam engines were first used as pumps to suck water out of flooded mines . . .

A rivulet of water ran down the wall beside him. He was perhaps three meters above the surface of the icy pool. He looked up and got a splat of cold water in the face. As he was clinging to the wall with one hand and wiping the water from his eyes with the other, he was drenched with bucketsful of water falling from above. He looked up again, in time to see torrents of white water erupt from the tops of the walls on every side. He barely had time to thrust his fist into a crack and twist it there, to jam himself fast. Then he was deluged. The water was pounding his shoulders, pounding the top of his head, thundering in his brain. All his weight was dependant on his right arm and fist and the bare toes of his left foot, which clung to a tiny ledge. He had to get out of the waterfall or give up and fall back into the pool. Bracing himself against the tons of water that descended every minute, he blindly felt for another handhold. His hand found a rough nob of cement, his toes reached another ledge. Carefully he transferred his weight sideways. The falling water was dense and blinding. He repeated the cautious process, moving sideways another half a meter. The sting of falling water on his head and shoulders seemed to lessen.

Another slow lateral move and he was in a dancing mist of water droplets, no longer absorbing the full force of the spillway. For the next few meters above him a vertical ridge of cement like a ship's prow cut through the cascading water on either side. He glanced around and saw tumbling water everywhere, streaming out of the glowing clouds under the roof. The pool was a seething, freezing caldron below.

Oddly, its level remained constant. Blake felt a shiver of respect for the designers of the ingenious hydraulic system of this labyrinth, which functioned as well as it had centuries ago when it was built.

He continued his climb, moving slowly from one finger- and toehold to the next. More than once he clung precariously to the wet cement after his foot slipped or his hooked fingers threatened to lose their grip. After half an hour's shivering climb he was twenty meters above the pool; even the huge central statue seemed tiny and far away.

He moved into the bright swirling mist. White light was everywhere, filtering through the blowing fog, but he could no longer see farther than the end of his arm. Fumbling in the mist, he came to the last of the bare concrete; the ridge he had been climbing tapered to a knife edge. Above it a smooth sheet of water spilled over the wall's unseen rim.

He felt for the wall under the falling water. His right hand found a crevice; he wedged his hand in and flexed his arm. His left hand found a knob; he lifted himself. The water poured thickly over his arms and shoulders. He was almost swimming vertically, an oversized salmon headed upstream without a running start. His feet found tiny ledges, enough to lift him to another handhold, and one more—

Then, suddenly, he was over the lip of the falls, lying flat. The force of the water threatened to roll him back, but he felt along the bottom for hand- and footholds and pulled himself along as the water sheeted over his face and forced itself into his eyes and nostrils.

The gasp and shudder of the great pumps ceased. Water drained swiftly away. He was lying in a channel of fitted stone, smoothly eroded by centuries of these artificial flash floods. The channel ran the circumference of the cylindrical room, under a corbeled ceiling slotted with great skylights which infused the mist with light. Somewhere above, the sun was shining.

He heard a rising whistle, and a lower, breathier, fluty sound. The wind came up. The mist stirred and formed into tendrils in which for a moment he fancied he saw human shapes. He stood. On both sides of the curving wall were enormous open drain spouts from which the floods had poured. Now they were exhausting warm air. The moving air was balmy after the freezing water; soon Blake's skin was dry, although his hair still dripped with moisture. The last of the bright mist cleared away.

The bare vertical ridge had debouched him near the only exit from the chamber of waters, an arched tunnel big enough to stand in. He climbed into the tunnel and clambered up its short, steep slope. The going was easy for a few meters. Then it ended abruptly.

He had entered the chamber of air.

He had been inside the clouds, and now he was above them. Unlike the other rooms, this "room" had no walls except those immediately beside him, glassy smooth, curving away beneath him into invisibility like the interior of a giant bell jar. A few meters down, the cloudscape unfurled, moving layers of cirrus and alto-cumulus stretching everywhere to a far horizon. In the east, if it were the true east, the sun had risen clear and was sending rosy streams of light to illuminate dark towers of cumulo-nimbus.

The illusion of limitless space was perfect; the technology of this chamber had leapfrogged to the early 21st century.

Lightning forked through a far-off thunderhead. Distant thunder pealed and crumpled. The wind freshened. Blake stood naked on the threshold of a door into the storm, a diver on the highest of platforms. He wondered what was expected of him now. Unless some flying machine or great bird were to rise through the clouds, he could think of no way forward.

The wind continued to rise. It whipped at his hair and pushed him staggering away from the edge. He got to his hands and knees and crept back, pushing his face into the wind. It was a hard, steady wind, as steady as the blast from a giant wind tunnel.

Once, when Blake was little and a late summer hurricane had whipped New York, he had been taken outside on the top of the skyscraper tower to feel eighty-knot winds from the safety of his father's arms. This wind was stronger.

The cloudscape continued to move serenely and majestically; its projected clouds were insubstantial creatures of light, unaffected by the fast-rising column of material air. The words of the invocation echoed in Blake's mind—". . . if he can master the fear of death, he will leave the Earth's bosom . . ."

Then he knew what he was supposed to do.

He crept back from the edge. Once more he tried to reassure himself of his hosts' sanity, or at least practicality. He raised his arms and ran forward. He dived away from the ledge as far as he could.

Skydiving was not one of his hobbies. He found himself tumbling and struggling, vainly beating the air with his arms and legs. The wind roared in his ears and the clouds rose past him at a terrifying rate—he fell through a layer of cirrus, plummeted haphazardly toward hazy stratus, saw himself drifting toward the skirts of a mushroom-capped thunderhead.

His athletic instincts came to his rescue, and he got his arms out and curved, his legs straightened and parted. Suddenly he found himself gliding like that great bird he had hoped would come to save him, although the roar of the wind reminded him that his speed through the vertical wind was still well over a hundred knots.

He scanned the clouds below. They were rising more slowly now—but it was all illusory. How far had he really fallen? How far down was the floor? What was down there, beside the whirling blades of a giant turbine?

A great canyon of cloud opened beneath him, its walls black with rain. As he gently descended into the airy canyon, he saw what he thought were birds spiraling on updrafts. But the shapes were not birdlike. With a start he realized they were human. They soared toward him, arms outstretched.

These were the initiates who had gone before

him. They climbed and dived past him, grinning gleefully. He recognized Bruni, Lokele, Salome, Leo, others, swooping and circling and tumbling naked in the air.

Blake caught himself smiling back. This wasn't so bad after all: in fact it was fun. He steered himself toward Lokele, who was climbing fast. At the last moment Blake veered and make a grab for Lokele's outstretched hand, but he miscalculated—and flew right through the man's body. Lokele kept grinning.

The fliers were as illusory as the clouds. Blake reminded himself of his true situation. He was suspended in a vast wind tunnel. He didn't know where the walls or floor were, and he had no idea how he was going to get out.

Another naked figure swooped down out of the clouds above him—not an initiate this time, an adept. It was Catherine. She flew toward him, smiling, her hands outstretched. He watched her image impassively, noting its realism.

She touched his hand. A palpable touch. She was real indeed. Still smiling, she gestured to Blake to follow her. She turned and dived away, into the black flanks of the nearest thunderhead.

He dived after her. As he flew into the cloud, rain brushed his skin and the light failed. A moment later he collided with a billowing surface that gave under him like an enormous breast. He bounced off it, into the air, but the roar of the wind dropped a notch and he fell back onto the fabric. Blake realized he was clinging to a huge, fine-meshed net. In the darkness he scrambled over its collapsing folds. He felt firmer air cushions underfoot, and then a hard surface. The sound of the wind faded with a dying whine of great rotors.

He was standing in virtual darkness, his ears still ringing from the wind. As his eyes grew accustomed to the dark he saw Catherine's figure ahead, rimmed in faint blue light. She beckoned, then turned and walked away.

His eyes straining, he followed her. As his hearing recovered he became conscious of another sound, the tremolo of a single note played on the organ.

As he walked, points of light appeared in the darkness, infinitely far away, above and below and on every side. The hard smooth surface on which he walked was invisible, giving off no reflection. Catherine's figure ahead of him was a black silhouette against the stars. The celestial sphere was no random sprinkle of lights, but a true map of the sky; constellations of the galactic plane arched overhead, Vela, Crux, Centaurus . . .

The organ note increased in volume, became a swelling chord, was underlined by throbbing strings and woodwinds, all holding to the single dominant. The sound filled all space, so rich and wide that Blake's chest reverberated as to the prolonged blast of a ship's whistle.

A figure in flowing white robes emerged from the distant darkness, walking slowly toward them on a floor of empty space. A dozen or more people in simple white robes appeared behind the leader, and behind them a dozen more, and then a hundred more.

The ethereal symphony burst into melody. Blake smiled at the cliché and the rightness of the choice; perhaps they had a sense of humor after all. It was the final movement of Saint-Saëns' Symphony No. 3, the organ symphony—a joyful hymn, militant in its joy. The trumpets blazed, the piano rippled like falling water, the strings soared in triumph.

The white-robed man in the lead nodded to Catherine and walked on past her; she joined the line behind him and was handed a robe to slip around her body.

The man in the lead was Lequeu. He drew near and halted. His dark eyes regarded Blake sympathetically; a smile played at the corners of his refined mouth. Without speaking he lifted a folded robe from his arm and held it out wordlessly. Blake stepped to him and let him fold the robe around his shoulders.

"Welcome, my young friend," Lequeu said then. Someone behind him handed him a bronze chalice surrounding a cup of carved amethyst, and he held it out with both hands. "Mnemosyne's potion. To help you forget your former life. Here all is well."

Blake took it and drank without hesitation. It tasted of nothing but cold water.

"Welcome to the sanctuary of the initiated, the content," Lequeu announced, loud enough for all to hear; his rich voice was warm with praise.

A star burst overhead, flooding space with a shell of light. In the moment of ensuing brightness, all the stars vanished. Hundreds of voices laughed and cheered, and Blake felt himself surrounded and pummeled by encouraging hands. When the lights came on again he saw that they were inside a modest and rather plain neoclassical hall, its sandstone walls relieved only by Doric pilasters. One feature made of the hall something unusual: the far end of it was dominated by a statue of helmeted Athena, enthroned, towering almost to the roof ten meters above. Blake peered at the bronze giantess in momentary confusion before he confirmed that the pedestal on which the goddess of wisdom sat really was a pipe organ. Into this 18th-century hall the 21st century had briefly imported the Galaxy, but the supreme technology of the past maintained its place.

He looked at the laughing faces closing in on him. Here were the real Leo, the real Salome, the real Lekole, the real Bruni, all showering him with congratulations, sincerely happy to see him—perhaps even a little madly happy to see him. Someone pressed a glass of wine into his hand.

His senses were already buzzing. The water in

the cup had been more than water, and something more than alcohol had fired his nervous system. He grinned madly back at those who grinned madly at him. His fellow initiates talked about old times. Old-timers talked about older times, their own experiences and what the records revealed of the initiation rites when the secret society's subterranean palace was new. Blake gathered that he had done no more or less than was expected of him—the society's pre-screening was that thorough. He was fascinated by the legends of novel solutions, tales of drastic errors.

The time passed in a blur. He retained a vague memory of encountering Catherine in a darkened room, with nothing between them but linen robes, and then nothing at all.

Later Blake could hardly recall coming up into the twilight air of the deserted Jardin des Plantes, whose gates had been closed when he had entered and were closed again. How many hours, days, had he been underground? Much less could he remember steering himself home to his rented room in Issy on his superped. He remembered only being summoned to Lequeu's office when he woke from what must have been a long sleep.

"Ah, Guy, good of you to be so prompt. Please have a seat." Lequeu, elegant as ever in gray summer-weight wool slacks and fine-checked cotton shirt, was seated on the edge of his desk, his customary casual perch. He pressed a finger lightly to his ear. "Join us, will you, Catherine?"

She entered from the adjacent office, demure in a floor-length green plastic skirt. She carried a large, thin portfolio.

"Guy, every initiate is honored to serve as he or she is best qualified," Lequeu continued. "You have a unique combination of talents—physical ability, quickness, and daring, of course, like all of us—but you also have a knack for ancient languages, as I've been privileged to observe. The progress you've made with hieroglyphics is quite remarkable. And you are also an excellent . . . actor.'' Lequeu held up a deprecating hand. "Meant as a compliment. I want you to join Catherine and me in one of our special projects.''

"Sure, how can I help you?'' said Blake.

"There are thousands of papyri in the basement of the Louvre which have been seen once or twice by scholars but never published,'' Lequeu said. "Some do not appear in the catalogues of Napoleon's expedition or any later expedition. Some, like this one''—he gestured to a hand-drawn reproduction of a papyrus scroll that Catherine had withdrawn from her portfolio—"are vital to our mission. Our job is to locate them and remove them to safety.''

"Remove?'' Guy asked. He peered curiously at the reproduction.

"To save them from mold and rot,'' Lequeu said. "And so that they may be returned to their rightful inheritors. I want you to familiarize yourself with this reproduction so that you will recognize the original when you see it. We can give you an approximate idea of its location, but you will have to find it yourself.''

Blake bent over the engraving that Catherine had laid on the desk. It consisted of numerous triangular drawings together with lengthy notation. "What's that supposed to be? It almost looks like instructions for building a pyramid.''

"You are partly right,'' said Lequeu. "Pyramids were actually models of the heavens, and one of their functions was to act as observatories. This papyrus apparently gives instructions for a model pyramid that could be used to locate a particular place in the Egyptian sky.''

"What place?''

"We're uncertain,'' Catherine said, speaking for the first time. "This copy contains many errors, but if the original is intact, I'll be able to reconstruct a star map from the information it contains.''

Blake looked at her curiously. ''You're a mathematician?''

She glanced at Lequeu, who smiled suavely. ''As I said, Guy, we all have multiple talents. You will have to exercise several of yours in locating the original of this papyrus.''

''And when I find it?'' Blake asked.

''Why then,'' Lequeu said, ''you will steal it.''

Blake hardly hesitated before he nodded. ''I'll be honored to help any way I can, sir.''

''Good man,'' Lequeu said, and he began to give Blake the details of how the theft was to be accomplished.

The very next afternoon Blake walked across the Ponts des Arts, dressed as an ordinary tourist, intending to visit the Louvre. His purpose was to scout the place for the mission he would undertake within the next few weeks. Inside the famous museum's crowded anteroom he stopped at a public information booth and made a quick transmission to his home in London. It had to be quick—any lengthy use of his home computer required cooling its central processor, and there was no way he could do that remotely.

There was a book in Blake's private collection, and yesterday he'd found a chip copy of it in the Bibliothèque Nationale. From it he derived a list of numbers. What he transmitted to his computer was that list.

Then he asked his computer to send a one-sentence faxgram to Port Hesperus, return code encrypted: ''Let's play hide-and-seek. . . .''

Blake thought he had been discreet. He also assumed that he was no longer under surveillance by the Athanasians. He was mistaken on both counts.

7

Two weeks later: after a fortnight's fast trip on a Space Board cutter, Sparta rode a shrieking shuttle into the atmosphere of Earth. The space plane winged out of its hot ionization blanket into a sky like a clear blue ballroom paved with veined marble.

Sparta peered out the passenger window. You could say a few things for Earth, she mused. It was bigger than Port Hesperus and had more trees, if less good living space *per capita*. It was cooler than Venus and warmer than most other places in the solar system, and it had air you could breathe— most of the time. But as the shuttle swiftly descended toward the cloud deck, the clouds that looked like milky marble came to resemble clotted cream, floating on weak coffee; the smog layer rose quickly, cutting off visibility.

Sparta's badge and her orders took her swiftly through customs. In twenty minutes she was on a magneplane, heading across the smoking Jersey marshes toward Manhattan. Its towers gleamed through the murk like the Emerald City.

Manhattan in August would test any space-wandering human's affection for the home world. Not that North America's premier demonstration city was dirty or inefficient; that would no more have been tolerated in 21st century Manhattan than in 20th century Disney World. It was the season, the latitude, the natural climate of the place that turned it into a late-summer steam bath.

Civilization made it worse: on the east coast of North America, as all over the globe, air pollution continued unabated into the fourth century of the industrial revolution, despite "clean" power from fusion reactors and orbiting solar-microwave stations. Many small nations were still dependent on coal and oil, and everywhere factory smokestacks continued to mainline carbon into the atmosphere. Light from the sun streamed in, but reradiant heat from the Earth was trapped; global temperatures inched upward, in a planetary greenhouse not unlike that which had melted and seared Venus a billion years ago.

There weren't many people in the canyons of midtown this afternoon; everybody was staying inside, where the climate was quite unnatural, and the temperature—traditional for summer in Manhattan—was near freezing. Calculate the power loss from all that heat exchange, convert it to its waste carbon equivalent, and observe the positive feedback loop: watch Earth trying to imitate Venus.

Sparta, stepping fresh from the air-conditioned magneplane, was sweat-soaked and giddy before she had made it through the revolving doors into the marble reception hall of the Board of Space Control's Earth Central headquarters. Inside, she shivered involuntarily. She had been in this building—the old United Nations building, overlooking the East River—just once before, the day the commander had packed her off to Port Hesperus.

That time too she'd come straight from Newark, where she'd been working undercover on the shuttleport docks as an agent for C & I branch—customs and immigration. That time, when she'd finally tracked down the commander, he'd been wearing his dress blues; she'd been wearing a dock rat's overalls. She hadn't been able to climb out of them until she was on her way to Venus. This time she was wearing *her* dress blues, determined to meet him on more nearly equal terms—even though the armpits of her blue worsted jacket were showing wet black patches.

She rode an elevator to the fortieth floor. She flashed her badge at the sergeant who guarded the commander's door. "Troy to see the commander."

"He's in the sports hall," said the sergeant, a rawboned Russian woman with a blond haystack hairdo. "Forty-four floors down. Ask at the desk."

"I'll wait here until he's through," Sparta said.

"Troy, yes? He specially wants to see you, as soon as you enter—'no matter what I am doing,' he said." The sergeant smirked at her. She was the type who enjoyed other people's troubles. "You had better go down now, Inspector."

When she got off the elevator in the basement, Sparta had to pause a moment to quell her rebellious stomach. The underground gym was rank with the odor of sweat and fungus, and the air was full of steam where the cold of the air conditioner met the heat of the saunas and pool and steam room.

The locker attendant pointed her in the direction of the pool. She walked down the corridor past dripping glass-walled handball and squash courts, where men and women were hurling themselves at the walls, trying to keep little black and blue rubber balls in the air. The tiled passageway turned a right angle and opened on the pool.

The far walls of the enormous room were obscured in mist; its pillars and terraces were opulently paved with blue and gold mosaics. Bare male and female bodies splashed in the chemical-blue water; their voices echoed from the hard walls. Sparta paced the poolside, peering into the mist. The blue-gold light was diffuse, coming out of the fog from everywhere at once, and her enhanced vision was useless.

She heard wet barefoot footsteps behind her and turned to find a lifeguard, dressed only in a white towel cinched around his muscular waist. "Can't be in here like that, Inspector. Dressing room's back and to your right."

"Would you find Commander . . ."

"We don't page people," he said, cutting her off. "Outside."

The big locker room was full of athletic men and women changing in and out of their clothes, using their lunch hour for exercise instead of food. Sparta found an unoccupied locker. Her dress uniform had already melted in the steam, surrendering its every carefully arranged crease. She stripped, hung up her clothes, and reprogrammed the locker's lock.

Back at the pool, she dove into the water, as bare as the rest of the lunch-hour crew but aware of herself as they were not, even though she knew her body's strangeness was not visible on its surface. She paddled slowly through the fog, keeping her nose a millimeter or two above water, searching for the commander. She moved the entire length of the Olympic pool in the slow lane, not exerting herself beyond a lazy dog paddle. As she neared the far end, she saw his blue eyes glint in the mist. His hands were clasped behind his head; his elbows were hooked on the ledge at waterline to keep him from sinking.

She swam within a meter of him, then back-paddled. "Commander."

"Troy. Took your time." His Canadian-accented voice was so hoarse it was almost a whisper, and his lean face was creased beyond his years. His skin was two-tone, burned mahogany at the wrists and from the neck up, a ruddy tan everywhere else she could see, even underwater. He'd been using the ultraviolet lamps in an attempt to even out his color, but it was hard to disguise that deep-space burn.

"What am I going to do with you, Troy?"

Uh, oh, she thought, that sounds like it's back to Newark after all. "That's what I'm here to find out, sir."

"You're not playing straight with me."

"Sir?"

"Think I kept you on Port Hesperus just to babysit a couple of archaeologists?"

"No, because the Space Board office was understaffed."

"Surprised you bought that phony excuse."

Sparta paddled to the wall and hooked an elbow on the ledge. "It seems that you're not playing straight with me either, sir."

"I sent you to Port Hesperus to look into the *Star Queen* incident. By the time you got through we had a couple of extra bodies, a wrecked ship, a hole in the station, and one of our own people turned into a human vegetable. After all the ruckus, I thought it was time I did a little investigation of my own. Without you around to edit the files for me." He looked at her sidelong. "One of your many peculiar talents."

She said nothing. To deny that she had frequently rewritten her own biography, keeping one step ahead of security checks and other inquiries, would be foolish.

The commander ran his hand through a brush of gray hair; each upright hair gleamed with a bead of condensed moisture. "So I interviewed your old bosses, your old teachers at business school, high school. None of them recognized your holo."

"I wasn't a memorable student."

"Although some of them recovered their memories when I showed them your transcripts. Or claimed they did. Then I tried your family."

"They're dead."

"Yes, that's what the death certificates say. I

went to that funeral home out on Long Island. Nobody could really remember, but sure enough, they had records too. And the urns are in the niche."

"Cremations are routine, I believe." Sparta was staring at the water. Her memories were different than she pretended, but not very different: her parents really had been cremated, in a manner of speaking, if what she'd been told was the truth.

"I had a chemical analysis done on the ashes," the commander said. "Some people would apologize for that, but I think you understand why I had to do it."

"I could say I understand," she said, "or I could say it makes me ill." But not, she thought, as sick as it made me to acquire those authentic human ashes. "You did all this investigation personally?"

"That's right. Got me out of the office for hours at a time."

"May I see your results?"

"Would it stop you if I said no?" His seamed face twisted in a predatory smile. "As a matter of fact you won't have access to my results, because they're not in the system. They're in here." He tapped his skull.

Neither of them said anything for half a minute. They both seemed intent on the plash and ripple of the pool, the grunts and splashes of the lap swimmers passing in adjacent lanes.

"Ever hear of the SPARTA project?" he asked.

"Yes, I've heard of it," Sparta said, "I read some things about it a few years ago, when I was in I.P. branch."

"What's your understanding of SPARTA?"

"Well, it stands for SPecified Aptitude Resource Training and Assessment. It was an educational program that was supposed to develop multiple intelligences—languages, math, music, social skills, so on. On Port Hesperus I met a guy who was actually in the project himself—"

"Blake Redfield."

"That's right."

"The expert on old books."

"That's right."

"You'd never met Blake Redfield before?"

Sparta expelled her breath, making the water ripple under her nose. "I have a good memory, Commander—"

"An extraordinary memory," he said.

"—and yes, when I saw him on Port Hesperus, I knew I'd seen him before. Two years ago he tried to pick me up on a street corner, here in Manhattan. He followed me for a couple of blocks. I lost him."

"What happened to SPARTA?"

"I heard it went out of business. The people who ran it died in a chopper crash."

"About the same time as Mr. and Mrs. Troy of West Quogue, New York, died in a car crash."

"I don't give much thought to meaningless coincidences," she said. "Why did you really bring me down here, sir?"

"I wanted to see if you were a real woman. You look like one, anyway." He appeared to be studying his toes, a meter and a half under the water. "Okay, here's what I want you to do. I want you to get a physical from the clinic here. I've set it up already—results for my eyes only. Then I want you to take some time off. R & R. Go anywhere you want. I'll reach you when I need you."

"Anywhere?"

"On Earth, I mean."

"Thanks. On my salary, I'll tour lower Manhattan."

"Expenses paid—within reason. Save your receipts."

"I'll have a ball."

"I thought maybe you'd like to check in with Blake Redfield in London."

"Why would I want to do that?" She stared at

him with the blankest expression she could muster.

Sapphire blue eyes set in a weathered mahogany face stared back at her. ''Because I think you like the guy, that's why.'' He drew up his knees and pushed his feet against the wall of the pool, launching himself outward, plowing the water in a fast, inelegant Australian crawl.

She watched him disappear in the mist. What was he up to, with his private investigations, with all those disingenuous questions about SPARTA, about Blake?

She resists our authority

William, she's a child

He could be one of them. He could have set her up for the *Star Queen* investigation—a setup it certainly had been. But if he knew who she was, why warn her? Why have her tested? If he knew who she was, he knew everything.

So he wasn't one of them—but maybe he was onto them. He could suspect that *she* was one of them. Or that Blake was. Or he could be merely curious.

Sparta was an anomaly, no doubt of that, despite her intention to maintain a low profile. Whatever was on the commander's mind, she had no doubt that she would be followed wherever she went on her ''R & R.''

Half an hour later she presented herself at the clinic on the thirty-fifth floor. What the commander was looking for, she didn't know; she herself didn't know everything she might have to hide. But she'd gotten used to medical examinations.

Clinics were friendlier than they had been once, a bit more civilized. You checked in at the little window and took a seat in the waiting room and skimmed the latest *Smithsonian* on the tabletop videoplate. When they called your name, you spent twenty minutes walking from one room to another, never taking your clothes off, never getting stuck with a needle, and then you were through. The data they got painlessly, had it been a century earlier, would have needed a week of insult and embarrassment at the Harvard Medical School.

Technicians still collected various bodily fluids for analysis, but most tests, and most treatments, involved no big machines, no nauseating drugs, no painful injections or traumatic incisions. Diagnostic gadgets that had weighed tons when they were invented were now hardly bigger than a dentist's chair, thanks to room-temperature superconductors and high-field-density magnets. Thanks to miniaturized supercomputers, they were also highly accurate.

In one room a magnetic imager made a couple of passes at your body showing your anatomical structures in detail and revealing your internal chemistries as well. In another room a nurse handed you a tasty radio-opaque cocktail; it entered your bloodstream in seconds and displayed the fine structure of your circulatory system—everywhere, even in the brain— to stimulated X-ray beams from a radiation-pipe the technician played over you. In a third room you were served another cocktail; the kicker in it was a mix of isotopes hooked to tailored enzymes that, once they got into you, swarmed to outline your nervous system before they died in a burst of radio emission. Your blood chemistry could be determined without drawing a visible amount of blood—but you still had to pee in a jar.

The supercomputers went to work on the data instantly, constructing layer upon layer of fine-grain images, columns of numbers, graphic curves—pictures of structures, functions, and purposes . . . and pathologies, if any.

The machines could not be completely fooled, but some tests could be avoided. Unless a person complains of arthritis, or has some other specific problem, the fingertips are not usually subject to inspection. Sparta had never mentioned her PIN spines; if they were discovered, she had a story ready—its cover already planted—about cut-rate cosmetic surgery. After all, PIN spines had actually become fashionable in certain circles; they weren't as easy to lose as standard I.D. slivers.

More to the point, Sparta had a degree of control over her metabolism that would have astounded her examiners. She was convincingly allergic to the more sensitive chemical probes, and as for the rest, the trick was to understand what the technicians were expecting to find and give it to them, with just enough variation from the norm to persuade them that they weren't inspecting a practice dummy.

Not all of Sparta's nonstandard anatomy needed hiding. Her right eye was a functional macrozoom not because of any detectable change in the structure of the eye itself, but because of cellular manipulations of her optic nerve and visual-association cortex. Her analytical sense of smell, her infrared vision, her tunable hearing were similarly due to neuronal "rewiring," not to detectable rebuilding. Her eidetic memory involved only changes in the neurochemical transmitters of the hippocampus, which were not accessible to standard diagnostics.

Only her raw number-crunching abilities involved a noticeable change in the density of forebrain tissue. Time after time, fascinated doctors had been convinced that the lump just beneath Sparta's forehead, just to the right of where Hindus and Buddhists locate the soul's eye, was a tumor. But repeated neurological tests had revealed no apparent effect on her perception, higher processes, or behavior, and the "tumor" had shown no change in several years; if it was a tumor, it was evidently benign.

On a grosser scale, the sheets of polymer structures under her diaphragm could not be hidden, only explained away. The "accident" she'd had when she was sixteen served that purpose. The polymer sheets were experimental tissue replacements, necessitated by abdominal trauma, and she had the scars to prove it. There was a steel staple in her breastbone, holding her once-crushed chest together. Her ribs and arms were threaded with grafts of artificial bone, of an experimental ceramic type.

Who, after all, would even have thought to ask if these crude structures were really batteries, an oscillator, a dipole microwave antennae . . . ?

Sparta suspected that one reason her explanations were persuasive was because the people who had implanted the real systems had taken care to disguise them. She had adopted the sort of cover story she was meant to have, although she couldn't recall ever have been rehearsed in it.

A half-hour after she entered the clinic, she walked out. She could have had the results an hour after that, if the commander hadn't put them under embargo. Sparta wouldn't know whether she'd gotten away with the deception again unless he chose to tell her.

She took an old-fashioned subway train to within a couple of blocks of the NoHo condo-apt she shared with two other women. She hadn't seen either of them in months, and rarely before that. When she let herself into the place neither of them was home. She barely glanced around before going straight to her own bedroom. It was as severely neat as she had left it, plantless, walls bare, bed made; only a fine coat of dust on every hard surface and a small stack of fax mail under the reader on her bureau hinted that she had been gone for months. The mail was advertising—she tossed the whole pile in the chute.

Five minutes later she had repacked her duffle and left the apartment. She had no idea when she would return.

* * *

Back on the subway platform, wilting in the heat, packed for the transatlantic supersonic jitney, on her way to London . . .

She wanted to see Blake. But she didn't want to see Blake. She liked Blake. She was afraid of Blake. Maybe she was in love with Blake.

She hated herself like this, when her brain went nothing but blah, blah, blah. She was hung on a cusp. She wanted to find out what had become of her parents, and Blake could have learned something. She wanted revenge for what had been done to her—or did she? She also wanted to survive. A few months on Port Hesperus, just being a cop, and her conviction had begun to dissolve.

Maybe the commander was right. Maybe she really needed a rest.

The antique subway train clattered into the station, glistening with bright yellow paint. She stepped onto the squeaky-clean car. It was empty except for a stylishly dressed young couple—on their way home from classes at NYU, to judge by the shiny black datapads they balanced on their knees.

Or they could be a tail.

Sparta sat by herself, beside the doors at the far end of the car. She pulled her jacket closer about her shoulders and brooded. The commander had boxed her in. She hardly had a choice but to go to Blake, to find out what Blake had to tell her. To be with him.

8

Sparta cautiously climbed the narrow, smelly stairs to Blake Redfield's flat in the City of London. In her trip from Manhattan she had taken every precaution to evade pursuit that was consistent with her pose of innocence. She had not tried to call Blake, either by personal commlink or public phonelink. She had made her travel arrangements as discreetly as she could, then changed them at the last minute, spending two days on a trip that could have been completed in an afternoon. All this would be child's play for the commander's people if they were tailing her, but she didn't dare try any fancy stuff.

London in the late summer was hardly better than Manhattan. Today the air was so saturated with humidity it had begun to rain. Drenched from within and without, she rapped on Blake's door.

There was no answer. She listened, then ran her hand lightly over the jambs. Her palm hovered above the alphanumeric keypad of his outdated magnetic lock, parsing its field patterns. In moments, guided by intuition, she had decoded its lengthy combination, $CH3C6H2N023246$. Which was very like Blake, thus predictable, and therefore rather stupid of him: minus subscripts, parentheses, and commas, it was the chemical formula of TNT.

Sparta's fingers danced on the keypad. Before she pushed the door open she hesitated. Blake wasn't stupid, of course. Blake was the sort to warn unexpected guests and, should they ignore his warning, leave them a little greeting card. A grain or two of TNT, or more likely nitroglycerin, that sort of thing. She bent her nose close to the strike plate and sniffed.

There was no sign of any chemical more unusual than light machine oil. There was no sign that the door had been used recently; in the infrared, it was cooler than the ambient air.

But the last person who had touched this doorknob was not Blake. Blake's unmistakably spicy aroma was overlaid by that of someone Sparta didn't recognize. A female.

Perhaps it was his landlady. Whoever she was, she was not inside now. Her prints were stone cold—more than a week old, Sparta guessed—and the lingering odor of perfume that came through the crack where the heavy door badly fitted its ancient frame was stale and so faint only someone with Sparta's sensitivity could have detected it. Nevertheless Sparta slipped her hands into her pockets and withdrew a pair of transparently thin polymer gloves. Someone had been in Blake's flat since he'd been there, and she could come back. Sparta had no intention of leaving traces of her own visit.

She pushed gently on the door and stepped back as it sprang open. There were no fireworks.

She peered cautiously into Blake's sitting room. She had never been here before. Her eager curiosity threatened to overwhelm her caution. But she sensed the current of the pressure-sensor wires under the kilim on the varnished oak floor, and she noted, mounted in the corners of the ceiling moldings, the movement detectors, invisibly small to anyone else.

She raised her arms, feeling for their wave patterns. Her belly burned for an instant, and three quick bursts disarmed Blake's alarms. Leaving her duffel bag in the hall, she stepped tentatively into the room.

There was a mullioned bay window to her left, shadowed by a big elm outside. Heavy rain continually rustled the elm leaves. The pallid green light of late afternoon filtered through the rain-streaked panes and gave the interior of the flat the watery feel of an aquarium.

The walls of the room were lined with bookshelves; the books were stacked on their shelves like vertical irregular bricks, their spines a faded spectrum from ruddy brown to slate-blue. There were albums of recent book chips and older books recorded on disk and tape, and an impressive number of real books made of paper and cloth and leather, many crumbling inside their clear plastic envelopes, others in pristine condition.

Where the walls were not obscured by bookshelves they were painted with creamy enamel and hung with framed manuscript pages and early 20th-century European oils.

Sparta retrieved her duffel and left it inside the door, which she closed carefully behind her. She moved through the quiet rooms. Blake lived well on his consulting fees, not to mention the income from a sizable trust fund; these gave ample play to his collector's passion and his taste in Chinese furniture and Oriental weavings.

Her eye zoomed in on surfaces and textures, probing shadowed crevices. Her ears listened beyond the human frequency range, below the human threshold of audibility. Her nose sniffed for chemical hints. If there were booby traps or hidden transmitters or receivers in the room, she would home in on them.

Blake had left his apartment at least two weeks ago, perhaps much longer. There was no sign that the circumstances of his leaving were unusual. But everywhere the prints of his woman visitor were more recent, if only by a few days; nowhere did his prints overlay hers.

Sparta looked into the bedroom. His bed was made with fresh sheets, and his closet was full of suits and shirts and shoes, everything from black leather pumps to red high-top moon boots. Blake was quite a dandy, but if anything was missing from this extensive wardrobe, Sparta would not know. She noted that the woman had pawed through his things.

His bathroom cabinet was fully stocked: Blake's cordless toothbrush was there, and a chemosonic shaver, and shelves full of deodorants and after-shaves and other nostrums. The woman had been here too, since Blake had left.

The refrigerator in the kitchen alcove held a six-pack of Czechoslovakian lager—his taste for cold beer confirmed that Blake was, after all, American—but it held no eggs or milk or vegetables or other perishables, only a few hard cheeses and a jar of mustard. The stove was spotless. There were no dirty dishes in the sink. The recycling chute hadn't been used for a week. Either Blake had planned his departure, or someone had cleaned up after him.

His back porch—a tiny enclosed landing, really—had been converted to a workshop; through its single window she could make out a row of brick-walled back gardens, trim and middle class. Rows of neatly labeled bottles of chemicals lined the wall above a table that was anything but neat; its surface was crowded with scraps of microlectronic substrate. There were traces of numerous nitrogen-based compounds and splashes of solified metal on the carbon-fiber work surface. All of the debris was cold.

The copper pipes of the kitchen plumbing to Blake's flat and the ones above and below his were exposed in one corner of the little workroom, next to a small laundry sink. But Blake didn't do his laundry here. The round metal gadget stuck on the end of the faucet was a mainframe computer, a micro-super smaller than the water filter it was packaged in. The computer worked through complexification and decomplexification of artificial enzymes; the thing got so hot when it was working at capacity that it needed a steady flow of coolant.

Blake's woman visitor had twisted the faucet handle, and she'd played with the remote keyboard on Blake's desk. Sparta wondered if she'd gained access to its memory.

Sparta turned on the cold water. She slipped the glove off her right hand and thrust her spines into the ports on the back of the keyboard. She got past the computer's quite competent security in a split second, and its informational guts started to spill faster than the steaming water that was already pouring into the sink. From one sprung booby trap in Blake's security—and several yet unsprung— Sparta knew that no snoopers had gained entry.

The flatscreen glowed. Anyone watching Sparta would have seen a woman staring as if hypnotized at a meaningless jumble of alphanumerics and scrambled graphics spilling across the flatscreen, but she was not seeing it; the data was flowing directly into her neural structures.

The little computer was so capacious that it took Sparta several seconds just to read the directory of its stored programs and files. There were knowledge-based programs for chemical analysis, some having to do with explosives, corrosives, incendiaries, poison gases, and other such pleasantries, others having to do with the analysis of papers and inks. There were powerful programs for modeling the complex interactions of shockwaves, programs so intricate they showed that Blake's interest in making things go boom was more than a mischievous hobby.

Of the files, the biggest were bibliographies. Sparta would not have been surprised if every edition of every book known to have been printed in English for the past three hundred years was listed here.

But one miniscule file called attention to itself. Its name was README.

She smiled. Blake knew Sparta as few others did. One thing he knew about her was that she could crack any computer almost effortlessly, although he didn't know *how* she did it, and she had no intention of telling him. She had no doubt that README was meant for her.

README, however, turned out to be unreadable. Not that it was inaccessible, but it contained nothing except an apparently meaningless list of numbers. The numbers were arranged in groups: 311, 314, 3222, 3325, 3447, 3519 . . . a total of 102 such groups in all, none with less than three numbers or more than six, and none repeated. The first few groups began with the numeral 3, the next few began with 4, and so on, in increasing numerical order. The last groups all began with 10.

Sparta smiled. She recognized the list for what it was and instantly committed it to memory.

So Blake wanted to play hide-and-seek, did he? She replaced her glove, turned off his computer, and left his workshop precisely as she had found it. She slipped quickly and quietly into the main room of the flat, moving like a shadow in the deepening shadows, grinning a cat's satisfied smile.

Outside, the rain still drummed on the elm leaves. The light was greener.

By pushing her nostrils close to the books on their shelves, she could inhale the residual odor of the hands that had touched them, the amino acids and other chemicals that were as distinctive to individuals as their fingerprints. Only Blake had handled

the plastic sleeves in which they were protected—
Blake and, in a few cases, the mysterious woman.

The woman had handled only a few books. She'd
pulled books from the shelves here and there, apparently at random—unlike Sparta, she had evidently had no idea what she was looking for.

Sparta was looking for a specific book. Blake had
left Sparta a message hidden in a book, a book he
knew Sparta would recognize as unique in a way
that one else could. The list of numbers in README
was a book cipher.

A book had drawn them both to Port Hesperus
and had served to reintroduce them, a copy of the
fabulously valuable privately printed first edition
of *The Seven Pillars of Wisdom*, by T. E. Lawrence.
There were no copies of any version of *The Seven
Pillars of Wisdom* on Blake's shelves, but they had
shared many other books in the past, when both
of them had been children in SPARTA. Among
Blake's collection of 19th- and 20th-century fiction,
memoirs, travel journals, essays, and other literary
letters, one book was an anomaly, an anomaly only
someone who knew Blake's collection intimately—
or someone who had been part of SPARTA—would
recognize.

She pulled it from the shelf and looked at it. The
eye printed on the jacket stared back at her. In the
more than one hundred years since it had been
published, the bright red of its dust jacket had faded
to pale pink, but its bold title was clearly visible
through the plastic: *Frames of Mind, The Theory of
Multiple Intelligences*, by Howard Gardner. It was a
gifted psychologist's exposition of what he called
"a new theory of intellectual competences," and it
had been a major influence on Sparta's parents
when they conceived the SPARTA project.

Sparta removed the book from its plastic sleeve,
studied its cover a moment, then carefully opened
it. She smiled at the dedication, "For Ellen." That
was a different Ellen in a different century—a real

Ellen, unlike the fictitious Ellen Troy—but she had no doubt that Blake meant her to take it personally.

Yes, she was now "in the mood"—the right frame of mind.

She turned to the first chapter, "The Idea of Multiple Intelligences." It began, "A young girl spends an hour with an examiner. . . ." Sparta knew the passage well, a brief parable of a youngster whose diverse gifts are summed up in a single round number, an I.Q. The thrust of Gardner's argument, and of the program Sparta's parents had created, was to lift the dead hand of I.Q.

The first page of this chapter was numbered 3 in the book. And the first letter of the first line was A. It was the letter to which README had directed her. The first group of numbers in README was 311, indicating page 3, line 1, letter 1. The next group of numbers in README was 314; it directed her to the fourth letter in the same line, which was u.

README's next group was 3222, which could be read as page 3, line 2, letter 22, but could also be read as page 3, line 22, letter 2, or even as page 32, line 2, letter 2. The steady increase of the initial digits told Sparta that Blake had used the simplest form of the cipher, taking each letter serially. Thus the first digit or two would always be the page number, from page 3 to page 10. The second one or two digits would count down the lines of the page, and the remaining digit or two would indicate the placement of the letter on the line.

There was little chance of ambiguity in this system—but it was bad cipher practice, the kind of regularity that instantly reveals the existence of a book cipher even to an amateur cryptanalyst. If the hidden message had been in plain language, the cipher could have been largely solved without even knowing which book was the key.

The message was not in plain language. When, after a few seconds of concentration and page flipping, Sparta had deciphered the last group, 102749, the entire message of 102 letters read thus:

aukcfkucaqnsrtgaldxqzlhofaiktbhobodkupkcdutse kavtvrbkqholskcdltpaudzdlybekybjtalqorvqmxhjzhudyfe siqzef.

Sparta was not surprised. In fact, this is what she had expected. Blake's invitation to play hide-and-seek had enjoined her to "play fair." The Playfair cipher was one of the most famous in history.

Even if a cryptanalyst knew that a message was enciphered in Playfair, the text was exceedingly difficult to decipher without the key. But Sparta already had the key. The key to Blake's every move in this game of hide-and-seek was their shared experience of SPARTA.

With this key she mentally constructed a Playfair alphabet square:

S	P	A	R	T
B	C	D	E	F
G	H	IJ	K	L
M	N	O	Q	U
V	W	X	Y	Z

She broke the string of book-cipher letters into pairs and swiftly performed the transformation. The first pair in the cipher was *au*. The line in the square that contained A intersected with the column containing U: the letter at the intersection was T. The line containing U intersected with the column containing A: the letter at the intersection was O. The first pair of letters in Blake's message was TO.

Pairs of cipher letters in the same line of the square were exchanged for the letters to their left. Pairs of cipher letters in the same column were exchanged for the letters above them. Soon Sparta had Blake's prepared plaintext: TO HE LE NF RO MP AR IS IF YO UF IN DT HI SF IN DM EI NT HE FO RT RE SX SZ SE EK IN GT HE FI RS TO FX FI

VE RE VE LA TI ON SY OU WI LX LN EX ED AG UY DE.

With the extra letters eliminated, the message read, TO HELEN FROM PARIS IF YOU FIND THIS FIND ME IN THE FORTRESS SEEKING THE FIRST OF FIVE REVELATIONS YOU WILL NEED A GUYDE.*

She laughed with delight. Blake was indeed leading her on a merry chase, and this time the clues were a little less obvious. She slipped *Frames of Mind* back into its protective envelope and replaced it on the shelf. She curled up in Blake's big red leather armchair and stared out the window at the falling rain, and the perpetually moving leaves and the shadows pooling in the branches of the elm, while she pondered the riddle.

TO HELEN FROM PARIS. Why Helen instead of Ellen? Because Helen of Troy was from Sparta—and Paris was her lover.

Where was this FORTRESS in which she was supposed to find him? Surely not Troy itself, the mound of Hissarlik on the Asian shore of the Dardanelles; two centuries after Heinrich Schliemann had devastated the ruins of ancient Troy, leaving what he found exposed to the elements, the towers of Ilium had melted to a featureless pile of mud. In this they shared the fate of almost every ancient site that eager archaeologists had laid bare in the 19th and 20th centuries.

The myth of Troy had nothing to do with it. Blake was not referring to himself as Paris, he was *in* Paris.

The Bastille having been torn down, the fortress of Paris, begun in the late 12th century, must be the Louvre. Blake was at the Louvre, SEEKING THE FIRST OF FIVE REVELATIONS. Sparta had heard of people seeking revelations, or enlightenment, or

*The Playfair cipher system is explained in the appendix.

whatever, but it seemed odd to seek five of them. And in order?

Her eye sought out the antique Bibles that rested on a bottom shelf of Blake's bookcase. In a moment she was out of the chair and had one of the weighty books open, turning the pages until she had found the Book of Revelation, chapter five, verse one. In the translation she had selected, the Jerusalem Bible, the verse read, "I saw that in the right hand of the One sitting on the throne there was a scroll that had writing on back and front and was sealed with seven seals." A footnote explained that the scroll was "a roll of papyrus in which God's hitherto secret decrees are written." It seemed doubtful that Blake was on the trail of God's secret decrees, but he might well be looking for a papyrus in the Louvre's vast collection of Egyptian antiquities.

But if Blake was in Paris, working in the Louvre's Egyptian collection, why would she NEED A GUYDE to find him? Why was GUYDE misspelled?

Perhaps somewhere in the process of switching one letter for another, tediously counting tiny letters in a big book, writing down all those numbers, Blake had made a mistake. But the Playfair system rendered an accidental substitution unlikely in this case, for in the alphabetical square based on the keyword SPARTA, the letter Y and the letter I are not in the same row or in the same column: moreover, one lies above and one lies below the other member of the plaintext pair, the letter U. Thus they could not have been mistaken for each other under any of the rules of transformation, which change the pair UY to *qz*, as found by Sparta, but would have changed the pair UI to *lo*.

So either Blake was being cute and fake-medieval, or he was telling her something. She knew she would not be able to push the last bit of the jigsaw puzzle into place just by sitting here and armchairing it. Sparta jumped up. She spent three minutes insuring that everything in Blake's apartment was exactly where she'd found it, then picked up her duffel, reset the alarms, and went out the door, hurrying to catch the next magneplane to Paris.

She had no way of knowing that she was already a week too late.

A week before Sparta left London, Blake spent the night in a Paris closet. . . .

Dawn seeped under the closet door in a thin gray plane of light. Through the thin wood panel Blake heard footsteps, a grumbled curse. He yawned and shook his head vigorously. He'd been awake for two hours, and before that he'd dozed fitfully among the mops and brooms. He was hungry and sleepy and stiff. He wished he had a cup of espresso, rank and black.

He was also nervous. He'd half-hoped Ellen would show up and extricate him from this fix, but it looked like he was going to have to go through with it.

He opened the door and backed carefully out of the closet, carrying a bucket of varnish remover and a fistful of rags and brushes. His long blue dustcoat was covered with paint smears. With his head down, fiddling with his grip on his thinner can, he fell in with the other painters and carpenters on their way down to the repository.

It was a Monday morning; the Louvre was closed to all but scholars, workers, and staff.

"Bon matin, Monsieur Guy," someone said to him.

"Matin," he grumbled. He didn't look at the man. Presumably he was the foreman with whom things had been "arranged," the man who'd been bribed—or blackmailed, or terrorized—not to notice the extra man on his crew.

The workers went down the broad sandstone stairs. There were five men and women ahead of him, all dressed as he was in blue smocks. A security guard followed, a gray-haired gentleman in an old-fashioned black uniform that was shiny with age. They walked down an echoing basement hall, three of them continuing toward rooms where stacks of stored paintings gathered dust, Blake and the others turning into a long, low-ceiling room, fitted with ancient incandescent light bulbs that burned yellow on the low current. Rows of heavy wooden cabinets stood in the center of the room. Fading lithographs of Egyptian ruins hung on the dingy walls.

After a few minutes of grumbling and stalling, the workers set about their task of removing three centuries of blackened varnish from the woodwork. Blake let his companions work their way away from him, toward the distant dark corners of the file room. The foreman ignored him.

An hour went by this way, and Blake fell further and further behind. No one really cared about the work; no one really thought it necessary. The government had provided authorization, and some bureaucrat had seen to it that the funds kept flowing, even into the deepest crypts of the Louvre.

The others were concentrating their effort at the end of the room, and Blake was down on the floor, half-hidden by the rows of massive oak cabinets. Blake looked up from the dirty baseboard. The bored security guard was somewhere in the hall.

Blake crept down an aisle between the cabinets. He found the drawer Lequeu had suggested, second from the top. He pulled it open. There, lying on cotton batting in crumbling cardboard trays, without other protection, lay a dozen scrolls of papyrus. Working as swiftly and as carefully as he could, he unrolled each of them far enough to determine if they matched the reproduction he had committed to memory.

None did. He closed that drawer and tried the next. He worked his way through the entire cabinet without success.

Blake peered nervously over the top of the cabinet. His fellow workers were still blithely ignoring him. He ducked down again, and pondered whether to try the cabinet to the right or the one to the left. Or had Lequeu gotten the wrong aisle entirely? It was like wondering what to do with a wrong phone number—probably only one digit was wrong, but which one?

For no good reason, Blake picked the cabinet to the left and started with the same drawer. Pinned to the cotton beside one of the scrolls, third from the left, was a faded notation in steel-point script, identifying its provenance: "*près de Heliopolis, 1799.*" Blake's hopes revived.

In 1801 the English army, after a three-year blockade, had at last landed troops on the coast of Egypt and forced the surrender of Napoleon's forces. The Man of Destiny himself had long departed, leaving among the old ruins the ruins of his dream of a new Egyptian empire under the flag of the French Revolution. He also left behind the magnificent Institut d'Egypte, its ranks of scholars, and its magnificent collection of antiquities, gathered in the course of three years of intense acquisition in the valley of the Nile. By the terms of the surrender the English took the lot, including the crown jewel, the as yet undeciphered Rosetta Stone.

The French tried to keep the Stone by claiming that it was the personal property of their commander, General Menou, and not subject to the terms of surrender, but the English would have none of it. The Rosetta Stone and much other booty was shipped off to the British Museum, where it still resides, "a glorious trophy of British arms," as the British commander phrased it.

Yet there were bits of carved and painted stone and a lot of fragmented old scrolls the British magnanimously allowed the French to keep. The fate of these cast-off treasures was also to be removed from the land where they had been made, some to be exhibited in that hoard of glorious trophies, the Louvre, some to languish in basement drawers, accessible only to determined scholars and to termites.

Blake carefully unrolled the brittle scroll, and immediately knew he had found what he'd come for. The scroll would not have recommended itself to a casual researcher. There were geometric sketches on it, but it was not a geometry text. There were references to Re, the god of the sun, but it was not a religious text. There were fragments of what surely were traveller's tales, but it was not a work of geography. The scroll was full of lacunae, and the surviving text was a puzzle.

Only a member of the *prophetae* would have recognized it for what it was. Blake was no professional mathematician or astronomer, but his visual and spatial intelligences were highly developed. Following Catherine's hint, he had spent private hours studying maps of the night sky, and he had deduced that the pyramid outlined in this scroll, if constructed during the era when the papyrus had been painted, would have pointed to a constellation in the southern hemisphere of the sky, not far above the horizon, a region which the Egyptians could only have seen in late summer.

Blake plucked the papyrus from its bed of cotton, opened his smock and lifted his thin pullover, and slid the scroll into the custom-sewn canvas sack that hung like a shoulder holster under his left armpit. He buttoned his smock, then slid the drawer closed. He crept back to his work.

At ten o'clock the workers took a break. Blake went to the toilet, which was down the hall, its door visible from the door of the papyrus room. The guard paid him no attention. Blake kept walking past the W.C. and turned and walked quietly up the stairs.

He walked past the closet in which he'd spent the night. He walked up another flight of stairs, across parqueted floors, past brooding sphinxes and stone sarcophagi, past painted limestone statues of scribes like the one whose black-inked brush had painted the scroll that rested against his side.

He walked into the palace's tall-windowed galleries and cast a glance over his shoulder, up the grand staircase, at Nike—the real stone Nike spreading her stone wings, striding forward upon a fiberglass cast of the stone trireme beak that resided where she herself should have resided, on Samothrace.

The black iron grille that barred the tall doors bore the laurel-wreathed imperial "N," but it had been placed there by a later, more bourgeois Napoleon. A mustached guard who could have been the brother of the one in the basement was talking into his commlink: trouble *en famille*.

"Open up, will you? I've got to get something from my 'ped."

The guard looked at him in irritation and went on talking while he keyed open the iron gate. The main doors already stood open on this humid summer morning. Blake walked through them and paused. He turned and stared at the guard, perplexed. It really wasn't supposed to have been this easy—why, he could just walk right out of here and nobody would ever know that anything was missing!

Which may have sat well with Lequeu and the rest of the Athanasians, but it was not part of Blake's plan. For a moment he stood still. Then he shouted at the guard, who was still on the commlink: *"Toi! Stupide!"*

The guard turned angrily. Blake let him get a good look and then shot him in the neck with a dart from the miniature tranquilizer gun that was strapped to his right wrist.

He walked quickly away, toward the leafy avenues of the Tuilleries. Around the corner, out of sight, he stripped off his smock and tossed it in a waste can.

Blake took his time crossing the river. He made a couple of lazy circuits around St. Germain des Pres before he returned to the rue Bonaparte and mounted the stairs to the offices of Editions Lequeu. He rapped twice, sharply.

"*Entrez.*"

Blake twisted the handle and walked into the airy room. Lequeu watched him from behind his desk, elegant as ever in a light blue polo short and linen slacks. Lequeu seemed distracted. His eyes were focusing on something outside the window.

"I have it," Blake said.

"Superb," said Lequeu, indifferently.

Blake lifted his sweat-stained shirt and carefully pulled the papyrus from its holster. Lequeu made no move in his direction so Blake stepped forward and laid the scroll upon Lequeu's desk with as much ceremony and decorum as he could muster.

Lequeu looked at it for a moment, then fingered the commlink. "Catherine, would you like to come in, please?" He looked at Blake. "While I'm thinking about it, I'd better have that dart gun back."

Blake unstrapped the gun and put it on the table. Lequeu picked it up and fingered it idly as Catherine entered. She came straight to the desk. Blake stepped away, watching her.

As she leaned over the papyrus she was silhouetted against the diffuse light from the tall windows. Deftly and cautiously she unrolled the first few centimeters of the scroll. She looked up at Lequeu. "Can you read it?"

He glanced down and began to recite: "*It is mighty pharoah's wish that his scribe set down the conversation of the veiled god-messengers . . . to do him honor. In the morning, while the warmth of Re stimulated our hearts to reason, the veiled god-messengers . . . from the home of Re . . . the gracious invitation of pharaoh approached his divine person, bringing gifts of god-metal and fine cloth, and oil and wine in great jars of glass, clear as water and hard as basalt*—this part is rather broken up—*at the gracious invitation of pharaoh . . . beyond the pillars of the sky. And they demonstrated with many demonstrations of the surveyor's art . . . stars steered by . . . journey to do honor to pharaoh . . .* and so forth and so on. It is the true papyrus," Lequeu said. "Take it. Go."

Without further discussion, Catherine rolled up the papyrus and swiftly left the room. Blake felt a twinge of alarm. "What's she . . . ?" he began, but Lequeu interrupted him.

"I was certain that my faith in you was not misplaced," said Lequeu, looking straight at him for the very first time. "But then no one possessed of your many and various fields of expertise could have gone wrong. Eh, Monsieur Blake Redfield?"

Someone else had come into the room as Catherine had left. Blake turned. Pierre, of course, hulking and impassive. There were several maneuvers Blake could have used to resist the inevitable, but he thought it better to save his strength in hopes of better odds.

"It is time we had a long talk, Blake, my friend," said Lequeu.

Blake turned back to him and smiled sunnily. "Certainly."

They took him down in the elevator. Pierre had him by the arm; Lequeu warily kept his distance. The contacts whistled softly as the car descended.

The basement was empty. Staff and "guests" had been ordered to find something to do for the day.

Pierre led Blake to his old cubicle and thrust him roughly inside. The door slammed behind him.

Blake knew the place well; he'd studied it in detail when he was living here. But he'd never thought to see the inside of this room again, and he knew that this time he would not be getting out until they decided to let him out.

PART 3

THREE-BODY PROBLEMS

9

Ninety percent of the way from Earth to the moon, at the L-1 transfer station, an agronomist named Clifford Leyland was beginning the final leg of his trip from the L-5 space settlement down to Farside Base. Cliff had one last stop before he could board the automated shuttle that would take him to the moon's surface.

Outside the station's docking bay there was a little booth, big enough for one person at a time. You went in there and took your clothes off and let the sensors sniff you and poke you and snap pictures of you in about four different wavelengths of radiation. Meanwhile you blew into the tube, a gas chromatograph mass spectrometer. The whole thing, not counting the time it took you to get undressed, lasted about five seconds. If you were clean, they let you put your spacesuit back on.

Drugs were a problem on L-1. Not a health problem but an administrative problem. Eighty per cent of all travellers to and from the moon went through the L-1 transfer station. So did half the freight. Drugs were very popular on the moon, especially among miners and the radiotelescope technicians stationed at Farside Base. Boredom had something to do with it. As a British wag once suggested—and it was as true of the moon's ice mines as it was of

English coal mines—if you were searching for a word to describe the conversation that went on down in the mines, *boring* would spring to your lips.

The top ten on the moon's hit parade of drugs constantly changed as newer and more clever designs for inducing euphoria in the suggestible human brain were invented by free lance chemists. The space settlement at L-5 had taken a commanding lead in the invention and manufacture of home-brew chemicals, partly because of local demand and partly because there was only one bottleneck between L-5 and the moon, L-1, whereas anything shipped from Earth had to make two or more transfers.

As for the authorities at Farside and Cayley, the major moon bases, there were some who said that they were less than diligent in policing the traffic. It was argued, off the record, that some illicit substances increased productivity, at least in the short run, and certainly stimulated the local economy—and how many people did they really harm? So the burden of enforcement fell on the security staff at L-1.

It was a staff of one, a man named Brick. He tended to be irritable, and today he was suffering from lack of sleep. "Go on through," he muttered to Cliff, and waved him past security check without bothering to look at the scans. Cliff, who'd made frequent trips to and from L-5 in the last few months, had always been clean.

Inside the docking bay, clothes in hand, Cliff encountered the other passenger he'd been told was accompanying him in the capsule to Farside, a Russian astronomer returning from leave in the Transcaucasus.

"You are Cliff?" she asked. "I'm Katrina. I'm glad to be meeting you—if you will excuse me just a moment." Katrina had just been through the inspection booth and was still getting dressed. She didn't bother to turn away as Cliff hastily struggled to get into his trousers and shirt. She took her time closing the seam of her coveralls over her own bare skin, then thrust out her hand and smiled.

He shook her hand. For a moment they rolled awkwardly in midair in the weightless bay. He cleared his throat and finally whispered, "Pleased, I'm sure."

Most men would have been delighted at their first sight of Katrina Balakian—she was a tall, leggy blonde with arresting gray eyes that twinkled with mischief—but she made Cliff instantly nervous. It was not only that she was an inch taller than the slight Englishman; it had more to do with the fact that Cliff had been away from his wife too long, and that the glimpse of Katrina's tan skin, that frank gaze of hers, were an unexpected challenge to his conscience. He was barely able to mumble the appropriate pleasantries as they climbed into the little capsule and strapped themselves down.

Launch came minutes later, and for thirty hours their capsule fell toward the moon in a long, smooth parabola. As it neared the end of its journey Cliff climbed out of the acceleration couch in which he'd spent most of his time since leaving L-1, sound asleep. Katrina was drowsily stirring in her couch.

Their sleep had been aided by prescription, for it seemed that only self-administered medication was objectionable to the authorities; drugging space travellers was standard practice, being ostensibly for their own good.

Cliff peered out the capsule's little triangular window and watched the splattered landscape come up fast.

"This part I always hate," said his colleague, lying rigid in her couch, her eyes now wide open. The two of them and their baggage took up most of the space in the capsule, though it was nominally designed to accommodate up to three passengers. "I watched once. It starts coming up fast like a big mud pie in the face. Always I'm sure we are going to miss the base.''

A visual-rules shuttle jockey trying to see his way to a landing on the moon might do all right on the Nearside, whose great dark plains and twisted, cratered uplands had long since imprinted an indelible image on the human memory, but the Farside was a featureless maze to all but the most experienced pilots. Farside had spectacular craters, to be sure, but they were more or less evenly scattered over the hemisphere, and all the space between was filled with other craters, craters within craters, right down to the limit of visibility.

"You were up here long before me. I should have thought you would have gotten used to it,'' Cliff said.

"Yes, but you travel more. I was not made for adventuring.''

This was Cliff's sixth trip to the lunar surface in the past half year, and for the first time he managed to spot his destination before the automatic shuttle put him right on top of it. "I can see Mount Tereshkova now. On the horizon, just to the left.''

"If you say. But how can you tell?''

It was near the end of a long lunar day. At night Farside Base's lights would have given it away; by day, unless the sun glinted off the field of metal sunflowers that was the telescope antenna farm, or the row upon row of solar panels that provided most of the power for the base, Farside was almost lost in a monotony of craters. Yet the base was inside one of the few recognizable landmarks in the terrain, the big lava-filled, mountain-ringed basin known as the Mare Moscoviense, the Sea of Moscow, whose existence was first hinted at in the smudged photos returned to Earth in 1959 by *Luna 3*. The base itself lay against the mountain walls to the west of the 200-kilometer-wide dark circular plain, at twenty-eight degrees north latitude and 156 degrees west longitude.

The other major outpost on the moon, Cayley Base, was near the dead center of the Nearside. In the early days its equatorial location had been vital for saving precious fuel; most traffic in the Earth-moon system still lay on the plane that sliced through both bodies and extended to the great space settlements.

Fifty years earlier Cayley Base had been built as an open-pit mine. The miners dug the metal-rich lunar dirt, compacted it into blocks, then shot it off the moon with an electromagnetic catapult to a transfer station at L-2 behind the moon and thence to the growing space settlement at L-5.

Farside Base was different, and its off-center position on the back of the moon was a compromise between competing demands. The dark lava of the floor of Mare Moscoviense concealed caves of frozen water—ice mines—the moon's most precious resource. The high ringwalls of the huge crater and the bulk of the moon itself isolated the base from radio pollution in near-Earth space, and a hundred radio telescopes lifted their dishes toward the uncluttered sky in an ongoing search for extraterrestrial intelligence.

As Cliff felt the solid thump of retrorockets under his feet, Katrina squealed, a little girl's squeal that issued incongruously from her Amazon's body, and at that moment they both felt their weight for the first time in days. The automated capsule slowed as it swept out over the plain, homing on the base. Cliff stayed on his feet, peering out the window.

Farside's most noticeable feature was the circular array of 200-meter radiotelescope dishes, more than a hundred of them covering thirty square kilometers of crater floor. Toward the edge of this perfect circle ran a tangent line, the base's forty-kilometer electromagnetic catapult; Katrina and Cliff were flying almost parallel to the launcher as they came in. Two white points marked the domes that were the inhabited center of the base, and beside them was the landing field. Beyond the field stretched a square plain of solar panels.

Farside's launcher had been built to throw entire space vehicles off the moon, not just ten-kilogram blocks of dirt—vehicles like the one in which Cliff and Katrina rode, capsules big enough to squeeze in three people with baggage and life-support or, stripped, a tonne of freight. After a lazy two-day trip to L-1, the capsules were outfitted with strap-on fuel tanks and sent back, braking their fall by burning abundant oxygen from the moon with rarer, more expensive hydrogen.

As the retrorocket lowered them onto the bare dirt landing pad, their cabin radio crackled: "Unit forty-two, that's Leyland and Balakian, right? The crummy's held up twenty minutes, Leyland, so you may as well plug into the bulkhead unit and save your suit O-two. Balakian, that tractor on the pad is for you."

The retrorockets cut and the shuttle fell the last half meter to the soft ground. Katrina sighed melodramatically and released her straps. "Want a lift? There's plenty of room in the big tractor."

Cliff tugged a large plastic case from the cargo net. "Thanks, I . . ."

"I'm such a sweety, yes?" Katrina batted her eyelashes.

Cliff smiled. "Indeed. I wouldn't mind getting these into some soil—or what passes for soil up here."

"What do you have in there, another bouquet of bird of paradise for the Grand Mall?"

"Rice shoots. L-5's best low-gee strain. Since the arrival of the new contingent from China, seems there's been an increased demand."

A yellow caution light came on, warning them to seal their helmets. The capsule's simple design wasted nothing on an airlock; when both passengers had sealed their helmets, Katrina keyed the computer and a pump pulled the cabin air into holding bottles. When the vacuum inside was as good as it could get, the little pressure hatch sprang open. Katrina squeezed through the circular hatch and Cliff slipped through after her.

The lower section of the capsule was surrounded by a doughnut-shaped strap-on fuel module; the capsule's retrorocket poked through the doughnut hole. Cliff and Katrina slid down the narrow ladder to the ground three meters below.

The loose moondust of the landing field was plowed in crazy waves of tire-tracks, crossing and recrossing in loops and tangles. A big-tired tractor from the antenna array was bounding over them like a motorboat over ships' wakes, leaving a wake of its own. The tractor skidded to a stop beside the shuttle in a cloud of quick-settling dust.

When the ready light came on over the tractor's rear hatch, Katrina pulled it open and shoved Cliff in ahead of her. She climbed in and pulled the hatch shut behind them.

"Ho, Piet," Katrina said on the suitcomm. "Did they demote you to tractor driving during my leave-taking?"

"Most amusing," the driver grumbled.

"This is Cliff," Katrina said. "I told him you'd drop him by Maintenance."

"Why not? As you point out, I'm simply a chauffeur."

"Piet is a signal analyst, actually," she said cheerfully. "My new chum Cliff here is in Agro. Cliff Leyland, Piet Gress."

Gress twisted in his seat to extend a gloved right hand. Cliff shook it. "Pleasure," Cliff said.

Gress grunted agreement. He shoved the throttle forward and the tractor bounded off again, throwing Cliff and Katrina against each other in the unpadded back of the tractor.

"I notice that your famous uncle's in the news again, Piet," said Katrina, when she'd recovered her poise.

"Really?"

"You of course never waste time watching the viddie." She turned to Cliff. "His uncle is Albers Merck."

Cliff was politely interested. "The archaeologist? The one they pulled off the surface of Venus a few weeks ago?"

"The very Merck. Him with the most definite ideas about extraterrestrial beings."

Cliff said, "He translated the thing they found on Mars?"

"Translated!" Katrina hooted. The suitcomms transmitted with equal volume in everyone's ears, painfully. "Certainly he did. And a most full and large translation it was. As you say, the 'last will and testament' of a dying civilization."

"You may save the irony, Katrina," said Gress. "That was a long time ago. He made a beginning. Several useful hypotheses."

Katrina laughed. "Translating a text in an unknown—not to mention an alien—language needs something more than a hypothesis. But far be it from those of us who actually know something about frequency analysis . . ."

"Who know rather less about natural languages, perhaps."

"Please do not misunderstand me, Piet. I'm glad they saved your uncle's life." She turned her helmet to look at Cliff. "It is a family tradition, you see. Piet's uncle digs up the past and imagines he reads messages in old bottles, while Piet looks to the future, eager to decipher the first message from the stars."

"There will be one," Gress said simply.

"If your uncle is right, there already was, but you missed it," Katrina responded. "Your Culture X has been dead a billion years."

Gress twisted his helmeted head and looked over his shoulder at Cliff. "You mustn't pay too much attention to her. She's not the cynic she pretends to be."

"Not a cynic at all," Katrina replied. "A realist. Never mind, we are sneaking in some good astronomy on these most expensive telescopes while you waste your time eavesdropping on a vacant phonelink."

The tractor was quickly approaching one of the big double-domes of the central base. A ring of vehicle-sized locks surrounded the base of the dome, and Gress headed toward the nearest open door. As the tractor rolled into the dusty lock, the clam-shell hatch automatically closed behind it. A pressure tube trundled out of the wall and fastened its aging polyrubber lips around the rim of the tractor's back hatch. The tractor spent a few moments stealing air from the dome; sensing pressure, the hatch popped. The riders unsealed their helmets.

"Thanks again," Cliff said. "See you around the Mall?"

"Me?" Katrina said. "Certainly. Not him, though. He spends all his spare time trying to extract meaning from nova blips and other such things."

Piet Gress shrugged, as if to say it was hardly worth replying to his colleague's distortions.

As if on an impulse, Katrina plucked at Cliff's sleeve. "Before you go . . ."

"Yes—"

"I am thinking of having some people over to my place later. To celebrate my safe return. Will you come? It is so nice to make new friends."

"Thanks, I . . . I'd better say no. I didn't sleep all that well on the way back."

"Just drop in. Do me a favor." She glanced sideways. "You're invited too, Piet."

Cliff looked at her. Her pale eyes were quite striking. He'd been trying not to admit that for the past couple of days, ever since chance had thrust them together on the same shuttle. He shrugged. "For you I'll stay awake a few hours."

"That's a promise, Cliff," she said. "About nineteen hundred, then." As she leaned away the change in her expression was subtle, carrying a hint of triumph.

Cliff clambered into the tube. He glanced backward. Piet Gress waved a brusque goodbye; Katrina was still staring at him with her soulful eyes.

When Cliff reached the inner door, the creaking mechanism bumped and wheezed and released its sucking grasp on the tractor. Through the thick glass port of the lock, Cliff watched the tractor back out into the lunar day and wheel around, heading for the distant antenna farm. He regretted his mock flirtation. He was, after all, a happily married man.

The big tractor sped along beside the linear launcher, toward the distant radiotelescopes.

"Quite a performance you just put on," Gress muttered. "Watch you don't overdo it."

Katrina yawned noisily, ostentatiously ignoring him. "Asleep for a whole day! I'm so full of energy."

"Did you really want to invite me to this party of yours?" Piet Gress asked.

"Don't be silly. You had your chance with me. More than once."

"I don't know whether to pity the poor man or envy him."

"If you had any imagination, Piet, you would envy him. But we've already established that you don't know what you're missing. He's rather cute, don't you think?"

Gress grunted gloomily and concentrated on his driving. After a while he asked, "Are you going to keep me in suspense forever?"

"Very well—since you are so impatient." Her tone became more serious. "The news is not exactly ideal."

"What sector?"

"As we suspected, the one we are scheduled to search next," she said. "Crux."

He drove silently for a moment. "You seem quite cheerful about it," he burst out bitterly. "Do you really care for the real purpose of this operation? Or is your interest really purely astrophysical, as you keep telling everyone who will listen?"

Katrina said gently, "I care, Piet. Doesn't it excite you to know we are that much closer to our goal? All of us?"

"Crux, then." His voice was filled with cool weariness. "I cannot say I was unprepared."

"Of course you are prepared. Don't worry, all will be well."

Cliff Leyland pulled his helmet off his head and tucked it under his arm. In his right hand he had a firm grip on the big briefcase he'd brought at considerable cost from L-5. He slid the case into a slot in the wall and waited for passive inspection. A second later the lock's inner door opened and Cliff stepped into the interior of the dome. That was all there was to it: there were no body searches at Farside.

The two big domes were the oldest structures on the base. Originally they had housed the construction workers and their machinery, but as soon as possible the people moved underground. The dome Cliff was in now was a garage, hangar, and repair shop for big equipment, busy with men and women swarming over broken moon buggies, defective transformers, sections of launcher track that needed repairing. The flash and glare of welding torches cast strange shadows on the curving interior of the dome, a colder place than its twin, which had been converted to a recreation area and garden and was thus filled with plants hardy enough to stand up to surface-level radiation, which could be intense where no atmosphere intercepted the solar wind and the constant bombardment of cosmic rays.

Cliff walked to the nearest trolley stop. In a few seconds one of the open cars rolled up, beeping a monotonous warning, and he climbed aboard, seating himself beside a couple of ice miners he recognized but had not met. Farside Base wasn't large even by small-town standards, but in a population of almost a thousand, most of them adults, newcomers can stay strangers for a long time.

The trolley hummed along through a low, wide corridor of compacted gray moon gravel, past smaller side corridors leading to dormitories, offices, dining halls, racquetball courts, restaurants, theaters, meeting halls. . . . Most of the base was like this, buried five meters underground, well shielded against the random energies of raw space. People got on and off at every stop, some in spacesuits, most in shirt-sleeves. The ice miners got off near their rooms; Cliff continued on to the agronomy station.

A man in transport technician's coveralls was waiting for him when he got off the trolley. "You're Leyland? I've got a load of the dry black stuff for you."

"You do? How'd you know I'd be here?"

"Don't be funny," he said. Cliff didn't recognize the fellow, although as he entered his acknowledgment on the manifest pad the man stared at him intently. He was a young man with thick black hair, carefully smoothed back, and the shadow of a dark beard beneath the transparent skin of his smoothly shaven jaw. He didn't look much like a low-grade technician.

Cliff handed the manifest back and started to turn away.

"Hey. You've got something for me," the man whispered urgently.

Cliff turned back. "What?"

"You've *got* something."

"Not that I know of," Cliff said, puzzled.

"Oh, man . . . You're Cliff Leyland, right?"

"Yes, I am."

The man leaned his head back, open-mouthed, disbelieving. "Leyland, don't you remember a little conversation we had in the lounge a couple of days before you left for L-5? You were going to look up a friend of some friends of mine."

"Oh." Cliff's face froze. "That was you. You look different when you're not wearing glitter."

"Save the comedy, man, just give me the stuff."

"I thought about the proposition. I decided against."

The disbelieving mouth threatened to fall open wider this time, before it snapped shut. "You what?"

"You heard me. Tell your friends, whoever they are, that I thought about their proposition and decided against."

"Do you know what you're saying, man?"

Cliff's face brightened with anger. "Yes, I think I do. Man."

The fellow appeared sincerely concerned. "No, man, do you know what this *means*?"

Cliff took a step forward. "Look, you, I want you out of here now. Stay away from me. Tell your friends to stay away from me, too. Or I'm turning you in."

"Oh, man . . ."

"You don't have anything to worry about if you just stay out of the way. Nothing that's been said to me will be repeated. But I want no one, no one at all, ever to bring this subject up to me again."

"Oh, man, you don't know what you're asking for . . ."

"Get out of here." Cliff turned back to his rows of plants.

"Oh, man, ohhh . . ." The words came out almost crooningly. The transport worker seemed as upset as if he were mourning the loss of a friend.

He gave Cliff one last stricken look and walked slowly away, leaving the shipment of night soil beside the door.

Cliff watched him go, then pushed his way through the double doors of Agro, into the square bright caves of the experimental greenhouses. Someone else could take care of the unsolicited black stuff.

By the time he'd planted the delicate shoots of the new rice strain, it was seventeen hundred hours; Cliff discovered he was hungry. He cleaned up and went to the dining hall favored by the other singles and separates. It was a luxurious place by the standards of similar facilities on Earth, with levels and alcoves and indirect lighting, and food superbly prepared even if it was served on a cafeteria line. Cliff ate by himself at a table for four; the linen and candles, the brocade and velvet walls, the deep pile carpet kept meticulously clean, the redwood-textured ceiling and the warm light only served to remind Cliff that he was trapped underground on an alien world.

After the hasty dinner he went to his shared cubicle and tapped out letters to be sent by radiolink to Myra and the children. He would have spoken to them by videolink if he could have afforded to do so, but the family resources were limited. So he painfully wrote out the words that would be transmitted in fragmented bits, bits that would be reassembled on a space-available basis at the fax unit at Cliff and Myra's apartment in Cairo. . . .

''My dear Myra. I've made another successful trip to L-5 and back. They have developed a high-yield strain of rice there that has done well for them and we are going to have a go at it here. The trip was uneventful I suppose although I must admit that after many such trips I have still not got used to the changes. Lonely as ever. I love you and I pray I will be with you soon. Love too to our newest, as only you can give it. With much love from your Clifford. . . .''

And in the second part of the message:

''Hello Brian and Susie! I have some good samples of moondust from many localities, Brian, and many rocks too that I have traded for with people who have been to other parts of the Moon, some of which you can see from where you live when the Moon is full, although you cannot see where I am living just now. Susie, when I can come home which will be soon I am bringing you some moon-silk, which is made by silkworms who live here on the Moon and is different from anything on Earth. I love both of you very much and it will not be as long as it seems until we are together again. Take care of your mother. I love you, your Dad.''

Cliff pressed the send key and pushed his back against his chair. He should get into his bunk now. He was certainly tired enough, if he would admit it to himself. His skin was gray, stretched like parchment from his cheekbones to his chin. But he'd promised Katrina he'd drop in on her party. And truth to tell, as tired as he was, he wasn't sleepy at all. All this shuttling back and forth between abstract points in space—he really didn't know what time it was anymore.

Something else was bothering him, too. It bothered him that he felt so very distant from his family. It bothered him that he could not think of his newest born with anything like the feelings a father should have. It bothered him that he was allowing himself to be more than merely cordial with Katrina—that he was allowing himself to be led on. Probably it would be better to stop before he started with her, but . . .

He slipped out of his chair and went into the tiny bathroom. He splashed his face with lazy water, water that fell slowly and clung to his skin until he pushed it away with the hand blower. He peered at himself in the mirror. He had not bothered to shave during the last day of his long trip from L-5. His skin was as pale as that of most moon-moles, perhaps even a little grayer, since the white skin was overlaid by the year-old faded melanin of a deep Sahara sunburn. Nonetheless he was still a good-looking man of thirty-four, dark haired, slender, precise in his appearance, precise in his movement even to the point of fussiness. He lingered a long time with his shaver, until his skin gleamed.

He took a crisp plastic jacket from his closet, slipped it on, and walked out the door.

It was a long underground tolley ride out to the antenna array, where the astronomers lived and worked; Cliff made the trip in silent contemplation. Almost before he knew it he found himself at the door of Katrina Balakian's apartment. He paused a moment, then took a deep breath and knocked.

The door opened on her wide bright smile. "Cliff." She was wearing a short black clingy dress, high on her thighs; a necklace of brushed aluminum and obsidian rested on her smooth artificially tan bosom. Her fingernails took his crinkly sleeve and drew him inside.

He found himself in another candlelit room. Candles burned brighter here because the air supply was oxygen-rich—oxygen was cheap and nitrogen was dear—but a room lit by candles was as much an invitation here as it was anywhere. A bottle of Luna Spumante was sweating in a bucket on the sideboard, with only two glasses beside it.

"Where's everybody?" Cliff asked.

"It's too early for the gang I am hanging out with. Let me have your jacket." She was behind him, already slipping it off his shoulders. "May I give you a drink?"

"I'm really quite lagged. . . . Tonight it had better be seltzer."

"Just try this." She removed the pressure stopper from the sparkling wine. "Guaranteed to be without hangover." She poured and handed him a glass. He hesitated but took it.

Gaily she poured her own, lifted it, and clinked it against his. "You see? You can be persuaded," she said.

He smacked his lips on the acidic sparkling wine. "It's nice." He was not used to this bubbly stuff. His habits were simple—not, he had to admit, wholly from choice. He found that he was still gazing into Katrina's wide gray eyes.

He glanced around her apartment, twice as big as the one he shared with another temporary bachelor. Her walls were hung with big color holos of places she'd worked before. There was a good shot of L-5's twin cylinders from five kilometers out, with a full Earth rising behind them; there was a shot of the Synthetic Aperture Array in the Khaaki steppes.

What had she done with her chairs? The only place to sit seemed to be the couch. I really shouldn't be here, Cliff was thinking as he sat down.

A moment later she was beside him, her bare knee not quite touching his, fixing him with those hypnotic eyes. Apparently she was well aware of their effect.

"You were on L-5?" he asked, his voice rising.

She smiled and decided to play her part a little longer. "It was my first assignment out of Novo Aktyubinsk. I helped set up the deep-space ULB antennas. And somehow I managed to get stuck in space."

"The first ULB antennas?" He tried to act impressed. "That must have been a challenge under those conditions. The station wasn't even half built, was it?"

For an answer he got her hand on his knee. "Let's not talk business, Cliff. Thanks for coming."

"Well, thanks for asking me," he said, feeling clumsy. He moved to face her, which had the effect of making his knee a barrier between them. Her fingers slipped lightly away.

"Tell me about yourself," she said. "You say you've been popping in and out of here for six months and we've never met? I haven't been gone *that* long. How were you avoiding me so skillfully?"

"Really, I wasn't. Honestly, I never saw you."

Her smile widened. "Am I so easy to ignore, then?"

"Of course not"—he blushed furiously—"Sorry. Frankly I never know what to say. Maybe because I don't know what I'm doing here, really."

She let it pass, sipping her champagne. "You miss Earth a lot?"

He nodded. "I miss the Nile. . . ." Cliff wanted to say he missed Myra and their children, but somehow the simple words didn't come out. "The Sahara project. Simply the scale of it—it'll be a century or two before we can ever experience that kind of landscape renewal anywhere but on Earth."

"Mars is as big a desert as all the land on Earth, and reclaiming that . . . I say that's where socialist man and woman will come into their own." She laughed. "See, you've got me talking business after all. Or politics, which is worse." She sipped her drink.

"You're thinking of moving to Mars."

"Perhaps I would like that. I said to you I am not an adventurer, but some things are worth adventure. To be an astronomer, yes. Even more, to someday be a pioneer of science in new lands." Her eyes were bright in the candlelight. "Let me tell you something, Cliff, it's hard being in the minority all the time. As a woman, I mean. I'm not the housekeeping, mothering type. I'm not one of your Christian nuns either, but the way the *men* plague a woman in these places—they expect us to pick one of them just to keep the others inside their caves." She stood up quickly, a practiced move in the low gravity, leaving her glass behind on the back of the couch. "Sorry. I am making you nervous."

Cliff's gaze had been captivated by a glimpse of Katrina's long, firm thighs beneath her floating skirt. "Why do you say that?" He tacked on a little hum to clear his throat.

She stared down at him. "You are not the type of man who likes to be told he is hard to resist."

Cliff sighed. "Katrina, you know very well that I'm . . ."

"You're married, you have little children, and you love your family. Yes, yes, you have told me. I *like* that."

"Well, mmm, you're really quite attractive too. That is . . ."

She moved to him and lifted him easily to his feet. She leaned her head against his shoulder. Her breasts gently nudged his chest. "No complications. One of these days I am going to Mars, and you are going back to the Sahara. Meanwhile we are very discreet. And the long nights aren't as long as they would be."

"Listen, I . . ." Cliff reddened. "Your friends will be along."

Her laugh was a purr. "No friends tonight, Cliff. You are the whole party."

"You said . . ."

"Relax, yes? Let's just talk a minute."

He took her by the arms and stepped back. "I don't think I have anything to talk about."

"Cliff . . ."

"Sorry. I really am sorry. I'm in love with my wife, I think. I mean, I'm not sorry about that, but . . . Katrina, you really are a very beautiful woman. It's simply that I really don't want to complicate my life—in, uh, the way you're suggesting."

She smiled her bright smile. "Okay! I get it—the message. Don't become strange with me. Sit down, finish your drink. Relax.'' She raised both hands. "I am keeping my mitts off.''

"I think . . . Thanks again. I must go.'' He crossed the room and retrieved his jacket from where she'd hung it.

Her smile vanished. "Are you so simple-minded as you pretend?''

"I suppose I must be.'' Cliff found himself still holding the wine glass. "Sorry, could you . . . ?'' He handed it to her, then struggled awkwardly into his jacket. "Look, well—''

"Become lost, why don't you?'' She threw the glass on the floor as hard as she could, hard enough to lift herself a millimeter or two off the carpet in reaction. Globules of liquid sprayed across the room. The glass hit slowly; unbroken, it sailed back into the air.

By the time the glass had settled gently to the floor, the door was closing behind him. Katrina shrugged and picked up the glass. In a few minutes she had rearranged the apartment; there was no sign she had had a visitor.

Cliff's mind was so full of confusion and guilt, not unmixed with frustrated desire, that he was hardly aware of the two men who followed him toward the main corridor. This sector was far from the busy halls of the central base. The ceilings were low, the walls close, and no one was around.

Except the two men behind him, whose echoing footsteps drew closer.

He turned another corner. They turned with him. His pace quickened until he was walking as fast as he could without actually running. When he heard them break stride and trot toward him, he tried to run.

They were on him in seconds. These men were used to the moon; their movements were quick and precise, unlike Cliff's overbalanced floundering. One of them grabbed his collar and yanked him back. The other kicked him hard in the back of the knees and he fell. The first pulled his jacket over his head, blinding him. His struggles were feeble, ineffectual; his terrified shouts were muffled. They hauled him, wriggling like a sack of fish, behind the steel doors of a utility substation.

Neither of them said a word at first. They just started hitting him: one held Cliff's elbows locked behind him while the other drove his fists into his stomach. When the first man got tired, they traded places. They scrupulously avoided hitting him where the bruises were likely to show.

Finally they let Cliff fall to the floor. He lay there retching.

"Next time we ask you to do something for us, don't say no," said one of them, between gulps of air. He shook out his arms and shoulders, loosening them; he'd been exercising stenuously. "Or it will be the last time you say anything."

Cliff lost consciousness, then. But his tormentor's voice was fixed in his memory.

10

Sparta's magneplane slid silently to a halt deep under the Gare St. Lazare after a brief supersonic trip through the Chunnel, the high-vacuum tunnel that crossed beneath the English Channel to link London with Paris. Sparta's Space Board credentials had been passed by the electronic *douane* at the London end, and she was able to step onto the crowded Paris platform with no more ceremony than if she'd been dismounting a Metro car. She rode the long elevator to street level and stepped off under the station's grandiose 19th-century cast-iron and glass roof.

A big flatscreen was mounted above the high iron arch opening onto the busy street, silently playing newsbites and viddie commercials. Sparta was almost out of the echoing station when a dancing newshead caught her eye:

LOUVRE'S PRECIOUS PAPYRUS STILL MISSING
POLICE MYSTIFIED
DRAGNET FOR MYSTERIOUS "GUY" ENTERS
SECOND WEEK

The flashing newsheads were accompanied by scenes of the crime, including an electronically aided reconstruction of "Guy's" appearance, presumably based on descriptions from witnesses.

144

Blake Redfield's mother probably would not have recognized his picture, but Sparta thought she could detect a distant resemblance.

It seemed she wouldn't need that GUYDE to the Louvre after all. Blake was not in the habit of drawing public attention to himself; he had obviously intended his disguise to be penetrated. He *wanted* to be recognized. But it was equally obvious that if he had wanted to be caught by the police, he would have been.

Blake had plainly hoped that Sparta would find him while he was still in the Louvre—before he'd been forced to reveal himself so spectacularly. What had he been doing there? Why was he trying to advertise it? And where was he now?

The door of Blake's cubicle banged open. Pierre walked in and grabbed him by the shoulder of his soiled shirt, pulling him roughly erect. Blake staggered and sagged against Pierre's grip. Half-supported, half-shoved by Pierre, he stumbled into the corridor.

Pierre aimed him toward the laundry at the end of the hall. Blake played his weakness for all it was worth, wishing he didn't feel almost as feeble as he pretended. The doors of the other cubicles stood ajar and their furnishings had been removed. In the preceding days of solitary confinement and starvation rations, Blake had heard voices and movement in the other rooms of the basement, but he hadn't been able to tell what was going on. Now it was apparent that the Athanasians had been moving. "Guy's" mishap could have had nothing to do with the move, which must have been planned in advance of the theft. But the discovery of Blake's real identity might have set the game afoot.

They reached the end of the hall. The laundry room was piled high with cartons and dirty linens; no one had done any laundry here recently. Over the smell of dirty linen there was the persistent moldy odor of ancient Paris drains.

Blake shook his head groggily. He noticed Lequeu for the first time. The older man sat on a pile of packing boxes beside the door, swinging an elegantly shod foot. He looked at Blake without expression and gave a quick nod to Pierre.

A wooden folding chair stood against one of the steel sinks. "Sit," Pierre said, pushing Blake toward the chair. Blake managed to bang his shin against the chair seat and stumble against the sink; his head bounced painfully on the edge of a shelve above it, and a big brown bottle of bleach tumbled into the sink, where it splintered with a crash.

Lequeu recoiled, clasping his nose, but Pierre had pinned Blake's arms and roughly shoved him into the seat.

"Stupid stunt, Redfield," said Lequeu, moving to the doorway. "You can sit there and breathe it in."

Blake glared back at him, red-eyed. The odor of sodium hypochlorite was strong near the sink, but Pierre braved it to stand menacingly over Blake.

Lequeu resumed his pose of casual dignity with some effort, then removed a tiny pistol-shaped drug injector from the breast pocket of his silk shirt. He held it up for Blake's inspection. "This is a neurostimulant cocktail targeted for Broca's Area and Wernicke's Area, the speech centers of the brain," Lequeu said evenly. "Within about five minutes of receiving a subcutaneous injection, you will begin to talk uncontrollably. If no one asks you a question, you will talk about anything that comes into your head. On the other hand, should I question you, you will talk about anything I ask you to talk about, with as many details as I ask you to provide. You will be fully conscious of what you are saying, and much of it you will regret. Some of it will be embarrassingly personal. Some of it will be disloyal. Nevertheless, you will withhold nothing."

Blake said, "It so happens I'm familiar with the technique."

"Then you know I'm not bluffing."

"I believe you, Lequeu."

"Perhaps you would rather talk without the aid of the stimulant?"

"What do you want to know?"

"There was a girl," Lequeu said casually. "Linda—the first subject of the program known as SPARTA. Where is she now?"

Blake listened carefully to Lequeu's intonation. He did not sound familiar with the SPARTA project, but perhaps he was being clever. "I don't know where she is. She looks different now. She calls herself something different."

"In fact she calls herself Ellen Troy. She is an inspector with the Board of Space Control."

"If you know, why bother to ask?"

"Come, Blake. . . . When did you last see her?"

"On Port Hesperus, as you surely know. The *Star Queen* case was exhaustively reported in all the media."

"And you had no doubt she was Linda?"

"I had seen her once before, in Manhattan. It was quite a surprise—I thought she was dead. At any rate, she clearly did not want to be recognized. I followed her a few blocks, but she lost me."

"Why did you think she was dead?"

"How much do you know about SPARTA, Lequeu?"

Lequeu's expression was as bland as ever. "Why don't you tell me what you think I ought to know?"

"Fine," said Blake. "I'll be giving away no secrets. You can read all about this in public records."

"I'll give you a chance to tell secrets later," said Lequeu. "For now, continue."

"Linda was SPARTA's only subject when she was an infant, when it was still a private affair between her and her parents. They were psychologists, Hungarian immigrants to North America. Their initial work was successful, they attracted attention, they got enough funding to mount a full-scale educational project at the New School."

"The New School?"

"The New School for Social Research, in Manhattan—Greenwich Village. It's about a hundred-and-fifty years old. Not as old as the Pont Neuf."

Lequeu granted him a wintry smile. "Continue."

"After Linda, I was one of the first to join. I was eight years old; my parents saw it as a chance to give me a head start on the rest of the world."

"You hardly needed it."

"My parents have never been inclined to take chances. In their opinion, if rich is good, smart and rich is better. Anyway, I'm just a year younger than Linda, closer to her age than any of the others. For six or seven years everything was great. Then the government took over SPARTA. Linda was sent away for 'special training.' A year later her parents died in a helicopter crash. SPARTA broke up. None of us ever saw Linda again, as far as I know—until that day in Manhattan."

"What happened to her?"

"When I saw her, I decided to find out. There were rumors that she had lost her mind, that she had died in a fire at the clinic where she was being treated."

"What else did you find out, Blake?"

Blake stared at Lequeu. If there were secrets Lequeu did not know—or did not know that Blake knew—they were getting to them now. But Blake had to tell the truth. He could not risk an injection that would leave him babbling aimlessly as he went about doing what he was about to do.

"The agency that took over SPARTA had changed its name to the Multiple Intelligences project. They classified it. Frankly, Lequeu, government files in what's left of the United States are cheesecloth. All it takes is a feel for bureaucratic turf wars. You can get a lot of 'need to know' information just from the overlap."

"What did you learn about this 'Multiple Intelligences' project, Blake?" said Lequeu.

"I learned the name of the man who ran it."

"Which is?"

"William Laird."

"And where is Laird now?"

Blake heard him say it from deep in his throat, and he knew that this was what Lequeu feared most. "I don't know," Blake said. "Shortly after the fire that supposedly killed Linda—and certainly killed someone who looked like her—he vanished. He didn't even bother to resign. I found his official biography—it was sketchy and vague, but one item caught my attention. As one of his memberships, Laird listed a philanthropic society."

"Yes?"

"The Tappers."

"Did you ever meet William Laird, Blake?"

"No."

"I thought not. If you had . . ."

But at that moment Blake turned his shoulder into Pierre's crotch. He twisted off his chair and shoved Pierre as hard as he could against the sink. Pierre bent over in pain, but he was quick enough to bring up his forearm to defend himself against Blake's thrusting arms. But Blake was not going for Pierre's face; he reached around and past him and grabbed a bottle of drain opener from the shelf over the steel sink. He brought the fragile plastic bottle down against the edge of the sink with all the strength he could muster, even as Pierre shoved him back. Blake's eyes and mouth were pursed tight and he was holding his breath; he yanked his shirt up over his face. Pierre swung as Blake ducked and dived. Pierre suddenly screamed.

Lequeu shrieked in pain and clutched at his throat. The bleach and the caustic, reacting in the drain, had expelled a heavy cloud of chlorine gas into the room, burning their eyes, their skin, their mucous membranes, their lungs.

Blake blundered toward the door with his eyes closed. He almost made it—but Lequeu threw out an arm and the injector brushed Blake's shoulder as he stumbled past, running blind. He left two disabled bodies gasping and writhing on the floor behind him.

The neurostimulant was real. Before he got out on the street Blake was babbling uncontrollably. He ran down the rue Jacob, tears streaming from his eyes, while he blurted an extemporaneous monologue: ". . . Pierre Pussycat, they ought to call you, all fake muscles from the exercise machine, never saw a day of real work in your life, you *type* . . ."

Blake had meant to head straight for police headquarters, but he knew it would be hours before he sounded sane. Until then, he had to go somewhere where no one would pay attention to his sudden attack of logorrhea.

He headed for the quays and riverbanks he had gotten to know well, where on sunny afternoons like this, under the chestnut trees, one or more of his former colleagues among the homeless could be found haranguing passers-by who did their best to pretend they heard nothing at all.

Meanwhile he kept talking nonsense: ". . . and as for you, Lequeu, who's your tailor? You ought to tell him to get into some other line of work. . . ."

"Frankly, Mademoiselle—"

"I'm an inspector, Lieutenant."

"Ah, yes," said the police officer, hooking a forefinger in his high stiff collar. "Inspector . . . Troy. At any rate, about this 'precious papyrus'—the director has admitted that the scroll would never have been missed had not the unfortunate incident with the guard forced the museum staff to do a thorough search and inventory of the area where this man Guy was working."

They were sitting in the lieutenant's cramped and crowded office at police headquarters on the Île de la Cité. Through the grimy window behind the lieutenant's head, Sparta could see leafy chestnuts and the mansard roofs of Right Bank apartments on the far side of the Seine.

"How was the guard attacked?" Sparta asked.

"With a minimal dose of tranquilizer, quite expertly applied via hypodermic dart to the neck."

"A dangerous area."

"Here is the dart." He held up a plastic package that contained a tiny glittering filament of metal. "Almost microscopic. It could have punctured the carotid artery without severe damage, although in fact it struck nowhere near the artery. In my estimation, Monsieur 'Guy' knew precisely what he was doing. What we don't know is why he was doing it. Can you help us, Inspector?"

"I can only tell you that 'Guy' is an agent engaged in research on a group known as the *prophetae* of the Free Spirit—at least, that is the name they were known by several centuries ago. We don't know what they call themselves these days. We've heard nothing from Guy in over four months."

"But here you are," the lieutenant remarked dryly.

"I received a coded message requesting me to meet . . . Guy . . . at the Louvre."

"He was engaged in research, you say?" The crisp, gray-haired Frenchman regarded her with professional suspicion and what she had learned to recognize as the endemic jaundice of the Paris *flic*. "What was the nature of this research? Who are these so-called Free Spirits?"

"I deeply regret that as a representative of the Board of Space Control, I am not at liberty to say more," Sparta remarked cooly. "I came to you because our man obviously intended to draw attention to himself. Otherwise the guard would not have been given an opportunity to recognize him."

"Possibly," said the lieutenant. He did not mention that the position of the guard's sleeping body indicated he had been shot *after* the thief had already escaped.

"And because I had hoped you would be able to provide some clue as to the importance of this papyrus."

"As to that, I can only repeat: the papyrus has little intrinsic value."

"Would you object to my visiting the Louvre personally?"

"Official Space Board business naturally takes precedence over our merely local concerns," the lieutenant replied, calling her bluff.

"Very well, if you would be so kind as to arrange a link with Earth Central," she said, calling his.

They watched each other from opposite sides of his cluttered desk. Then, with an almost imperceptible sigh, the lieutenant reached for his old-fashioned phonelink console.

Before his fingers reached the pad, however, the console chimed. He hesitated, then keyed the link. *"Qu'est-ce que c'est?"*

"Pour l'Inspecteur, Monsieur. De la Terre Centrale."

He looked up at Sparta. "They are saving us the trouble, it seems." He handed her the link's hand unit.

"Troy here," said Sparta.

"Troy," said a gravelly voice.

"Commander," she said, surprised. "How did . . . ?"

"Never mind that. I'm calling from an infobooth on the Quai d'Orsay."

"Out of the office again," she said dryly. "Anyway, I have important information concerning our friend that . . ."

"It will have to wait, Troy. Sorry to cut your fun and games short—whatever line you've been feeding that French cop—but I just got a commwhistle from Central. Something's come up."

"Yes? Where?"

"On the moon."

PART
4

MAELSTROM

11

He was not the first man, Cliff Leyland told himself bitterly, to know the exact second and the precise manner of his death. Times beyond number, condemned criminals had waited for their last dawn. Yet until the very end they could hope for a reprieve; human judges can show mercy. But against the laws of nature, there is no appeal.

Only six hours ago he had been whistling happily while he packed his ten kilos of personal baggage for the long fall home. Blessed surprise! He'd been released early from his tour of duty on the Moon: he was needed back on the Sahara project, as quickly as possible. He reserved his place on the first available manned capsule from Farside and sincerely hoped he would never be coming back.

He could still remember (even now, after all that had happened) how he had dreamed that Myra was already in his arms, that he was taking Brian and Sue on that promised cruise down the Nile. In a few minutes, as Earth rose above the horizon, he might see the Nile again; but memory alone could bring back the faces of his wife and children.

He'd had the usual moment of nervousness as he climbed aboard, of course; he'd never really gotten used to living on the moon, or to traveling in space.

He was one of those people who would have been delighted to stay on Earth his whole life. Nevertheless, in the course of his frequent business trips between Farside and L-5, he'd gotten used to the automatic capsules that shuttled him back and forth from the transfer station at L-1. He still didn't trust the heavy modular tugs that worked the traffic trajectories between the libration points and low-Earth orbit. And he'd long been inwardly terrified at the prospect of re-entering Earth's atmosphere on one of the fiery winged shuttles.

Cliff had ridden the catapult often enough, in fact, that people like Katrina considered him something of an expert. The first time, having heard many tall tales of electromagnetic "bumpiness," he'd expected the launch to be rough. But so rigidly was the capsule suspended by the magnetic fields surrounding its own on-board superconducting magnets that in fact he felt no lateral movement at all as he was whipped along thirty kilometers of so-called "rough acceleration" track.

Nor had he been looking forward to the ten gees of acceleration he would have to endure for twenty-four long seconds before the capsule reached the Moon's escape velocity of some 2,400 meters per second. Yet when the acceleration had gripped the capsule, he had hardly been aware of the immense forces acting upon him. At its worst it was like lying under a pile of mattresses on the floor of a swiftly ascending elevator.

The only sound had been a faint creaking from the metal walls: to anyone who had endured the thunder of a rocket launch from Earth, the silence was uncanny. And when the weary voice of the launch director came over his helmet radio to announce, "T plus five seconds; velocity 500 meters per second," he could scarcely believe it. In the traditional English units still natural to Cliff, he was going over a thousand miles an hour!

A thousand miles an hour in five seconds from a

standing start—with nineteen seconds still to go as the generators smashed their thunderbolts of power into the launcher. He was riding the lightning across the face of the moon. And when the acceleration finally ceased and Cliff was suddenly weightless, it was as if a giant hand had opened and released him gently into space.

He'd ridden the lightning five times in six months, and although he was far from blasé upon this sixth and final occasion, he was resting almost comfortably in the accelerating capsule. But this time, at T plus twenty-two seconds, the lightning failed.

Even in the womblike shelter of his acceleration couch, Cliff knew instantly that something was wrong. The capsule had not ceased hurtling along the track, but in this final kilometer before acceleration was to cease there came a moment of stomach-lifting drag.

He had no time to feel fear or even to wonder what had happened. Free-fall lasted less than half a second, before acceleration resumed with a jolt. A corner of the cargo net tore loose and one of his bags walloped onto the floor beside him. The final burst of acceleration lasted only one more second, and then he was weightless again. Through the little triangular windows forward, which were no longer "overhead," Cliff saw the peaks of the ringwall of Mare Moscoviense flicker past in a wink. Was it his imagination? They had never seemed so close.

"Launch control," he said urgently into his radiolink, "what the devil happened?"

The launch director's midwestern American voice held no hint of boredom. "Still checking. Call you back in half a minute." Then he added belatedly, "Glad you're okay."

Cliff yanked at the buckles of the webbing that held him to his seat and stood up, weightless, peering through the windows. Was the moonscape really significantly closer, or did it just seem that way? Through the window the surface of the moon was falling smoothly away, and the field of view was filling with stars. At least he had taken off with most of his planned speed, and there was no danger he would crash back to the surface immediately.

But he would crash back sooner or later. He could not possibly have reached escape velocity. He was rising into space along a great ellipse—and in a few hours he would be back at his starting point. Or would be except that he'd never get through that last little bit of solid rock.

"Hello Cliff, Frank Penney talking to you." The launch controller sounded almost cheerful. "We've got a first fix on it—we got a transient phase reversal in the fine acceleration sector, God knows why. It put enough drag on you to lop about a thousand klicks off your final velocity. That orbit would bring you right back down on top of us in a little under five hours if you couldn't change it, but no sweat. Your onboard retro's got enough delta-vees stored to kick you into a stable orbit—heck, you could even make it on verniers alone. Your consumables are fat, you've got air enough in there for three people plus safety margins. All you'll have to do is sit tight until we can get a tug from L-1 into your neighborhood."

"Yes of course . . . that doesn't sound too complicated."

Slowly Cliff allowed himself to relax. In his panic he'd forgotten all about the retrorocket, although he didn't intend to admit that to launch control. Low-powered as they were, even the maneuvering rockets could easily put him into a rounder orbit that would clear the moon by a comfortable margin. Though he might fall back closer to the surface than he'd ever flown—except when landing—the view as he skimmed over the mountains and plains would be breathtaking. He'd be perfectly safe. He just had to keep telling himself that.

"So if you've got nothing better to do, why don't you let us talk you through the procedure," said Penney cheerily. "You see a panel marked B-2 on the left of the main instrument board?"

"Yes."

"Find the big T-bar toggle in the middle of it, which is in the down position, ENG, engaged that is, and push it to the up position, which is DISENG, disengaged. A red light should come on."

Cliff found the chrome handle and pushed it up. It went smoothly but with a reassuring firmness of action. "All right, I have a red light in the disengage position."

"Good, that means whatever we do here is off-line. Nothing's gonna go boom before we're ready. Now I want you to find the toggle marked MAN/AUTO, at the top right of the panel, and confirm that it's on AUTO. The toggle's got a light in it, and that light should be yellow."

"Yes, I've got it. It's on AUTO and the light is yellow."

"Right next to it is a similar toggle labeled LOC/REM, which should be yellow and in the REM position, the remote position."

"That's confirmed."

"Good. What we're going to do here is insert a new program so that when we engage again, the maneuver-control system will initiate a burn at our command. We're looking at sort of a minimax situation here, Cliff. The later we burn, the better we can fine-tune your orbit. But at the same time we prefer to do this by line-of-sight transmission rather than routing through the transfer stations—I won't bore you with the technicalities. So anyway, let's first confirm that the MCS is receiving our transmissions as it should. Is the BC narrowband flat-screen showing a green light? That's a little square liquid crystal window down at the lower left of the panel, and it's labeled BC NARROW.''

"Yes, the light's green."

"Okay, we're going to squirt up a little harmless information here, and that should show up on the flat-screen as a bunch of squiggles followed by a message, just the word RECEIVED. You got that?"

Cliff said, "Yes, I understand. I'm standing by."

There was a pause. "What do you have on the LC, Cliff?"

"Nothing. Go ahead when you're ready."

This time the pause was longer. "How about now?"

"There's no change," said Cliff.

"Okay, Cliff . . ." The air was dead a moment. "Looks like we'll be going to manual on this. The narrowband does not seem to be fully up to snuff."

"Please say again," Cliff requested.

"Well, we sent our test message three times and apparently you did not get it. We've queried your narrowband with telemetry and we are not getting anything but noise—sounds like the sizzling rice dish in the dining hall last night. So tell you what, just shove that REM/LOC toggle over to LOC, would you, buddy?"

Cliff did so. "It's on LOC. Now the light is red."

"Great, don't worry about it, we're still disengaged. Now just find that PROG button on row three, second from the left, and tell me if you get a little blue light."

"It's blue."

"Good, that means the computer is ready for instructions. So I'm going to read you a list of numbers, not too long, and you will key them in by hand, okay?"

"Okay. Yes." Let's get on with it, Cliff thought, beginning to get a bit irritated. The launch controller was acting so calm he almost seemed condescending.

"Okay, Cliff, here they come."

Penney read off a list of coordinates in three axes, plus specifications for the intensity and duration of the burn. Cliff read them back as he punched them in.

"Right, Cliff, now just press ENTER and you're all set. That blue light will flicker and turn green."

"I just pressed ENTER. The light flickered, but it's still blue."

"That rascal . . . So, just confirming that we have the T-bar in DISENGAGE, the pilot on AUTO, and the control LOCAL . . ."

"That's all confirmed."

"Give us a sec."

For a long time Cliff stared out the window as the horizon rolled away beneath him.

"I'll tell you what, Cliff"—Penney's voice was, if anything, cheerier yet—"why don't we stick this thing in MAN and ENGAGE and see if we can't just go around the barn. I mean, cut the computer out of the command loop."

"Right now?"

"Sure, buddy. Let's blow you into a higher orbit right now—what the hell, we'll figure the trajectory later. Won't take but a few seconds once we get a couple of Dopplers on you."

"If I'm off will the tug be able to reach me?" Cliff hoped his voice didn't betray the depth of his fear.

"Hell, you're not going anywhere near *that* far out. Trajectory might not be ideal, but you can afford to wait a little longer to rendezvous."

Better than not being able to wait any longer at all, Cliff thought. "What do I do?"

"Just flip her into manual. . . ."

He pushed the toggle to red. "Done."

"Now engage the controls."

He pulled the T-bar down and the light went green. "Done."

"Okay, Cliff, now grab something and hold on. The acceleration's going to be the usual retrofire, about half a gee, but we don't want you barking a shin or something.'' By now Frank Penney was positively jovial.

Cliff twisted his left hand in a firm grip on the cargo net. "Right, then," he croaked.

"Look over to panel B-1, Cliff. There's a big red button with a safety cover on it. Flip up the cover and push the button. Do it now."

The safety cover was painted in diagonal black and yellow stripes; the stenciled label beneath said MAIN ENG. With his right hand Cliff reached out and flipped it up. His left hand gripped the cargo net harder. The fingers of his right were trembling when he pushed the big red button.

Nothing happened.

"Nothing happened," Cliff whispered.

"Ain't that somethin', buddy?" Penney whooped. "Ya know, Cliff . . ." Then the controller's glee suddenly drained away. "You're just going to have to give us a few minutes with this. We'll get back to you."

Cliff barely restrained himself from screaming, begging the controller not to go away. But the man wasn't going anywhere, and there wasn't anything for them to talk about. For whatever reason the capsule's rockets, which a moment ago Cliff had believed would carry him to safety, were utterly useless. In five hours he would complete his orbit—and return to his launching point.

Cliff floated weightless in the tiny tin can, peering out its window as the moon receded. I wonder if they'll name the new crater after me, thought Cliff. I suppose I could ask them to. My last request: "Crater Leyland: diameter . . ." What diameter? Better not exaggerate—I don't suppose it will be more than a couple of hundred meters across. Hardly worth putting on the map.

Launch control was still silent, but that was not surprising. They clearly didn't have any bright ideas, and what do you say to a man who's already as good as dead? And yet, though he knew that nothing could alter his trajectory, even now Cliff could not believe that he would soon be scattered over most of Farside. If that were true, they would have more to be worried about than he did. He was still soaring away from the moon, snug and comfortable in this little cabin. The idea of death was incongruous—as it is to all men, even those who seek it, until the final second.

For a moment Cliff forgot his own problem. The horizon ahead was no longer a mottled curve of cratered rock. Something more brilliant even than the blazing sunlit lunar landscape was lifting itself against the stars. As the capsule curved around the edge of the moon, it was creating the only kind of earthrise possible, an artificial one, no less beautiful for being a product of human technology. In a minute it was all over, such was Cliff's speed in orbit. As his capsule climbed above the moon, the Earth leaped clear of the horizon and swam swiftly up the sky.

It was three-quarters full and almost too bright to look upon. Here was a cosmic mirror made not of dull rocks and dusty plains but of snow and cloud and sea. Indeed it was almost all sea, for the Pacific Ocean was turned toward Cliff, and the blinding reflection of the sun covered the Hawaiian Islands. The haze of the atmosphere—that soft blanket that was to have uplifted the wings of the atmospheric shuttle bringing him home—obliterated all geographic details; perhaps that darker patch emerging from night was New Guinea, but he could not be sure.

There was bitter irony in the knowledge that he was heading straight toward that lovely, gleaming apparition. Another thousand kilometers an hour and he would have made it. One thousand kilometers per hour—that was all. He might as well ask for a billion.

The sight of the rising Earth brought home to him with irresistible force the duty he feared but could postpone no longer. "Launch control," he said, holding his voice steady with great effort, "please give me a circuit to Earth."

"You've got it, buddy."

Cliff told launch control whom he wanted to talk to. For a moment the aether was filled with echoes and clicks.

This was one of the stranger things he had done in his life: to sit here above the moon and listen to the ringing of the phonelink in his own home, 400 thousand kilometers away on the opposite side of Earth. To save money he'd only written faxgrams before; a direct phonelink was an expensive luxury.

The phone kept ringing. It was near midnight down there in Africa, and it would be sometime before there would be any answer. Myra would stir sleepily; then, because she'd been on edge ever since he'd gone into space, she'd wake instantly, fearing disaster.

But they both hated to have a phone in the bedroom, much less wear an earlink like half the self-important people in the world did these days. So it would be at least fifteen seconds before she could switch on the light, pull a wrapper around her bare shoulders, close the nursery door to avoid disturbing the baby, get to the end of the hall, and . . .

"Hello?"

Her voice came clear and sweet across the emptiness of space; he would recognize it anywhere in the universe. He detected at once the undertone of anxiety.

"Mrs. Leyland?" said the Earthside operator. "I have a call from your husband. Please remember the two-second time lag."

Cliff wondered how many people were listening to this call on the moon, on Earth, or, through the relays, throughout the rest of the inhabited solar system. It was hard to talk to your loved ones for the last time when you didn't know how many eavesdroppers were listening in, especially the mediahounds who could soon be splashing your dialogue all over tonight's viddie news.

"Cliff? Are you there?"

As soon as he began to speak, no one else existed but Myra and himself. "Yes darling, this is Cliff. I'm afraid I won't be coming home as I promised. There's been a . . . a technical slip. I'm quite all right at the moment, but I'm in big trouble."

He swallowed, trying to overcome the dryness in his mouth, then went on quickly, overriding her time-lagged interruption—"Cliff, I don't know what you . . ."—before it reached him.

"Myra, listen for a moment. Then we'll talk." As briefly as he could he explained the situation. For his own sake as well as hers, he did not abandon all hope. "Everyone's doing their best," he said. "Maybe they can get a high-orbit tug to me in time. But in case . . . well, I wanted to speak to you and the children."

She took it well, as he'd known she would. He felt pride as well as love when her answer came back from the dark side of Earth.

"Don't worry, Cliff. I'm sure they'll get you back, and we'll have our holiday after all. Exactly the way we planned."

"I think so too," he lied. "But just in case, would you wake the children? Don't tell them that anything's wrong."

There was a hiss of aether before she said, "Wait."

It was an endless half-minute before he heard their sleepy yet excited voices. "Daddy! Daddy!" "Hi, Dad, where are you?"

Cliff would willingly have traded these last few hours of his life to have seen their faces once again, but the capsule was not equipped with such luxuries as a videoplate. Perhaps it was just as well, for he could not have hidden the truth had he looked into their eyes. They would know it soon enough, but not from him. He wanted to give them only happiness in these last moments together.

"Are you in *space*?"

"When are you going to be here?"

It was hard to answer their questions, to tell them that he would soon be seeing them, to make promises that he could not keep.

"Dad, have you *really* got the moondust with you? You never sent it."

"I've got it, Brian; it's right here in my kit." It needed all his self-control to add, "Soon you'll be able to show it to your friends." (No, soon it will be back on the world from which it came.) "And Susie—be a good girl and do everyth—"

"Yes, Daddy?"

"And do everything that Mummy tells you. Your last school report . . ."

"I will, Daddy, I promise. I *promise*."

". . . wasn't too good, you know, especially those remarks about behavior . . ."

"Dad," Brian said.

"But I'll be *better*, Daddy," Susie said, "I promise I will."

"I know you will, darling . . ."

"Dad, did you get those holos of the ice caves you said you would?"

"Yes, Brian, I have them. And the piece of rock from Aristarchus. It's the heaviest thing in my kit . . ."

He tried to put a smile in his voice. It was hard to die at thirty-five, but it was hard, too, for a boy to lose his father at ten. How would Brian remember him in the years ahead? Perhaps as no more than a fading voice from space. Six months was a long time to be away from a ten-year-old.

In the last few minutes, as he swung outward and then back to the moon, there was little enough that he could do except project his love and his hopes across the emptiness that he would never span again. The rest was up to Myra. "Let me talk

to Mom now, will you Brian? I love you, son. I
love you, Susie. Goodbye now.''

He waited out the heartbeats until they said,
'' 'Bye, Dad.''

''I love you too, Daddy.''

When the children had gone, happy but puzzled,
it was time to do some work—the time to keep
one's head, to be businesslike and practical.

''Cliff?''

''Myra, there are some things we should talk
about. . . .''

Myra would have to face the future without him,
but at least he could make the transition easier.
Whatever happens to the individual, life goes on;
and in this century that still involved mortgages
and installments due, insurance policies and joint
bank accounts. Almost impersonally, as if they
concerned someone else—which would soon be
true enough—Cliff began to talk about these things.
There was a time for the heart and a time for the
brain. The heart would have its final say three
hours from now, when he began his last approach
to the surface of the moon.

No one interrupted them. There must have been
silent monitors maintaining the link between two
worlds, but the two of them might have been the
only people alive. While he was speaking Cliff's
eyes remained fix on the dazzling Earth, now more
than halfway up the sky. It was impossible to believe that it was home for seven billion souls. Only
three mattered to him now.

It should have been four, but with the best will
in the world he could not put the baby on the same
footing as the others. He had never seen his
younger son; now he never would.

''. . . I guess I've run out of things to say.'' For
some things a lifetime was not enough, but an hour
was too much.

''I understand, Cliff.''

He felt physically and emotionally exhausted,

and the strain on Myra must have been equally great. He wanted to be alone with his thoughts and with the stars, to compose his mind and to make his peace with the universe. "I'd like to sign off for an hour or so, darling," he said. There was no need for explanations; they understood each other too well. "I'll call you back—in plenty of time."

He waited the long seconds until she said, "Goodbye, love."

"Goodbye for now." He cut the circuit and stared blankly at the tiny control panel. Quite unexpectedly, without desire or volition, tears sprang from his eyes, and suddenly he was weeping like a child.

He wept for his family, and for himself. He wept for his mistakes and for the second chance he wouldn't get. He wept for the future that might have been and the hopes that would soon be incandescent vapor, drifting among the stars. And he wept because there was nothing else to do.

After a while he felt much better. Indeed, he realized that he was extremely hungry. Normally he would have saved his hunger by sleeping until the capsule docked at L-1, but there were emergency rations in the capsule and no conceivable reason for dying on an empty stomach. He rummaged in one of the nets and found the food kit. While he was squeezing a tube of chicken-and-ham paste into his mouth, launch control called.

"Leyland, do you read me?"

"I'm here."

"This is Ven Kessel, Chief of Operations." The voice on the link was a new one—an energetic, competent voice that sounded as if it would brook no nonsense from inanimate machinery. "Listen carefully, Leyland. We think we've found a way out. It's a long shot—but it's the only chance you have."

Alternations of hope and despair are hard on the nervous system. Cliff felt a sudden dizziness; if there had been anywhere to fall he might have stumbled. "Go ahead," he said faintly, when he'd recovered.

"All right, we think there's still some room for an orbital adjustment when you reach apogee. . . ."

Cliff listened to Van Kessel with an eagerness that slowly changed to incredulity. "I don't believe it!" he said at last. "It just doesn't make sense!"

"Can't argue with the computers," answered Van Kessel. "We've checked the figures about twenty different ways, and it *does* make sense. You won't be moving fast at apogee; it doesn't take much of a kick at that point to change your orbit substantially. You've never taken a space walk?"

"No, of course not."

"Pity—but never mind, it just takes a bit of a psychological adjustment. No real difference from walking around outside on the moon. Safer, really. The main thing is you'll be on suit oxygen for a while. So go to the emergency locker in the floor and break out a portable oxygen system."

Cliff found the square hatch stenciled with a blue 02 and a bright red EMERGENCY ONLY. Inside was an oxygen package that clipped into a valve on the front of his suit and augmented his suit's built-in supply. It was a procedure he had practiced in drills.

"Okay, I've got it hooked up."

"Don't open the valve now. Just don't forget to open it once you're outside. Now let's go through the procedure for the hatch trigger."

Cliff's stomach began floating in a different direction from the rest of him when he confronted the big red double-action handle beside the hatch. DANGER, EXPLOSIVE BOLTS.

"That handle pulls straight out and twists up to the left. The pressure hatch blows away. There's going to be decompression, so the proper procedure is to brace your feet on either side of the hatch before you blow it, so you don't bang something vital going out.''

"I understand," Cliff said softly.

"You've got about ten minutes until apogee. We want to keep you on cabin air until then. When we give you the signal, seal your helmet, blow the hatch, climb out there and *jump*."

The implications of the word "jump" finally penetrated. Cliff looked around the familiar, comforting little cabin and thought of the lonely emptiness between the stars—the unreverberant abyss through which a man could fall until the end of time. He had never been in free space; there was no reason why he should have been. He was just a farmer's boy with a master's degree in agronomy, seconded from the Sahara Reclamation Project and trying to grow crops on the moon. Space was not for him; he belonged to the worlds of soil and rock, of moondust and vacuum-formed pumice. Most of all, he longed for the rich loam of the Nile.

"I can't do it," he whispered. "Isn't there any other way?"

"There's not," snapped Van Kessel. "We're doing our damnedest to save you. This is not the time to go neurotic on us. Dozens of men have been in far worse situations, Leyland—badly injured, trapped in wreckage a million miles from help. You're not even scratched and already you're squealing! Pull yourself together right now or we'll sign off and leave you to stew."

Cliff slowly turned red. Several seconds passed before he answered. "I'm all right," he said at last. "Let's go through the instructions again."

"That's better," said Van Kessel with evident approval. "Ten minutes from now, when you're at apogee, seal your helmet, clip your safety, brace yourself, blow the hatch, and climb out there. We won't have communication with you; unfortunately the relay goes through the out-of-commission narrowband. But we'll be tracking you on radar and we'll be able to speak to you directly when you pass over us again. Now remember, when you're out there . . .''

The ten minutes went quickly enough. At the end of that time, Cliff knew exactly what he had to do. He had even come to believe it might work.

''Time to bail out,'' said Van Kessel. ''The capsule's still in a nose-up position and it hasn't rolled— the pressure hatch is pointed pretty much the way you want to go. The precise direction isn't critical. *Speed* is what matters. Put everything you've got into that jump! And good luck.''

''Thanks,'' said Cliff, feeling inadequate. ''Sorry that I . . .''

''Forget it,'' Van Kessel interrupted. ''Now seal up and get moving.''

Cliff sealed his helmet. For the last time he glanced around the tiny cabin, wondering if there was anything he'd forgotten. All his personal belongings would have to be abandoned, but they could be replaced easily enough. Then he remembered the little package of moondust he had promised Brian.

This time he would not let the boy down. He dived to the cargo net and ripped open the seam of his bag. He pushed aside his clothes and toilet gear until he found the plastic package. The minute mass of the sample—only a few ounces—would make no difference to his fate. He pushed it into his thigh pocket. There was something in the pocket he didn't remember putting there, but this was not the time to worry about it. He sealed the seam.

He clipped his safety line to the stanchion. He took hold of the emergency handle with both hands and squatted over the hatch, one boot on either side. Before he twisted the lever he craned his helmeted head over his shoulders to see whether there was anything floating loose in the cabin. Everything seemed secure.

He pulled. The lever didn't budge. He didn't pause to worry; he yanked with all his might. It popped out and he twisted it. There was a simultaneous blast of six bolts that he felt through his feet. The pressure hatch vanished in a stream of vapor.

Decompression was gentler than he expected. The volume of air in the capsule was small and the hatch relatively large, the outflow of wind dwindled quickly to nothing.

With his gloved fingers, suddenly all thumbs, he hauled himself out of the hatch and carefully stood upright on the steeply curved hull of the little tin can, bracing himself tightly against it with the safety line. The splendor of the scene held him paralyzed. Fear of vertigo vanished; even his insecurity deserted him as he gazed around, his vision no longer constrained by the narrow field of the tiny windows.

The moon was a gigantic crescent, the dividing line between its night and day a jagged arch sweeping across a quarter of the sky. Down there the sun was setting and the long lunar night was beginning, but the summits of isolated peaks were still blazing with the last light of day, defying the darkness that had already encircled them.

That darkness was not complete. Though the sun had gone from the land below, the almost-full Earth flooded it with glory. Cliff could see, faint but clear in the glimmering earthlight, the outlines of "seas" and highlands, the dim stars of mountain peaks, the dark circles of craters. Directly below, its lights pricking cheerily through the gloom, was the tiny outline of Cayley Base. Except for that single sign of humanity, he was flying above a ghostly, sleeping land—a land that was trying to drag him to his death.

And far above his head was the life-ring he could not reach, the spidery L-1 space station, its sunlit struts and cables too far away to be visible against the stars.

Now Cliff was poised at the highest point of his orbit, exactly on the line between moon and Earth. It was time to go.

He bent his legs, crouching against the hull. Then, with every bit of strength he could muster, he launched himself toward the stars and the invisible space station far overhead. His safety line uncoiled swiftly behind him; until the length of polyfiber was completely payed out, he could still change his mind.

The capsule dwindled with surprising speed, until it was a mere shadowy speck against the earthlit moon below. As it receded, Cliff felt a most unexpected sensation. He had anticipated terror, or at least vertigo, but not this unmistakable, haunting sense of déjà vu. All this had happened before. Not to him, of course, but to someone else. He could not pinpoint the memory, and there was no time to hunt for it now.

He flashed a quick glance at Earth, moon, and what he could see of the receding shuttle, and he arrived at a decision without conscious thought. He snapped the quick-release. His safety line whipped away and vanished.

He was alone, more than 3,000 kilometers above the moon, 400 thousand kilometers from Earth. He could do nothing but wait; it would be two-and-a-half hours before he would know if he could live. If his own muscles had performed the task that rockets had failed to do.

And as the stars slowly revolved around him, he suddenly recalled the origin of that haunting memory. It was many years since he'd encountered the stories of Edgar Allan Poe, but who could ever forget them?

He too was trapped in a maelstrom, being whirled down to his doom; he too hoped to escape by abandoning his vessel. Though the forces involved were totally different, the parallel was striking. Poe's fisherman had lashed himself to a barrel because stubby, cylindrical objects were sucked down into the great whirlpool more slowly than his ship. It was a brilliant application of the laws of hydrodynamics. Cliff could only hope that his use of celestial mechanics would be equally inspired.

How fast had he jumped away from the capsule? His total delta-vees were a good two meters per second—five miles an hour at most—trivial by astronomical standards, but enough to inject him into a new orbit, one that, Van Kessel had promised him, would clear the Moon by several kilometers. Not much of a margin, but it would be enough on this airless world, where there was no atmosphere to claw him down.

With a sudden spasm of guilt, Cliff remembered that he'd never made that second call to Myra. It was Van Kessel's fault; the engineer had kept him on the move, made sure he had no time to brood on his own affairs. Van Kessel was right, of course: in a situation like this, a man could think only of himself. All his resources, mental and physical, must be concentrated on survival. This was no time or place for the distracting and weakening ties of love.

He was racing now toward the night side of the moon, and the daylit crescent was shrinking as he watched. The intolerable disk of the sun, at which he dare not look directly, was falling swiftly toward the curved horizon. The crescent moonscape dwindled to a burning line of light, a bow of fire set against the stars. Then the bow fragmented into a dozen shining beads, which one by one winked out as he shot into the shadow of the moon.

With the going of the sun, the earthlight seemed more brilliant than ever, frosting his suit with silver as he slowly rotated front to back along his orbit. It took about ten seconds for him to make each revolution; there was nothing he could do to check his spin, and indeed he welcomed the constantly changing view. Now that his eyes were no longer distracted by occasional glimpses of the sun he could see the stars in thousands, where there had been only hundreds before. The familiar constellations were drowned, and even the brightest of planets was hard to find in the blaze of sellar light.

The dark disk of the lunar-night landscape lay across the star field like an eclipsing shadow, and it was slowly growing as he fell toward it. At every instant some star, bright or faint, would pass behind its edge and wink out of existence. It was almost as if a hole were growing in space, eating up the heavens.

There was no other indication of his movement, or of the passage of time, except for his regular ten-second spin. When he looked at the chronometer display on the forearm of his suit he was astonished to see that a half an hour had already passed since he'd left the capsule. He searched for it among the stars, without success. By now it would be several kilometers behind him. But according to Van Kessel it would presently draw ahead as it moved on its lower orbit, and would be the first to reach the moon.

Cliff was still puzzling over this seeming paradox—the equations of celestial mechanics which physicists found so simple were opaque to him, who was at home with the complexity of diploidy and triploidy and selection principles that the same physicists invariably got inside out—when the strain of the past hours, combined with the euphoria of unending weightlessness, produced a result he would hardly have believed possible. Lulled by the gentle susurration of the air inlet, floating lighter than any feather as he turned beneath the stars, Cliff fell into a dreamless sleep. . . .

12

The underground control room of the electromagnetic launcher was a cramped room with two banks of flatscreen consoles facing a wall of larger screens. Half a dozen human controllers could monitor power supply, power control systems, track alignment, cargo loading, space vehicle maintenance—all the other complex subsystems of the launcher.

Topside, work was normally done by radiation-hardened robots and teleoperators; the launcher operated continuously, and radiation from space precluded humans from holding steady jobs on the surface. But for now the launcher had been shut down. The auxiliary reactors that had provided power during the long lunar night were cooling as rapidly as safety permitted. Power from the solar panels, once more flowing in the lunar morning, was shunted to capacitors and banks of monstrous flywheels. The launcher would remain out of commission until its failure was understood and resolved.

On the big wall screens, huge videoplates showed the surface of Farside Base in crisp detail: the launcher track stretched in an uncannily straight line to the east, vanishing at an infinity defined only by the distant peaks of the Mare Moscoviense ringwall. To one side the radio-telescopes were rimmed in the backlight of the low sun, a hundred round ears forming one big ear.

The alarm had gone out by suitlink to everyone working on the surface in the vicinity of Farside Base. Spacesuited men and women dropped what they were doing and trudged away. Tractors and moon buggies turned in their tracks and rolled in stately slow-motion toward the base's central domes and hangars.

Inside the domes and in the labyrinth of underground facilities, yellow warning lights flashed and low sirens moaned in every bay and corridor. Damage-control crews gathered their equipment and reported to standby positions. Everyone whose work was not essential to life support, communications, and emergency services was ordered to head for the deep shelters that had been established in the ice mines.

The inhabited areas of the base were buried under enough regolith to provide plenty of protection against meteorites, from cosmic dust specks on up to massive, thousand-kilogram giants—the sort of monster that might hit somewhere inside the base perimeter once every ten million years, but would likely miss any important structure even then.

The errant launch capsule was far more massive than even a giant meteorite. A bit more acceleration and the derelict would have sailed safely overhead; a bit less and it would have impacted with the moon well before reaching the Mare Moscoviense. But through a chance so unlikely it had been dismissed as neglible when the linear accelerator was designed and built, it was aimed right for the base. The only shred of optimism in this bleak scenario was that, with very minor uncertainties, the moment of impact was predictable.

Van Kessel and a knot of worried controllers clustered around the duty officer's desk at the top of the room. Van Kessel's shiny pate was ringed with unruly gray fuzz, giving him a faintly comic appearance that was flatly contradicted by his hard gray eyes and the firm set of his mouth. He and the others were paying no attention to the base's emergency drill. They were staring at a computer flatscreen that fed out continuously updated data on the capsule's trajectory. Wherever radars on the moon could get a fix on the falling object they monitored its progress, comparing projections of its path against its actual track.

"Still doesn't look very good," muttered Frank Penney. He was a handsome, athletic young man with a deep artificial tan, incongruous among the pale faces of the other controllers.

"No significant deviation," Van Kessel agreed. "It's going to be messy."

"Does Leyland have any idea what's actually going to happen to him?" Penny asked.

"Absolutely not," Van Kessel replied. "I didn't dare tell him. He almost fainted on us as it was."

"Let's hope it wasn't all for nothing."

"At least we kept the poor devil busy for a few minutes. Whatever else, it's going to be a hell of a sightseeing tour."

At some prompting from his subconscious, the "poor devil" woke up. Where was he? Where were the walls of his home? No, of his room on the moon. Of the space capsule. He could see nothing but stars and . . .

Then Cliff remembered. That was the moon down there. He was flying naked, but for a few layers of canvas, through hard vacuum.

The blue-white Earth was sinking toward the moon's horizon. The sight almost brought on another wave of self-pity; for a moment Cliff had to fight for control of his emotions. This was the very last he might ever see of Earth, as his orbit took him back over Farside into the land where earthlight never shone. The brilliant antarctic ice caps, the equatorial cloud belts, the scintillation of the sun upon the Pacific—all were sinking swiftly behind the lunar mountains. Then they were gone; he had neither sun nor Earth to light him now, and the invisible land below was so black that his eyes ached when he peered into it.

A cluster of stars had appeared *inside* the darkened disk where no stars could be. In his still drowsy state, Cliff stared at them puzzled until he realized he was passing above one of the outlying Farside research posts. Down there beneath their portable pressure domes, men and women were waiting out the lunar night—sleeping, working, resting, perhaps quarreling or making love. Did they know that he was speeding like an invisible meteor through their sky, racing above their heads at more than 6,000 kilometers an hour? Almost certainly; for by now the whole moon and the whole Earth must know of his predicament. Already those below must be tracking him on radar, and some might even be searching with telescopes, but they would have little time to find him. Within seconds, the unknown research station had dropped out of sight, and he was once more alone above the dark side of the moon.

It was impossible to judge his altitude above the blank emptiness speeding below, for there was no sense of scale or perspective. Sometimes it seemed that he could reach out and touch the darkness across which he was racing; yet he knew that in reality it must still be many kilometers beneath him.

But he also knew that he was still descending, and that at any moment one of the crater walls or mountain peaks that strained invisibly toward him might claw him from the sky.

In the darkness somewhere ahead was the final obstacle—the hazard he feared most of all. Around the Mare Moscoviense loomed a ringwall of mountains two kilometers high. Those familiar peaks, over which he had passed so often in recent months as automated capsules shuttled him back and forth, were deceptively smooth of surface; like all the hills and valleys of the moon, they had been sanded by countless micrometeorite impacts over billions of years, their defiles filled with the debris. But they were as steep as mountains on Earth, and high enough to snag him at the last instant before he sailed over the base.

The first eruption of dawn took him completely by surprise. Light exploded ahead of him, leaping from peak to peak until the whole arc of the horizon was lined with flame. He was hurtling out of the lunar night, directly into the face of the sun. He would not die in darkness.

The greatest danger was fast approaching. He glanced at his suit chronometer and saw that five full hours had passed: he was almost back where he had started, nearing the lowest point of his orbit. Within moments he would hit the moon—or skim it and pass safely out into space.

As far as he could judge, he was some thirty kilometers above the surface and still descending, though very slowly now. Beneath him the long shadows of the lunar dawn were daggers of blackness, stabbing into the night land. The steeply slanting sunlight exaggerated every rise in the ground, making mountains of the smallest hills.

And now, unmistakably, the ground ahead was wrinkling into the pattern it had taken him so many trips to learn to recognize. Rolling into view, ahead and off to his right, was the deep crater Shatalov, an outlier of the bigger crater Belyaev in the foothills of the mountains. The great western ringwall of the Mare was rising ahead, still more than 150 kilometers away but approaching at well over a kilometer per second. It was a wave of rock, climbing from the face of the moon.

There was nothing he could do to avoid it; his

path was fixed, unalterable. All that could be done had already been done, two-and-a-half hours ago.

It became apparent that what had been done was not enough. He was not going to rise above these mountains; they were rising above him. Straight ahead he could make out the distinctive shape of Mount Tereshkova, the highest peak on the crater's western rim.

Cliff regretted his failure to make that second call to the woman who still waited so many thousands of kilometers away. Yet perhaps it was just as well; perhaps there had been nothing more to say.

Other voices filled the aether as his suit receiver came within range of the base, calling to each other, not to him. They waxed, then waned again as he entered the radio shadow of the ringwall, and some of them were talking about him, although the fact hardly registered. He listened with an impersonal interest, as if to messages from some remote point of space or time, of no concern to him.

He heard Van Kessel's voice say, quite distinctly: ". . . confirming you will receive intercept orbit immediately after Leyland passes perigee. Your rendezvous time now estimated at minus one hour, five minutes."

I hate to disappoint you, thought Cliff, but that's one appointment I'll never keep.

Now the wall of rock was only eighty kilometers away, and each time he spun helplessly around in space to face it, it was fifteen kilometers closer. There was no more room for optimism. He sped more swiftly than a rifle bullet toward that implacable barrier, and it suddenly became of great importance to know whether he would meet it face first, with open eyes, or with his back turned like a coward.

No memories of his past life flashed through Cliff's mind as he counted the seconds that remained. The swiftly unrolling moonscape rotated beneath him, every detail sharp and clear in the harsh light of dawn. No more than three of his ten-second days were left to him. He was turned away from the onrushing mountains, looking back on the path he had traveled, the path that should have led to Earth, when to his astonishment—

—*the moonscape beneath him exploded in silent flame.* Somewhere behind his back a light as fierce as that of the sun instantly banished the long shadows, struck fire from the crests of the surrounding peaks, rimmed the craters which were spread below him in searing brightness. The light lasted only a fraction of a second, and by the time he had turned toward its source it had faded completely.

Directly ahead of him, only thirty kilometers away, a vast cloud of dust was expanding toward the stars. It was as if a volcano had erupted on the flank of Mount Tereshkova—but that, of course, was impossible. Equally absurd was Cliff's second thought: that by some fantastic feat of organization and logistics the Farside engineering division had blasted away the obstacle in his path.

For it was gone. A huge, crescent-shaped bite had been taken out of the approaching skyline; rocks and debris were still rising from a crater that had not existed five minutes ago. Only the energy of an atomic bomb, exploded at precisely the right moment in his path, could have wrought such a miracle. And Cliff did not believe in miracles.

The bizarre vision slid from his sight as he twisted away into another revolution. He had come all the way around and was almost upon the mountains when he remembered that all this while there had been a cosmic bulldozer moving invisibly ahead of him. The kinetic energy of the abandoned capsule—many tonnes, traveling at almost a kilometer-and-a-half every second—was quite sufficient to have blasted the gap through which he now flashed. Appalled at the scope of the destruction, Cliff wondered what havoc the impact of the man-made meteor had wrought on Farside Base.

Cliff's luck held. There was a brief patter of dust particles against his suit, but none punctured it—most of the debris had been propelled outward and forward—and he caught a brief glimpse of glowing rocks and swiftly dispersing smoke falling away beneath him. How strange to see a cloud upon the moon!

Then he was through the western mountains, with nothing ahead but empty black sky. For the moment.

Less than a kilometer away, below and to the left of his path, he saw the track of the electromagnetic launcher whipping past like a picket fence beside a racing car. The launcher was a hairline scribed at great length across the floor of the Mare. Here and there a flash of light and a puff of dust erupted in the regolith below, marking the track of flying debris from the explosion.

Cliff twisted through another lazy revolution and when he came around, half the track was behind him and half still ahead. The twin domes above the most densely inhabited parts of the base flicked away under his feet, well off to his right. Straight ahead of him, fifteen kilometers away, were the hundred silver paraboloids of the antenna farm. Suddenly they lit up with little sparks of light, like a momentary Christmas display. . . .

One more turn. Cliff's view panned like a camera as the base receded behind him, and if Farside had suffered damage, none was visible in his odd and hasty grab shot. But as his eyes came front again, he was passing directly over the great antennas. They were rimmed in sunlight and seemed as broad and round and structurally sound as ever. But Cliff had just the faintest impression that they had been peppered with something black—

—then he was past them. Were those really black spots on the bright dishes? Or were they holes in the shining aluminum? Those bright sparks . . . The lighter shrapnel from the blast had to go somewhere, and the antennas were directly in harm's way.

"Leyland, come in. Leyland, do you read?"

Cliff was suddenly conscious that Van Kessel's voice had been sounding in his ears for several seconds now. "This is Leyland. I hear you. I hear you."

There was just the briefest hesitation before Van Kessel said, even more gruffly than before, "It's about time. Take it you're all right?"

"Fine. Under the circumstances," said Cliff. "Was that bit of fireworks part of the plan all along?"

"Frankly I didn't think it was a good idea to lay it out for you too plainly, Leyland. The whole thing was a long shot."

"Yes, I gather."

Van Kessel's tone shifted; he was strictly business now. "While we've got you in line-of-sight: in less than an hour you'll rendezvous with the tug *Callisto* out of L-1. They'll send a man out on a long tether to grab you. Be aware that there will still be some delta-vee. It should be an easy catch, but for God's sake pay attention and don't mess up the contact. Because this really will be your last chance."

"Don't worry, Van Kessel, I won't mess it up. And thanks."

"Don't mention it," Van Kessel said. "By the way, if you think you've got any panic left in you, you better close your eyes now. . . ."

Cliff was coming around to another head-on confrontation with the lunar mountains, this time the eastern rim of the Mare Moscoviense. He had not really forgotten them, but neither had he really wanted to think about them; they loomed as high, as ominous as the western rim, and suddenly his heart was racing again. What would clear the way for him this time?

He was a fragile spacesuited human hurtling toward the sheer, falsely soft cliffs. Surely he would strike the rim. . . . But this time there was no Mount Tereshkova to bar the way. Cliff flicked past the jagged rim with tens of meters to spare.

A moment later he resumed something like his regular breathing. "One more surprise, Van Kessel, and I swear I'll strangle you."

"No more surprises, Leyl—" Then Van Kessel's hearty voice was swallowed by interference as Cliff passed into the radio shadow of the eastern rim.

Cliff wasted no anxiety on the loss of radio contact. Somewhere up there among the stars, an hour in the future along the beginning of his second orbit, a tug would be waiting to meet him. But there was no hurry now; he had escaped from the maelstrom. For better or worse, he had been granted the gift of life.

And when he had finally climbed aboard that tug he could make that second call to Earth, to that woman, his wife, who was still waiting in the African night.

13

The usual shuttles and tugs took more than a week to reach the L-1 transfer station from low Earth orbit, but a Space Board cutter on an emergency run could make the distance in a day.

Sparta's cutter shut down its plasma torch and sidled up to a ramshackle collection of cylinders and struts and solar panels. The airlock popped and Sparta went through the docking tube into the station, towing two duffel bags behind her. Her ears were ringing and she had a headache that threatened to push her eyes out of her head.

"Welcome, Inspector Troy. I'm Brick, Security." Brick was black, North American-born like Sparta but with the physical grace of a man who'd spent his life in space.

She let the duffels float while she touched his hand lightly, hovering in the cylindrical, padded gate area. "Mr. Brick."

Only a flicker of his lashes betrayed his surprise at her youth and slight build. "Do you want to see Leyland right away?"

"I need to get my bearings first. Is there somewhere we can talk?"

"My office. Give me that—so you'll have a hand to steer with." He took one of her bags and set off toward the core of the station. They squeezed past other station workers, coming and going. Many of L-1's inhabited areas were interconnecting steel and fiberglass cylinders, the original fuel-tank casings from which the station had been built fifty years earlier. "This your first visit?" he asked over his shoulder.

"Yes, and not just to L-1. It's my first trip to the moon."

"But you're one of, what, only nine people ever to land on the surface of Venus?"

"Not a distinction I was seeking."

"Quite a piece of work, if half the viddie stories are true."

"Less than half," she said. "Tell me something about L-1, Mr. Brick."

"You want the standard spiel, or are you changing the subject so I'll shut up?"

"I'm serious."

"Okay, the standard spiel. Back in the 1770s, Joseph Louis Lagrange was studying the so-called three-body problem, and he discovered that in a system of two masses orbiting each other—the Earth and the moon, say—there would be certain points in space around them of gravitational stability, such that an object placed there would tend to remain." Brick paused. "Stop me if you've heard all this before."

"A long time ago. I can use the refresher."

"Okay, three of these so-called Lagrangian points lie on the axis between the two masses and are only partially stable: an object at one of these points—us, for example—if disturbed along the axis, would tend to fall. In our case, toward the Earth or the moon. Two other points, lying on the smaller mass's orbit around the larger but sixty degrees ahead and behind, are very stable indeed. These points, L-4 and L-5, are some of the most valuable 'real estate' in Earth-moon space."

"The space settlements."

"Yes. Of course because of the sun's influence,

the settlements don't sit right on L-4 and L-5, they follow orbits around them.''

''So the Earth and the sun orbit each other, the moon and the Earth orbit each other, and the L-5 settlement orbits L-5. Orbits on orbits on orbits.''

''Yeah, Ptolemy called them epicycles, but these are real, not imaginary. They give shape to space. L-3 is on the opposite side of the Earth from the moon and is of no use to anybody, but L-1 and L-2, the quasi-stable Lagrangian points near the moon, are different. Here at L-1, with a little maneuvering fuel, we maintain a strategic position smack above the center of the Nearside. That's where most of the lunar population is, especially at Cayley. We monitor surface and cislunar navigation and communications. L-2, beyond the moon, was well situated for the transfer of lunar building materials from the mines of Cayley when they were building L-5.''

''Was?''

''That station was mostly dismantled when the heavy work at L-5 was finished. When they built the launcher at Farside Base, the spider webs from L-2 were moved here.''

''The spider webs?''

''Come over here.''

He led her to the nearest thick glass port in the cylindrical station wall. She could see, silhouetted against the stars, two huge, delicate-seeming structures, strange tangles of rails and webbing.

''Basically, they're big cargo nets. You see, we're about half an orbit away from the Farside launcher. They shoot up a dead load and it gets here going about 200 meters per second. Radar tracks it in and those nets whip around the tracks and grab it out of space and slow it down so it can be unloaded. Sixty nets on each set of tracks. Real Rube Goldberg, aren't they? They had five sets at L-2, working around the clock, grabbing moon rocks shot up from Cayley. They were always getting tangled, so a couple were always out of commission. We don't handle nearly as much cargo, mostly liquid oxygen and ice from the mines at Farside." He turned from the window. "So, at the moment we're the moon's only space station. Everything goes through here, up and down. Including illegal drugs. Sometimes I think, *especially* drugs."

Brick led Sparta through several more right-angle turns in narrow corridors to a cramped office with curving walls, his own; it took up a quarter of a slice through one of the cylinders. "Tiny, but it's got a great view. Any more questions I can answer?"

"What shape was Leyland in when he got to you?"

"Pretty cheerful. The skipper of the tug said he chattered for a couple of hours. Couldn't sleep, just wanted to talk. He gave him a physical when he arrived and found him in excellent shape, nothing in his system that wasn't supposed to be there."

"Who has he talked to?"

"Crew of the *Callisto*, me. Other than official business he's been incommunicado. Except I let him talk to his wife. We clamped a command-channel coder on that so he could get through without every viddie reporter in the solar system listening in."

"Good. I assume you listened in, though."

"Standard operating procedure."

"And?"

Brick shrugged. "No new facts. His mood was relief—and maybe a little guilt. Nothing he said. The way he said it."

"Just a *little* guilt?"

"That's right, Inspector. He didn't sound like a man who'd just been caught carrying half a kilo of very expensive white powder in the thigh pocket of his spacesuit."

"What was the analysis?"

"Gabaphoric acid."

"That's a new one to me."

"Fairly new to us, too. Made on L-5, most likely. Apparently very popular on the moon. Keeps you happy as a clam for six months or so. Then your hippocampus turns to oatmeal—couldn't recognize your own mother. We've had two cases like that."

"Why was he smuggling it *off* the moon?"

"Mmm." Brick spread the fingers of one hand and bent them down with the other, one by one, as he ticked off the possibilities. "Because he's hooked on the stuff and doesn't have a source on Earth. Because whoever was using him as a mule paid him off in kind. Because they wanted him to open a new market Earthside . . ." Brick hesitated.

"Go on," Sparta said.

"Because somebody planted it on him."

"And if you had to guess?"

Brick shrugged. "Lots of possibilities. I'll leave it to you."

"I'll talk to him now. Alone would be best."

"Wait here a minute, I'll send him in."

"And Brick—the embargo is still on. Except for those of us who are already in on it, I don't want anyone anywhere to know what you found on Leyland."

When Leyland appeared he was dressed in borrowed coveralls a size too big for him. His expression was grim. "You're from the Board of Space Control?"

"Yes, Mr. Leyland. I'm Inspector Troy."

"You're an inspector?" Cliff glared at her. "I'd have taken you for a clerk."

"I don't blame you for being unhappy, Mr. Leyland. I got here as fast as possible and I won't keep you any longer than absolutely necessary."

"A day in the tug, a day in this smelly tin can. Perhaps I'd rather be orbiting the moon."

Sparta studied him intently, in ways he could not have suspected. Her macrozoom eye inspected the irises of his brown eyes, the pores of his pale exposed skin. His chemical signature was borne to her through the air; she stored it for further reference. His odor, like his voice, carried overtones of exasperation but not of fear or deceit.

She handed him one the duffels. "They gave me these before I left. Said they were your size."

He took the bundled clothes she held out to him. "Well—that was thoughtful of somebody."

"Do you want time to put them on?"

"No, let's get this over with. I must say, I can't understand why this couldn't have waited until I got to Earth."

Because if you give me the wrong answers you're not going to Earth, Sparta wanted to scream at him. She rubbed her neck with one hand and said, quietly, "There are good reasons, Mr. Leyland. Drugs in your pocket, for one."

"As I've repeatedly explained, anyone could have put that in my suit. It was in an outside pocket! If I were a smuggler, I certainly wouldn't have carried it where it would be spotted straightaway when I stepped into L-1, now would I?"

"But of course you would have had two days to make other arrangements. Your journey was interrupted. In the excitement you could have forgotten what you were carrying."

"Am I under arrest, then?" he said defiantly.

"There's no need for that, unless you insist. But there are other reasons for keeping you here, which I think will be clear to you shortly."

"Please do carry on, then," he said, trying his best to be sarcastic.

"First tell me exactly what happened. I need to hear it . . ."

"I've been over that repeatedly with . . ."

". . . from you. In person. Starting with the moment you began packing for the trip."

"Oh all right, then." Cliff sighed. Sullenly he began to retell the tale. The farther he got, the more he became involved in reliving his own experience.

Motionless in the tiny office, Sparta listened to him, rapt with concentration, although every detail of the events he recited was already familiar to her—every detail except the timbre of his own voice, revealing his emotions at each stage of his terrifying descent and his eventual deliverance from gravity's maelstrom.

She was quiet a moment when he finished. Then she said, "How many people might want to kill you, Mr. Leyland?"

"*Kill* me?" Cliff was shocked. "You mean . . . ?"

"Murder you. Because of something you did. Or didn't do. Or might still do. Or as an example to others."

Cliff looked at her with wounded innocence. She almost laughed at him, then; had she grown so cynical in so short a time?

"My background is with the customs and immigration branch, Mr. Leyland. The first thing that occurred to me when I reviewed your records was that your shuttling back and forth between L-5 and Farside carrying agricultural samples would make you a perfect mule."

"A what?"

"A mule is a smuggler's courier. In your agricultural specimen cases you could have secreted any number of small objects. Forged I.D. slivers. Nanochips. Micromachine cultures. Secrets. Jewels. Drugs being the most obvious and most likely. Clearly this also occurred to someone at Farside."

Leyland flushed.

"Drugs it was," she said, reading his expression. "Were you a mule, Mr. Leyland? Or did you turn them down?"

"I refused," he whispered. "I thought I had made it clear to them. Even after they beat me." His voice was rich with self-pity.

"Well, that's a start, isn't it?" she said, trying to

encourage him. "Give me the names and circumstances, please."

"I don't know the names, not certainly. One of them I could recognize, but he's of no importance. . . ."

"I'll judge that," Sparta said.

Leyland hesitated. "Just a moment. The voice . . ."

"What is it, Leyland?"

"The launch attendant—the one who strapped me in just before the capsule went into the launcher. I'm sure it was the same voice. One of the men who beat me up."

"Do you think he could have planted the acid on you?"

"He could have done—while he was checking the seat straps. I didn't notice anything."

"Okay, he'll be easy enough to identify."

"The man who planted the drugs on me certainly didn't try to kill me. What good would it have done him?"

"Quite right. Who else? Who could conceivably have had a motive for revenge?" Floating weightless, she leaned forward to press the question. "Anything, Mr. Leyland. No matter how trivial." He said nothing, merely shrugged, and she knew he was hiding something. "You're an attractive man, Mr. Leyland," (some people might think so), "didn't any of the women at the base tell you that?"

"There was a woman," he whispered. "I don't know how . . ."

"Her name?"

"Katrina Balakian. An astronomer at the telescope facility."

"So she was attracted to you. She made it obvious."

He nodded. Sparta was amused to see Leyland's reaction to what he evidently took to be her intuition.

"And you spurned Ms. Balakian," she said. "Or maybe you didn't. But at any rate, you were going home to your wife and children."

"I saw her only one more time. Do I . . . ?"

"I have no intention of embarrassing you or violating your confidence, Mr. Leyland. But I have to have all the facts."

Reluctantly Cliff told his story. When he was done, Sparta said, "It will be a fairly simple matter to find out whether Balakian had the means and opportunity to sabotage the launcher. It won't be necessary to drag you into it."

"Why do you insist it was sabotaged, Inspector?" he protested. "Why not an accident? These things have failed before, haven't they?"

"Occasionally." It was an understatement. Sparta knew that the electromagnetic launcher at Cayley had suffered glitches aplenty in the early days. Firing five ten-kilogram blocks of sintered moon rock every second for days at a time, the stress on the Cayley launcher was great enough to cause numerous power-control failures. While the area downrange was somewhat safer than a shooting gallery, a thin swath of the moon to the east of Cayley was peppered with meter-wide craters, punched by blocks that fell short.

The engineers who built the big launcher at Farside had benefited from Cayley's experience. Cliff Leyland's accident was the first time Farside's launcher had ever failed during a launch.

"I can't prove it was deliberate or that you were singled out," she said, and smiled. "In fact, I admit it doesn't seem likely, unless this woman you tangled with is the archetype of a vengeful harpy—but I'm simple-minded. I have to start the investigation somewhere."

Leyland, almost against his wishes, smiled with her. "Well—if someone *is* trying to kill me—perhaps I should actually thank you for keeping me here."

"I hoped you'd understand. Just a few more questions, Mr. Leyland. . . ."

An hour later she was falling toward Farside, a passive rider in a capsule like the one that Clifford Leyland had abandoned in mid-flight; rather than ride a Space Board cutter to the surface, she wanted to sample as much of Leyland's experience as possible.

She'd cleared him to continue his interrupted journey to Earth. The poor man's long-awaited homecoming was about to be spoiled by howling newshounds, one reason the Space Board had kept him at L-1—not to protect him from murderers but from the media.

For her, it would be a sleepy ride, and then she would set foot on the busy moon for the first time. . . .

PART
5

AT THE CROSSROADS

14

They sent a moon buggy to fetch her from the landing field. She spent half-an-hour in the tiny office of Farside Security, querying the computer files, before she phoned Van Kessel at launch control. "Inspector Troy, Board of Space Control. Let's see if we can find out what's bugging your system, Mr. Van Kessel."

"I'll be there to pick you up in twenty minutes," Van Kessel replied.

"This is where we control the whole operation," Van Kessel said importantly, as men and women squeezed past him to take their places at their consoles or to get out the door to the trolley stop; Van Kessel and Sparta had arrived in the narrow-tiered control room just as the shift was changing. "Most systems are fully automated," he said, "but we humans like to keep an eye on what our robot friends are doing."

Sparta listened without comment as he explained at length the functions of each console station, even though most were self-evident at a glance. This was the first stop on what already promised to be a long tour of the electromagnetic launcher; her head was throbbing again. She focused her attention on the big videoplate screens on the forward wall. They showed that, except for the inactive launcher itself, Farside Base had returned to normal activities.

The only things visibly out of the ordinary were the occasional coruscations of light that played over the concave shadows of the distant radiotelescope antennas. The monitoring camera that viewed the eastern portion of the landscape was mounted halfway down the launcher track; the track stretched away for twenty kilometers toward the sun, and the antennas to one side of it were barely visible in the picture, a wide, flat row of rim-lit circles, like a raft of soap bubbles viewed edge on. The big screen had plenty of resolution, and Sparta's right eye zoomed in on the sector, enlarging the image of the telescopes. They were racked low, pointing to the southern sky, with their line of aim presently crossing the launch track. The sparks were from electric welders; spacesuited humans and bare metal servos were crawling over the faces of some dishes, patching the damage caused by the debris from "Crater Leyland."

"Frank, I want you to meet Inspector Troy," Van Kessel said.

Sparta turned her attention back to the control room. A sandy-haired man in his mid-thirties was smiling at her out of a handsome, artificially tanned face.

"This is Frank Penney, Inspector," Van Kessel said. "He's in charge this shift. Frank was the launch director on duty when we encountered our little glitch."

"You rescued those guys on Venus, didn't you?" he said with boyish enthusiasm as he reached for her hand. "That was really something."

"Mr. Penney." When she shook his hand his grin got wider, showing lots of perfect white teeth. Frank Penney on parade. She couldn't help but notice his deep chest rippling under his thin short-sleeved shirt, his muscular forearms, the firmness of his grip.

"Hey, it's really an honor." His eye held hers. He was pouring on the charm—out of habit.

Sparta tugged her hand free. Her interest in him was not what he hoped. As she watched him she inhaled his faint odor. Under the aftershave perfume and ordinary human sweat there was an odd aroma; its formula popped into her mind unbidden, a complex steroid with unusual side chains. Was Penney hyped on adrenalin? Nothing about him suggested fear or excitement; in fact he seemed quite a cool character.

Van Kessel said, "We're going to look over the site, Frank, how'd you like to come with us?"

"Great, if you don't mind."

"Don't be silly," said Van Kessel, playing the gracious boss to Penney's favored employee. "Let's get suits on and get out there."

"That's the end of the rough acceleration track—twenty-seven kilometers of it—and now we're coming into the three-kilometer stretch of track for fine-tuned acceleration."

Van Kessel filled the driver's seat of the moon buggy to overflowing, with Sparta and Penney squeezed in behind. They were bounding along beside the massive structure of the launcher track, which seemed to stretch endlessly across the level floor of the Mare Moscoviense, and every time Van Kessel raised a gloved hand to gesticulate, the buggy swung dangerously toward the track supports. He was not a good driver. Sparta itched to grab the moon buggy's controls.

"How rough is rough?" she asked, hoarsely.

"The whole track is built from independently-powered sections, each ten meters long," he shouted over his shoulder. "Over the whole length of the rough acceleration track we can let them get out of line by up to four or five millimeters. More than that and you get oscillations in the capsule that would shake the teeth out of your head. Also we're less concerned with the precise acceleration rate here—we let it vary up to a centimeter per second-squared. In the fine-tuned section we tolerate no more than a millimeter variation from a perfectly straight line and no more than a millimeter per second-squared off the ideal acceleration.''

"How do you keep three kilometers of track straight to within one millimeter?'' She addressed the question to Penney. Her headache had subsided and she was managing to sound more persuasively interested now, but in fact she had memorized the plans and technical specifications of the Farside launcher before leaving Earth and could call them to consciousness instantly. It was not the sort of knowledge she wanted anyone to know she had.

"The variations aren't too bad to begin with,'' Penney explained. ''Mostly expansion and contraction with lunar night and day. And we get a bit of sag between the track supports. The active-alignment technology itself is practically ancient, developed last century for particle accelerators, compound optical telescopes, that stuff.''

Van Kessel broke in. He liked to talk better than he liked to listen. ''Basically we're dealing with laser beams and active track elements—those pistons, you can see them on the supports, that continually push the track this way and that if the beam starts to wander off target. Acceleration is actively controlled by the capsule itself, broadcasting accelerometer readings to the power-control units on the upcoming section of track.''

"What's the reason for the fine-tuning?''

"Aim,'' said Penney.

"Right,'' Van Kessel shouted. ''If a load leaves the launcher a centimeter to one side of its true path, or a centimeter per second too fast, it's going to be hundreds of meters wide by the time it reaches apogee. It could miss the spider web at L-1 altogether. We're talking dead loads, of course.

The capsules can adjust their flight path after they leave the launcher.''

''If the first thirty kilometers of track accelerate the load, what're the last ten for?'' Sparta asked.

''Drift track,'' said Penney. ''The load is already at escape velocity—that is, it's supposed to be—and it just glides along without friction while we make final adjustments in aim. At the end the track curves gently away beneath, following the curve of the moon, and the load keeps going straight over the mountains into space, neat as you please.''

Just then Van Kessel jerked the buggy's yoke to one side and they skidded to a stop. ''We're here. This section is where the phase reversal occurred. Let's seal up.''

They sealed their helmets. Van Kessel hit the pumps to suck the cockpit air into storage tanks. The buggy's bubble popped up and they climbed out onto the dark gray rubble that covered the crater floor.

Van Kessel scrambled up one of the squat, sawhorse-like legs that supported the accelerating track. ''Watch your step.'' Sparta followed him, and Penney came after her.

Sparta stood on the track with the two men. It was lunar morning, and the gleaming, uneroded, unoxidized metal of the quiescent launcher pointed directly at the sun. The loops of the guide magnets circled the three of them. The gleaming loops receded on both sides, seemingly to infinity, constricting until they seemed to become a solid bright tube of metal, finally vanishing in a bright point. It was like looking through a newly cleaned rifle barrel. When she turned and looked in the opposite direction, the sensation was the same.

Torrents of electric current flowed through the accelerating track when it was operating, but for the moment they could walk the track without fear.

''We've been over this piece damned carefully,'' said Van Kessel. ''I don't think you'll find much.''

Sparta didn't answer, only nodded. Then she said,

"Wait here, please." She left the men standing and paced the length of the section, half a kilometer long.

The launcher was a linear induction accelerator—in effect an electric motor unrolled lengthwise. The moving capsule played the role of rotor, while the track played the role of stator. As the capsule, levitated on strong fields generated by its own superconducting magnets, passed from one section of track to the next, the track's electric fields switched phase behind it and in front of it, pulling it forward ever faster, just as in an electric motor the rotor spins faster as current to the stator is alternated faster.

But if the alternation reverses phase, the rotor can be dragged to a violent halt. Before Sparta visited the control room she examined recordings of the near-fatal launch sequence; they confirmed Van Kessel's report that the phase had been reversed in these several sections of track during Cliff Leyland's launch, slowing his capsule so that it failed to achieve escape velocity.

It had taken the trackside monitors a split second to note the failure and switch the track off altogether, preserving the capsule's momentum. Another fraction of a second passed, and the fields came back on, restoring acceleration to the capsule—but it was too little and too late to boost the capsule to escape velocity.

As Sparta walked the track, inspecting it with senses that would have astonished the two engineers, Sparta could see no sign of damage or tampering. She paused at the accident site and stood quietly a minute. She was about to turn back when suddenly she felt a queer sensation, a kind of queasiness accompanied by an inaudible chittering in her head. She looked around but could see nothing unusual. The sensation passed as quickly as it had come.

Slowly Sparta walked back to where the engineers waited.

"That's the power-control station for this section?'' she asked, nodding to a black box on a post beside the track, bristling with antennas.

"Yes. It's functioning perfectly. We checked."

"Bear with me while I make sure I've got this straight: as it accelerates, the capsule—or the bucket, for dead loads—transmits coded information about its exact position and rate of acceleration to these power-control stations, telling them what phase and field strength and when to turn the track sections on?"

"Correct."

"Could the capsule transmit erroneous information? Could it have sent a signal reversing the phase of this section of track?"

"That's supposed to be impossible. Before the signals are sent, three onboard processors make independent judgments based on the accelerometer readings. Then they vote."

"So if the capsule sent an erroneous signal," Sparta said, "either all three processors went crazy in the same way at precisely the same instant, or somebody programmed them to lie."

Van Kessel nodded solemnly.

Sparta gave him a spare smile. "Mr. Van Kessel, you're not a reticent man. But you haven't once mentioned the word sabotage."

He grinned broadly. "I figured you'd reach that conclusion on your own."

"I didn't have to come all the way to the moon to reach that conclusion. Sabotage was apparent from the facts."

"Oh?" Frank Penney chirped. "You were ahead of us, then."

"I doubt that. It wasn't that the launch *failed*," she said. "It was the way it failed."

"Strange, wasn't it?" Van Kessel said, nodding again. "An adjustment in launch velocity so precise that Leyland's orbit would bring him right back down where he started. The odds against it are almost impossibly large."

"And the failure occurred right where you could do nothing to prevent it—not enough track left to accelerate the capsule to launch velocity, and not enough left to stop it without crushing Leyland."

"Right," Penney said with relish. "If we'd tried to decelerate him in the drift section, he would have been all over the inside of that thing like a bug on a windshield."

"I did think it was sabotage," Van Kessel said, "but old engineers are superstitious. We know that sooner or later anything that can go wrong *will* go wrong. Murphy's Law."

"Yes, and it's sound statistical thinking. It's why I wanted to see the hardware for myself." Sparta was silent a moment, staring in the direction of what everyone was already calling Crater Leyland, far away on the slopes of Mount Tereshkova. She turned. "Can we have a look at the loading shed?"

They climbed down from the launcher and packed themselves into the vehicle. Van Kessel shoved the throttle forward and the big-wheeled buggy wheeled around and galloped off across the moon.

A few minutes later Sparta and Van Kessel were peering through a thick glass window at the interior of the loading shed. The graceless steel barn, lit by rows of bare blue light tubes, stretched for almost half a kilometer beside the launcher track at ground level; a forest of steel posts supported its flat roof.

Penney had gone on to the control room, but the loquacious Van Kessel was delighted to continue squiring Sparta around. "You should see the place when it's working," he said. "All those tracks are full of capsules shunting along like cars on a carnival ride."

The floor of the huge shed was a switching yard, a spaghetti platter of magnetic tracks, laid out so that empty capsules and buckets for dead loads could be loaded at the far side of the shed and shunted forward gradually, one at a time, steered to their designated places in line. As the capsules approached the launcher they were grabbed by stronger fields and shoved into its breech.

"The launcher can handle up to one capsule or bucket a second," Van Kessel said. "Since the track is built in sections, each load is independently accelerated even if thirty loads are all traveling down it at once."

Dead loads and inert freight capsules were handled by robot trucks and overhead cranes, but for human passengers and other fragile cargo a pressurized room with docking tubes was provided at one end of the shed. Sparta and Van Kessel were in it now, standing before its big window, still suited, their helmets unlatched. Waiting capsules were lined up at platform's edge. The place had all the charm of a subway platform.

Out in the shed nothing moved accept dancing shadows cast by a lone robot's welding torch. Sparta turned away from the window. She ducked through one of the docking tubes and squeezed through the hatch into an empty capsule.

She spent a moment confirming that the interior layout was identical to that of the capsule she'd ridden to the Moon—control panel, acceleration couches, baggage nets, emergency supplies and all. "How long do you give passengers to get aboard?" she called to Van Kessel.

"We like them here an hour early, but people who travel a lot can usually get themselves strapped in and do a system check pretty quickly—ten minutes or so." Van Kessel extended his hand to help her as she climbed back out of the docking tube. "We have manned-launch attendants here to assist."

"So passengers don't walk in and take any available capsule?"

"No, the capsule's are designated in advance, usually the day before. We don't like to send up any extra mass that has to come back down again, so we talk to L-1 and try to calculate the return trip fuel requirements at this end."

"Whoever sabotaged the capsule could have known a day in advance that Cliff Leyland was going to be in it alone?"

"That's right. Like now—we've got a dozen people waiting right now for us to clear the launcher. Every one of these capsules is earmarked in launch order."

"Yet we're free to climb in and out of them?"

"If we weren't who we are, Inspector, I assure you we couldn't have gotten into this area. It's well guarded—by robot systems that don't stop to ask questions."

Sparta said nothing, but continued to watch Van Kessel.

Nervously he twisted a strand of his gray fringe. "Is something wrong?"

"Do you know who the manned-launch attendants in this area were on the day of Leyland's mishap?"

"Penney will have that info. As I said, it was his shift."

"Penney, Inspector Troy needs some information," said Van Kessel.

"Inspector?" Frank Penney swiveled his chair toward her. He brushed his fingers lightly through his hair.

"I understand you have customers standing by for the launcher to resume operation."

"That's an understatement." Penney smiled his charming smile. "You can see the manifest here— all on hold." He gestured to a flatscreen packed with names and cargo numbers.

She glanced at it, and in that instant committed it to memory.

"As you can tell, the economy of Farside Base hangs upon your whim, Inspector," Penney said lightly. "We're all waiting for you to let us get back to our jobs."

Sparta looked around the room. All the controllers were watching her. She turned to Van Kessel.

"We'll handle that as soon as possible. One thing you can do for me."

"What's that?"

"I'll need the use of a moon buggy," she said.

"I'll be happy to drive you where . . ."

"That's okay, I'll drive myself. I'm checked out."

It occurred to Van Kessel that a woman who could drive a Venus rover could drive a moon buggy. "Take the one we used before."

"Thanks. By the way, Mr. Van Kessel, I noticed you're set up so that anyone in the room can unilaterally execute an override instruction without corroboration from the robot systems."

"Manual override? That's an emergency measure. We've never used it."

"We never had a failure before Leyland's," Penney put in. "Manual override wouldn't have done us any good there anyway."

"You might consider putting fail-safe locks on your directed override procedures," Sparta suggested.

"Is that an official recommendation?"

"No, do what you think best, it's your department. As far as the Board of Space Control is concerned, you can resume operations at your discretion. I'm satisfied you don't have an equipment problem."

"We'll give the override matter some study."

"Let me know what you decide." She turned toward the door.

"Oh, Inspector," said Van Kessel, "weren't you going to ask Frank about . . . ?"

"About the launch attendants the day of the failure? No, Mr. Van Kessel, I already know their names. Pontus Istrati. Margo Kerth. Luisa Oddone. I asked if *you* knew who they were."

Van Kessel watched Sparta leave the control room. His expression was unusually thoughtful. The normally cheerful Penney was staring morosely at his console.

15

The night of his escape, Blake had spent hours haranguing the flowing waters of the Seine from the cobblestones of the Quai d'Orsay before his irresistible urge to talk finally faded into mutterings, and he was able to sink exhausted to the ground in sleep.

The coppery light of morning was reflecting from the ripples in the oily river before he thought he could trust his own mouth. At last he walked to a cafe and made an anonymous call to the police to report an "accident" in the basement of Editions Lequeu on the Rue Bonaparte.

In his present mood he would not have deeply mourned the death by chlorine gas of Lequeu and Pierre, but he knew too much about toxins and dosage to believe that the two men would suffer anything worse from the episode than lingering coughs. He had no doubt they had long since made good their escape; still, it wouldn't hurt to let the police paw through whatever remnants of the Athanasian Society had been left behind.

Blake hung up the phonelink and quickly moved to another cafe, where he dosed himself with expresso while he considered his next move. He realized he was in great physical danger, perhaps as much danger as Sparta. He knew too much; indeed, he knew even more than the Free Spirit knew he knew.

Although Blake had no surgically enhanced memory or calculating skills, the SPARTA project had developed his natural abilities to their peak. He had had an opportunity to study the stolen papyrus thoroughly before handing it over to Lequeu, and he had had more than a week to think about its significance in the light of the teachings of the Free Spirit.

The papyrus was a star map. Evidently the Free Spirit were interested in a particular star, and Catherine had been assigned to find out which star it was. More than that, she had been sent to do something about it.

What could anyone *do* about a star? Nothing but observe it. And what could be revealed by observation? Blake could think of only one thing that would be of interest to the Free Spirit. The Free Spirit believed in the return of the Golden Age. No doubt they hoped to find out where it was returning *from*.

In his days of solitude and introspection, Blake had mentally reconstructed the pyramid described in the ancient papyrus. The text of the scroll had named the days when the pyramid would specify a line through the heavens that would point the way, as the papyrus phrased it, to the stars the "god-messengers" had "steered by." The relation of visible sky and Earth and the count of days by calendar had changed much in the past few thousands of years; without access to the right computer programs Blake could not pick a star, but he could pick a group of likely candidates. And he knew exactly what constellation to look in.

Blake found another infobooth and linked himself to his computer in London. In a few seconds he had determined that someone, presumably Sparta, had accessed the README file. If she'd read the file, surely she'd found and deciphered his message. Why hadn't she followed him?

He broke the link before his computer overheated, promising himself to rig a means of remote-controlling its cooling system just as soon as he got home. Then he placed another call, still routed through his London address, to the Earth Central headquarters of the Board of Space Patrol. "My name is Blake Redfield. I have a message for Inspector Ellen Troy."

"Where are you now, Mr. Redfield?"

"I can't tell you that. My life could be in danger."

"Stand by, Mr. Redfield."

"I'll call back," he said quickly. "Please locate Troy and tell her I'm trying to reach her." He keyed off the phonelink and walked quickly away.

Blake was on his way up the Boul Mich to find a different infobooth when a gray electric sedan glided silently to the curb a few paces in front of him. A tall man with blue eyes and iron-gray hair, his skin so dark Blake momentarily took him for an Arab, alighted from the passenger side of the sedan in a movement of quick athletic grace. His left hand was held away from his side, palm out to show that it was empty, while in his right hand he held an open badge case displaying the gold star of the Board of Space Patrol.

"You must be Redfield," he said, forcing the words out of his throat in a harsh whisper. "Troy's out of touch, but I happened to be in the neighborhood."

"Who are you?" Blake demanded.

"Sorry, no time to get acquainted," the blue-eyed man whispered. "Whatever you have to say to Troy, I'll see she gets the message."

Blake had turned sideways, reducing the size of the target he presented, and his weight was balanced to run. "What I have to say is for her alone."

The blue-eyed man nodded. "That can be arranged."

"How?" Blake demanded.

"I'll let you handle this on your own, if that's the way you want it. But be cautious, Redfield. We traced your call right through London and back to you in five seconds flat. You're lucky Troy left me here with instructions to find you."

"You work for her?"

"You could put it that way. If you want to talk to her, you can come with me now—or if you prefer, get to DeGaulle on your own. Tonight at twenty-two hundred. C terminal, shuttle gate nine. We'll get you to her. If you don't show, forget it."

"Where is she?" Blake asked.

"You'll recognize the place when you get there."

"All right," Blake said, allowing himself to relax. "I guess I may as well let you give me a lift."

The man with the gravelly voice left Blake at the shuttle gate. The Space Board shuttle lifted off minutes later.

In less than an hour Blake was being escorted through the weightless corridors of the Space Board station in low-Earth orbit, onto another ship. Everyone treated him with cool courtesy, although even his most casual questions went unanswered. When Blake realized they had put him on a Space Board cutter, something like awe crept in under his nonchalant manner. Immense resources had been placed at Sparta's disposal. He had no way of knowing that Sparta would have been as awed and puzzled as he. . . .

The cutter left orbit under brutal acceleration, and in little over a day Blake saw their destination on the cabin screens. Yes, he recognized the place. The cutter was diving for Farside Base on the moon.

* * *

''You are Inspector Troy?'' Katrina Balakian's eyes took in Sparta's small frame. ''You are the Inspector Troy who saved the lives of Forster and Merck on the surface of Venus?''

''I was lucky,'' Sparta mumbled. She was not delighted to be so famous, but she supposed she'd better get used to it.

''I am honored to meet you,'' said the astronomer, extending her gloved hand to Sparta. Both women were still wearing their pressure suits; Katrina had just come from inspecting the progress of the antenna repairs.

Katrina led Sparta to a little coffee area at one end of a brightly lit corridor in the telescope facility's central operations bunker. She seemed not to care about privacy; men and women passed frequently, bestowing curious glances on them as they sat down. The underground was redolent of body odors, and among them Sparta noted a tantalizing suggestion of a personal aroma she had encountered somewhere before.

''My colleague Piet Gress will be envious of me,'' Katrina said.

''Oh?'' Sparta spent a fraction of a second searching her memory for the name; she realized that she'd seen it on the manifest of passengers and cargo standing by to use the launcher.

''Albers Merck is his uncle.'' Katrina grinned broadly; her high cheekbones glowed. ''He will be envious that I have met you. And he is already mad enough at me.''

''Why is he mad at you?'' Sparta asked. Katrina seemed remarkably ready to share her thoughts, whether or not they had anything to do with the business at hand.

''He is a signal analyst; he develops programs to study the radio signals we receive—to look for patterns. His passionate dream is to receive a message from a distant civilization, to be the first to decipher it. He is mad at me because our search program is looking in areas he does not consider fruitful. And I support the current program.''

''Does he take it so personally?''

''He is eager to make his great discovery. Meanwhile the telescopes are pointed somewhere of more interest to us astronomers.''

''That would be the constellation Crux at present, is that right?'' Of course it was right.

''You've made yourself familiar with our work, I see. Not that we will do any astronomy for a while—not until the antennas are repaired. They suffered superficial damage from debris when Leyland's abandoned capsule impacted.''

''Yes, I know. The principal purpose of this facility is to search for extraterrestrial civilizations, isn't it?''

''We are looking for signs of intelligent communication, yes. From the media stories, you would think that is our only purpose. But I assure you that we manage to do some basic science on the side.''

''Well, I hope Mr. Gress will not stay mad at you.''

''Once I cared what he thought. He didn't care that I cared.'' She shrugged. ''Now it does not matter. We are not doing astronomy and we are not listening for aliens, not until the antennas are patched.'' Katrina smiled. ''Listen to me talk and talk! You came to ask questions.'' Apparently the prospect of being questioned by the law did not bother Katrina Balakian in the least.

''Someone tried to kill Clifford Leyland,'' Sparta went on. ''You knew him. . . .''

Katrina laughed, a loud, rich laugh, filled with genuine good humor. ''You think I would bother? He is a *worm*.''

''Leyland said that after his first meeting with you—a drink at your apartment, I believe—he decided to ask you for another meeting.'' Actually he'd said considerably more, that he couldn't get Katrina out of his mind, perhaps it was the sheer strangeness and novelty of her, so big and bold and straightforward: the strapping astronomer was not at all like his wife. Whatever Katrina's attraction, Cliff said, he had found that he couldn't walk away from it.

"A meeting, yes. If that is the word for it." Katrina still seemed amused. "The next day after I tried to wrestle him, he called. He apologized to me and said he needed to talk to someone, that I was the only friend he had made on the moon. He asked me to meet him for dinner. I said yes, okay, let's have a drink first, my room. He came over and told me that some men had beaten him up the night before, after he left my room. I convinced him to show me his bruises. They were tender, but they weren't really serious." She grinned wolfishly. "We never went to dinner."

Sparta nodded solemnly. According to what Leyland had told her, he'd spent the night with Katrina, and when he went to work the next day he was still dazed with fatigue, plagued with guilt—only to find out that he'd suddenly been transferred back to Earth—back to his family. He didn't even bother to inform Katrina. Terrified by what he'd done, he turned off his commlink and for the next few days refused to answer her messages.

"Let a man sleep with you, then he pretends you don't exist, refuses to talk to you, not even to say 'no more'—how would *you* feel?" Katrina's grin had faded, and her pink skin was bright with remembered indignation.

Sparta had never been in such a situation and could not imagine it. For a moment she felt more like an eavesdropper—a rather eager one—than a somber investigator. She became aware that she was sympathizing with Katrina. There was something about Cliff Leyland, something *sneaking* masquerading as shyness, that might fool a woman once or twice but would finally, inevitably, infuriate her. He seemed to Sparta like a victim walking around waiting for disaster to strike. She didn't reveal her feelings to Katrina, however. "You admit you had a motive, then?"

"Yes," Katrina said fiercely. "If you think that is a strong motive. But in the end, what importance? Besides, if I had killed him, everyone would know it. I would have broken his neck."

"I see."

Katrina's hands were hidden by the gloves of her pressure suit, but her arms were long and her shoulders were wide; she looked as if she'd been made to tame horses—perhaps her ancestors had been among the legendary Scythians. At any rate, Katrina seemed like a woman who acted upon her desires right away, if she intended to act on them at all, the kind of woman who would write off her losses, not endlessly brood over them.

Cliff Leyland's launch failure had occurred the day Sparta had traveled from London to Paris in search of Blake—shortly after Cliff had met Katrina Balakian as she was returning from her extended leave. If Katrina had wanted to, she'd had the time she needed to plot his demise—although, privately, Sparta doubted she'd had anything to do with it. "If necessary, can you establish where you were for the twenty-four hours preceding the launch?"

Katrina smiled. "In a place this small, everyone knows where everyone else is all the time. Or thinks they do."

"Assuming you *didn't* try to kill Leyland . . ."

"Sorry, I don't know who did. He said the men who beat him up wanted him to smuggle for them, and he refused. Perhaps they decided to go farther, to make sure he would stop spreading tales."

"Do you know who they were?"

"One hears names." She leaned away.

"Is one of the names Pontus Istrati?"

"Perhaps."

"Others?"

"Many people here use drugs, it is not hard to find a source. I don't like repeating hearsay," Katrina said.

"This isn't the 20th century," Sparta replied. "We don't throw people in jail without sufficient evidence, properly come by. Tell me the names."

Katrina took a second to think about it. She expelled her breath through flared nostrils. "Okay," she said—and gave Sparta a half-dozen names. "But Inspector, don't you think it might have been an accident after all?"

"The capsule was almost certainly sabotaged."

"I mean it was an accident that Cliff was aboard that capsule. Perhaps the guilty party wished to destroy the capsule itself. Or something in it."

Sparta smiled. "An interesting hypothesis."

"But to you, obviously, not a new idea."

"I'll let you know how it all comes out." Sparta rose easily in the fractional gravity. "Thanks for your help."

Katrina got to her feet and this time stripped off her glove, shaking hands with Sparta vigorously. Then she hesitated, looking past Sparta's shoulder.

Sparta turned to see a sad-eyed, tall young man, passing in the hall. He was dressed in a pressure suit and carried a suitcase.

"Goodbye, Piet," Katrina said to him quietly.

The man said nothing, only nodded briefly and kept walking.

Katrina looked back at Sparta, then smiled and turned away.

Sparta thought her parting smile was rather sad. But that was only one of the startling facts she had registered in the brief exchange. In touching the bare skin of Katrina's hand she had analyzed the woman's amino-acid signature and had suddenly identified the aroma, mixed until now with the human reek of the crowded corridor, that had eluded her.

Katrina Balakian was the woman who had searched Blake Redfield's apartment.

The retrorockets of an incoming spacecraft burst into flame over Sparta's head as her moon buggy sped across the gray plain. The white ship with the blue band and gold star settled gently toward the landing field beyond the domes. Sparta wondered what could have brought the cutter back to the moon so soon after she'd left it at L-1.

16

After twenty kilometers of bumpy, dusty driving beside the endless launcher track, Sparta was approaching the center of the base. For most of the distance she'd been pondering what connection could possibly exist between Blake Redfield and Katrina Balakian. What Sparta knew of Balakian from the files indicated that the astronomer had been on Earth on a three-month leave of absence, all of which had been spent on the shores of the Caspian Sea. No one knew better than Sparta how easily such records could be faked.

Could there be some innocent explanation for why Balakian's mark had been on Blake's apartment? Sparta could think of none. On the other hand, Balakian's relationship with Blake had nothing to do with Cliff Leyland's near-fatal non-accident, of that she was certain, because the answer to the Leyland mystery was already clear. . . .

Her commlink hissed. "Van Kessel here, Inspector Troy. We've installed the fail-safe devices you suggested."

"That was quick."

"It was an easy circuit change. A unilateral manual command now requires the agreement of at least one power-control computer."

"Good. When are you restarting the launcher?"

"On your right."

Sparta looked up as a bucket carrying a dead load flashed silently toward her and disappeared past her, down the track. A second later another bucket streaked by. Then another. And another. Soon an invisible beaded string of tiny projectiles was stretching into space behind her.

Sparta skidded the awkward buggy to a halt outside the maintenance dome. She didn't bother with the vehicle airlocks; her helmet was locked and she'd left the buggy's interior in vacuum. She hopped out and walked toward the dome's nearest personnel entrance.

Her commlink hissed again. "Landing field dispatch, Inspector Troy. A Space Board cutter just sat down out here. Pilot says she wants you to come out and pick up a passenger."

"Patch me through, please."

"She's on the link."

"Who's your passenger, pilot?" Sparta demanded.

"I'm not at liberty to divulge that," the pilot replied. "My orders are to deliver the passenger to you and nobody else."

Sparta recognized the woman. "How much of a hurry are you in, Captain Walsh?"

"We'll be refueling for an hour," the pilot replied. "Then we're gone."

"I have business. I'll get out to you before you're topped off."

"Fine with me, Inspector Troy."

Sparta's business was an unscheduled interview with a launch technician, whom she intended to escort to Base Security before the next shift change at the launcher. The name Pontus Istrati had been high on Sparta's list of suspects since shortly after she'd set foot on the moon. She'd gotten the name directly from personnel files: Istrati was one of the three people on duty as launch attendants the day of Clifford Leyland's near-fatal launch. The other two were women. The voice Cliff Leyland heard before the hatch closed on him was a man's.

And it was a distinctive voice. Sparta had been grimly amused to find, after a bit of cross-checking, that Istrati didn't bother to hide the mellifluous tones Leyland had found so noticeable—Istrati had a local reputation around the base as singer in a jazz combo.

As for the Farside smuggling ring of which Istrati was such an incautious member, Sparta had little doubt it was run by Frank Penney. Penney had more than means and opportunity; he had the entire launch operation under his control. He even *smelled* of drugs. Katrina Balakian was not the only person who had named Penney as one of the people who supposedly could get you what you wanted.

None of which was proof, or even admissible evidence. Sparta hoped Mr. Istrati would lead her to that. More than a smuggling ring was at stake. Sparta was sure that Frank Penney—in a moment of panic, and thinking himself overly clever—had tried to kill Cliff Leyland.

Sparta entered the outside chamber of the nearest personnel airlock. Air rushed in and she opened her helmet. She was shaking the moondust from her boots, waiting for the robot gatekeeper to confirm her identity, when emergency sirens started to wail.

"What's the problem?" Sparta demanded.

"Clear channels, please," said the robot voice of the base's central computer.

Sparta ripped the glove from her right hand. She shove her PIN spines into the information slot and squirted the central computer with her identity code. "This is Troy. Command channel!"

"Command access acknowledged," said the robot.

"Nature of emergency?" Sparta demanded.

"Apparent attempted hijack of orbital tug now in progress."

"Status," Sparta barked.

"Tug is disabled. Alleged hijacker is not in possession of appropriate lift codes."

"Identity of hijacker?"

"Alleged perpetrator of apparent attempted hijack is tentatively identified as Mr. Pontus Istrati. He may be armed and should be considered dangerous."

Sparta pulled her spines from the slot, tugged her gloves on, and sealed her helmet. She popped the door of the airlock without waiting for the gradual decompression of the vacuum pumps. She was almost blown out the door, but she kept on her feet as she leaped in great moon-strides toward her waiting buggy.

In moments she was barreling toward the landing field.

You had to be told an emergency was in progress to recognize the situation at the field. At one end of the field the tall white cutter was being serviced by a rolling gantry, while the fat cislunar tug which was allegedly being hijacked was sitting all by itself at the opposite corner of the field, illuminated by floodlights. A few seconds ahead of Sparta, a single unarmed moon buggy with a red light flashing on top of its bubble plowed to a stop a safe distance away from the tug's engines. That flashing red light represented one third of Farside Base's total mobile security force.

Sparta hauled her buggy to a stop beside it. Over her helmet link she said, "Farside Security, this is Inspector Troy of the Board of Space Control. Request permission to approach the tug."

There was a moment of hesitation. A man's gruff voice said, "The man may be armed, Inspector."

"What makes you think so?"

"Uh . . . just that it's possible."

"Is that an informed guess?"

This time the pause was longer. ''We really don't know a whole lot, Inspector.''

''You know Istrati, don't you? Is he the type to use a weapon?''

''Uh . . . there's no record of that, Inspector.''

''Repeat: your authorization to approach the tug?''

The patroller breathed disgustedly into his commlink. ''It's your neck.''

''Thanks,'' she muttered. She popped the lid of the moon buggy and climbed out. Moon gravity was still new to her, and she hopped cautiously past the security buggy with its flashing red light, toward the tug.

No one challenged her as she easily climbed the ladder, nine stories up the floodlit side of the tug's bundled fuel tanks, until she reached its slender command module. The hatch was locked tight from inside. She thrust her gloved hand into the emergency release and the hatch sprang open, adding its oxygen to the ephemeral lunar atmosphere. She quickly climbed inside.

She set about decoding the magnetic lock to the tug's interior, a task she estimated would take about fifteen seconds. ''If you are really in there, Istrati,'' she breathed into her suit's commlink, ''you'd better have your suit on, because I'm coming in. And when . . .''

The hatch exploded in her face, the inner hatch cover slamming into her, all its bolts blown. She was hurled back against one wall of the airlock and out through the outer hatch. Wheeling and clutching the vacuum, she fell.

She fell thirty meters. Someone falling off a nine-story building on Earth hits the ground in less than two-and-a-half seconds, hard enough to burst. Someone falling the same height on the moon doesn't hit the ground for an agonizing six seconds. The impact, when it comes, is substantial—like a hard parachute landing on Earth—but if met heads up with knees flexed, it can be walked away from. Sparta's twisting and flailing had a purpose. Like a cat, she landed on her feet.

Above her, Istrati was sliding down the ladder. When he saw that she'd recovered her balance, he put his feet on a rung and he leaped as hard as he could, a soaring leap that took him well above her head. He hit the ground some seconds later, rolled twice, and bounced to his feet. He ran in great long jumps across the plain.

In the adrenalin rush of the moment, Sparta almost ran after him, but she stopped herself. She wheeled toward the security buggy. "Where's he going?" she demanded.

The patroller's voice in her helmet sounded baffled. "Nowhere. There's nothing in that direction. We'd better go pick him up before he hurts himself."

"I'll handle that. You're needed at the launch control room."

"We are?"

"You will be, I guarantee it. Get over there and wait for me."

"If you say so, Inspector." The security buggy immediately wheeled around and headed back.

She brushed the moon dust from her suit and walked back to her buggy. She drove off at a leisurely pace, following the now dwindling white figure of Istrati, who was still springing along toward the distant rimwall, a hundred kilometers away.

They covered two or three kilometers this way. At first Sparta expected the man would come to his senses and realize he had no choice but to give up. Another two kilometers passed beneath her oversized tires, and she began to grow weary of the chase. She accelerated.

As she gradually closed on Istrati, she tried talking to him on the commlink. "Mr. Istrati, I'm getting tired of this game and I'm not even exerting myself. How about you? You've been running for over five minutes now. Why don't you save your strength. Slow down, let's talk. I won't come any closer than you want me to.''

His suitcomm was open, but all she could hear was his ragged breath.

She drove with one hand, steering the buggy into the larger craters that pocked the floor of the Mare and up their far rims, wheeling smoothly around the smaller ones. The buggy's electric wheel motors whined softly under the crackle of the radio. ''You know there's nowhere for you to go. Let's make this easy, okay? You stop running, I'll stop following you.''

Ahead of her, the running man took a ten-meter wide crater in one great bound, and disappeared beyond its far lip. She nosed the moon buggy into the crater—it was deeper than it looked—and with wheels spinning she climbed the far wall. She cleared the top of the rim with all four wheels in the air, and landed in a cloud of dust. ''Say the word, Mr. Istrati. I'll be glad to give you a lift back to the . . .''

He wasn't there. She skidded to a stop.

Something slammed into the plastic bubble over her head. Istrati had jumped from behind the buggy, gripping a meter-wide basalt boulder in his two hands, and crashed it against the vehicle's roof. He still held the massive rock; he hit the bubble again. He was trying to smash his way into the cab.

Sparta saw his red-rimmed, glaring eyes through the plate of his spacesuit and saw the froth on his lips. Istrati was gripped by no simple panic. He was in a state of chemically induced rage.

She threw the buggy into reverse and backed off, slapping at the catches of her safety belt to release them. Istrati was about to leap again when she threw open the bubble and jumped for him. He swung the sharp-edged boulder at her and missed—

but in the tricky gravity she missed her intended tackle.

Istrati had held onto his weapon, and the momentum of the swing had pulled him off his feet. He tumbled onto his shoulder and rolled, then skidded in the dust. He struggled slowly to his knees and onto his feet. Sparta poised to jump again, but again he anticipated, hurling himself forward as hard as he could. . . .

In horror she watched him throw himself purposely onto the rock he still held between his gloved hands. An edge of basalt as sharp as a primitive hand-axe shattered his faceplate. He was still alive when Sparta reached him, but there was nothing she could do for him. His red eyes turned redder as the blood rushed into them. He shuddered violently as the last of his breath frothed into the vacuum, and then he died.

Sparta knelt helplessly beside the body for several long seconds. She was conscious of her commlink crackling with static, but she didn't call in. This stinging sensation in her eyes was tears, an inchoate upwelling of angry sadness. She was not made for this business. Whatever they had made her for, it wasn't this.

She let the sadness fill her and slowly ebb, until she was left exhausted and sore all over. The whole yoke of her shoulders burned with stiff pain. Slowly she stood and lifted Istrati's big, lightweight body in her arms.

She carried it to the moon buggy. She arranged Istrati in the back seat, as straight as she could manage, and strapped him in. She climbed into the driver's seat, lowered the canopy, and pressurized the cabin from the stored air. When pressure was normal she unlatched her helmet and sniffed the air.

Long chemical formulas appeared on the interior screen of Sparta's consciousness—a complex cocktail of cortico-adrenal drugs of which Istrati's body still reeked, although it was at the end of its breath.

She engaged the buggy's motors and headed slowly back toward the base. "Troy to Farside Security. Command channel." There was no answer. Sparta looked up and saw that Istrati's initial attack had sheared the antennas. Her commlink was dead.

She drove toward the distant base, sunk in a black depression. She'd come to Farside to investigate an attempted murder. Now she had a successful murder on her hands. Istrati had been deliberately overdosed—and the same man was responsible, for the same reason. Penney was desperately trying to cover his tracks. . . .

Sparta's introspection was interrupted by an eerie sight. Sharply visible in the Moon's hazeless non-atmosphere, on the near side of the landing field where the bright spike of the white cutter blazed against the star-filled sky, a brightly backlit spacesuited figure was walking toward her, gesturing. She zoomed her eye in on the distant figure, still five kilometers away, bringing it close in her field of view. . . .

It was Blake Redfield.

She sealed her helmet and depressurized the cab. A few minutes later she skidded to a halt beside him. When she popped the bubble she saw his big grin through his faceplate.

Her suit radio crackled. "You're the passenger I was supposed to pick up?"

"The same. I persuaded them to let me off the ship." He was mightily pleased at the effect he'd created.

"Do you mind sharing the back seat?"

"Not at . . ." His grin dissolved when he realized that the man in back had a smashed helmet.

"Until I can get Security to take him off my hands." Her tone was edgy, challenging him: make a joke of *this*.

"In that case . . ."

He settled himself quickly in the back, leaning against his straps away from Istrati's body. She lowered the bubble. The buggy resumed its journey toward the base.

After several moments of silence, she said, "What are you doing on a cutter? That's for triple-A-priority cases."

"I had the impression you sent it for me."

"Who gave you that impression?" she asked sharply.

"Tall guy, gray hair, blue eyes, a voice like high tide on a pebble beach. He wouldn't give me his name, but he said he worked for you."

Sparta almost choked; she turned it into a throat-clearing sound. "Right," she wheezed. "I found your message, Blake, and I got to Paris, but I was too late. Then this business came up."

"What business? Nobody's told me what's going on. Or why you're here."

"The Farside launcher failed a few days ago and almost killed the farmer who was riding in the capsule. They sent me up here to find out whether it was an accident. It wasn't. Right now I'm on my way to arrest the guy who did it."

"Oh," Blake said. "I guess you've been pretty busy."

There was silence in the cab except for the whine of the wheel motors, conducted through the frame.

"Ellen, are you unhappy to see me?"

She stared sullenly ahead for a long moment, then shook her head. "I'm sorry. I just—I have so much to deal with. I'm running low on energy."

"One of the things I wanted to tell you—I found William Laird. Or whatever his name is."

She swallowed and found that her throat was like sand. Laird. The man who'd tried to kill her. The man who, if they were dead, must have killed her parents. "Where?" she whispered.

"In Paris," he said. "He was calling himself Lequeu. He found out who I was before it occurred to me who *he* was—they had me locked up for more than a week before I got away."

"Why did you steal that scroll?"

"I'm a member of the Free Spirit now. It was my first assignment. I was hoping you'd show up in time to save me from a life of crime. I came as close to botching it as I could, and I laid a trail back to Lequeu. But he was too smart for the *flics.*"

"Blake, do you know a woman named Katrina Balakian?"

"No. What about her?"

"Her fingerprints were all over your apartment. She searched the place after you left it."

"Damn. They must have caught me sending the hide-and-seek message," he said. "What do you know about Balakian?"

"She's an astronomer here at Farside. Soviet. A big, muscular blonde, gray eyes . . ."

"Catherine!" Blake exclaimed.

"Who?"

"Lequeu's sidekick, Catherine. You say she's Russian?"

"Transcaucasian. A real man-eater. Charming accent."

"Catherine speaks flawless French," Blake said. Then, softly, he added, "And *of course* she's an astronomer. . . ."

"Of course?"

Blake leaned forward excitedly. "What I really wanted to tell you—I found out what they were trying to do with you. With all of us in SPARTA. I know what their program is."

"What's Catherine/Katrina got to do with it?"

"Lequeu—Laird, I mean—he and the rest of them believe that gods have been among us, watching evolution for a billion years, watching human progress, waiting until the time is ripe. The *prophetae* have appointed themselves the high priests of the whole human race. They think it's their task to create the perfect human, the human equivalent of the gods, the perfect emissary. To put it the way they do, they intended to raise up the Emperor of the Last Days, whose role it would be to greet the descending Hosts of Heaven as they ushered in Paradise. . . .''

"You're making me dizzy. Get to the point."

"This is the point, Ellen: *you* were supposed to be the Emperor—the Empress, I guess—of the Last Days. That's what they tried to do to you. Humanity's envoy."

She laughed bitterly. "They botched that, all right."

"All of which might sound very vague and nutty, except they know where these so-called gods came from."

"Blake," she said, exasperated, "what possible . . . ?"

"Their home star is in Crux."

"Crux!"

"Why the surprise?"

"How do you know it's in Crux?" she demanded.

"They have what they call the Knowledge— original records of visits from these gods of theirs, in historical time! This papyrus, for example—it identifies Crux for anybody who can build a pyramid and recognize a star map."

The buggy skidded as she turned sharply, throwing Blake against his harness. He found himself staring into Istrati's dead eyes. "What's going . . . ?"

"The Farside antennas were aimed at Crux when Leyland's capsule crashed. They still are." The moon buggy was walloping across the lunar landscape as fast as its motors would drive it, heading away from the domes of the distant base and the loading shed of the electromagnetic launcher, toward the far end of the launcher track. Sparta was headed on a straight line toward the radiotelescopes. "It's about to happen again. There's going to be another launch failure."

"There *is*? How do you . . ."

"Be quiet, Blake. Let me think."

"Call the launcher, if you're so certain," he said. "Make them shut it down!"

"The guy beside you chopped off my antenna. If I'm counting the seconds correctly"—she had no doubt that she was counting the seconds correctly—"the capsule that's being loaded into the breech of the launcher at this moment is the one that's slated to hit Farside."

"Dammit, Ellen, how can you possibly know that?"

"Because I know who's in it."

17

The launcher stretched away to both sides in front of them. A dead-load bucket flashed past at a thousand meters per second, still energetically accelerating. It vanished down the track.

One second later, another bucket flashed past. A second after that came another bucket—and they kept coming, regular as a clock, a clock that kept time by firing rifle bullets. But the sound of firing was eerily absent.

"We're in the middle of nowhere!" Blake protested. "Where are you going?"

Sparta was silent, concentrating. The moon buggy whined toward the track for another half a kilometer. "Ten seconds until we're in range," she said. "You steer. Keep us going on a straight line."

Blake slipped his harness and leaned forward over the seat. Sparta let go of the yoke as he grabbed it. "What—uhh—are you doing—aagh—*now* . . . ?" His stomach repeatedly slammed into the seat back as the bucking moon buggy lurched on across the cratered plain.

"Brace yourself."

"Oh—ugh—sure . . ."

Sparta had the dome open. The buggy's big front tires were spraying moondust straight into the airless vacuum like rooster tails behind a speedboat.

"In two seconds I'm going to jump. Try not to flip this thing."

"Do my . . . ?"

But she was gone. As she'd finished speaking she'd leaped from the buggy. Blake caught a blurred glimpse of her flying away from him, her arms spread in the vacuum as if she were a winged creature, while a manned capsule was flying down the launcher track toward them. Sparta curved her arms and hands into hooks. For a moment she was a levitating goddess. . . .

The bubble of the moon buggy slammed down. Blake reached for the throttle as the mounded dust of the well-used buggy road beside the track caught one wheel. Blake felt the yoke slip from his hand. The buggy skidded and lurched. The back end slipped around and the vehicle bucked to a stop. It slid practically under the launcher track before it came to rest.

Blake leaned back and closed his eyes, gulping suit air.

When his eyes opened he screeched. He'd forgotten he still had company in the buggy: Istrati's dead red eyes were glaring at him in frozen rage.

Blake slammed open the bubble and staggered out of the moon buggy, his knees shaky from too much adrenalin. Then he saw Sparta. She was lying crumpled in the dust beside the track. He started to run toward her, but his leap was long and he came down off balance, sliding to his knees beside her.

She raised herself halfway. "Settle down before you hurt yourself," she said hoarsely.

"Are you all right?"

"I'm terrific." She did a quick push-up and bounded erect. "We'd better head for launch control. Can you stand up by yourself?"

"Yes, I can stand up," he said petulantly. He demonstrated it, wobbling to his feet. "What happened?"

"I'll tell you about it later. Let's get this dust off." She began beating at the caked and clinging moon-dust that covered her spacesuit.

She had no intention of telling him everything there was to tell.

When Sparta and Blake arrived in the launch control room, most of the talking seemed to be over. Some controllers were anxiously querying their computers; some were staring vacantly at their screens. Frank Penney sat at the launch director's console.

Van Kessel glared starkly at Sparta. He opened his mouth, but seemed unable to think of anything to say. Then he bleated, "Again, Troy! A manned-launch failure."

Sparta didn't look at Van Kessel. "Frank Penney"—he turned to face her—"you are under arrest for conspiracy to commit murder, and for the murder of Pontus Istrati, and for illegal traffic in drugs in violation of numerous Council of Worlds statutes. You have the right to remain silent. You have the right to retain counsel, who shall be present at any official interview. Meanwhile, anything you say may be used against you in a court of law. Do you understand your rights under the Council of Worlds charter?"

Penney's tan face flushed deep red. The man who liked attention was aware that all the controllers in the place were staring at him in amazement.

"Or would you rather run, Frank? Like Istrati," she whispered, unable to contain the malice. "I won't try to stop *you*."

"I want to contact my attorney," Penney said huskily.

"Do it somewhere out of the way. We have things to take care of here."

Penney got stiffly out of his chair and walked out of the room. Two security patrollers were standing at the door to meet him. Every eye followed his retreat.

Blake raised an eyebrow. "How did they know?"

"I told them I'd need them here, before I went after Istrati."

"Inspector Troy!" Van Kessel roared at her.

"Yes, Mr. Van Kessel," she said mildly. "The launch failure. I'm aware of it. We have a few hours to do something about it, don't we?"

"You're *aware* of it! How can you be *aware* of it?"

"Because, Mr. Van Kessel, I was sent here to learn why Cliff Leyland's launch failed, and I've been thinking about little else since I arrived. Had I not been thinking of it, I would not have prearranged the arrest of Mr. Penney."

"What does *that* have to do with anything?" Van Kessel exploded. "Everybody *knows* Frank and Istrati were into something together!" He fell suddenly silent. His flushed face paled.

Sparta smiled tiredly. "Well, you might have told me, but you didn't need to. Now you might tell me this: did you know that Istrati tried to recruit Cliff Leyland into Penney's operation?"

"If you knew the way things were up here . . ." Van Kessel said huskily. "We don't pry."

"I'm not a judge or a prosecutor," she said, trying to reassure him. "Istrati worked as a launch loader. It was his idea to recruit Cliff Leyland, because Leyland made frequent trips to L-5 and back. Leyland refused, even after he was beaten up, but he didn't turn Istrati in—not his only failure of judgment, but almost his last. Istrati thought it would be a cute idea to teach him a lesson, by planting drugs on him where L-1 security was sure to find them."

She looked around the room; she had a rapt audience. "As you all seem to know," she said, "Penney was the boss of the ring, and he was the launch controller that day. Istrati must have bragged to him about what he'd done as soon as Leyland's capsule was on the track. It would have been obvious to Penney that it was more than a stupid mistake, it was a disaster that could blow his whole operation. So, I reasoned, Penney decided to destroy Leyland's capsule—a capsule that was only halfway down the track. If Penney killed the power right then and sent it short, the launch would abort; the capsule would never leave the track.''

''How could he have killed . . . ?''

''There was no fail-safe on your direct override, Mr. Van Kessel,'' she said firmly. ''Any person in this control room could have sabotaged the capsule. Penney had the motive. And he had the means to send it long, into deep space, or short, into the moon.'' She paused. ''Sending it long was no option, of course: Penney didn't care what happened to Leyland, but he couldn't let the capsule be recovered, ever. So he waited until the computer told him it was too late to abort; but in the last split second he could still make the capsule crash. That gave it a peculiar orbit, an orbit that would bring the capsule back practically on top of the base. While pretending to try to help Leyland, he made sure to send signals that put the capsule's maneuvering system out of commission.''

Van Kessel grumbled, ''You figured all this out. . . .''

''I hypothesized it before I came to the Moon. I had most of the facts I needed.''

Van Kessel took a deep breath. ''I suppose I should congratulate you.''

''Don't. I was dead wrong,'' Sparta said. ''Penney had nothing to do with Leyland's launch failure.''

''He *didn't*?'' Van Kessel was more confused than ever.

''Penney's a killer, all right—I don't think it will be hard to establish that Istrati went crazy and committed suicide because Penney deliberately dosed him with hypersteroids, just before he reported for this shift. He knew I was closing in on him. But he was not responsible for the launch failure.''

''Then who was?'' Van Kessel demanded.

''Piet Gress.''

''*Gress!*'' Van Kessel barked. ''He's in the . . . !''

Sparta nodded. ''The man in the capsule right now. He's an analyst from the antenna facility. Their job is to search for extraterrestrial intelligence, but it's apparent that Piet Gress is willing to give his life to make sure they never find it.''

''You mean he was trying to destroy the antennas?'' Blake asked.

''Who are you?'' Van Kessel said, glaring at Blake as if noticing him for the first time.

''This is Blake Redfield, my associate,'' Sparta said, not bothering to complete the introduction. ''Because they were about to begin looking in Crux,'' she said to Blake. ''Where, according to you, they may find the home star of the 'gods'—of Culture X.''

''Culture X? Culture *X*. What in hell does a bunch of scribbling on old plates have to do with this?'' Van Kessel demanded, but no one paid him any attention.

''But then he's already tried once and failed,'' Blake protested to Sparta. ''You told me Leyland's capsule hit the mountains. The antennas are protected by the ringwall.''

''Not any more.''

Blake saw it then.

So, even though he was at a loss for the meaning of it all, did Van Kessel.

''Crater Leyland,'' Van Kessel moaned.

Gress had somehow used Leyland's capsule to blast a hole in the ring of mountains that protected the Farside Base antennas. A second capsule on the same trajectory would fly through the gap—and make a direct hit.

"What's the orbit on Gress's capsule?" Sparta asked Van Kessel.

"Too early to be precise. Failure occurred in exactly the same section of launch track as Leyland's. First approximation is that Gress is following the same trajectory."

"Have you contacted him?"

"He doesn't respond. His radio must be dead."

"Let me try."

She sat at the launch director's console and keyed the commlink. "Piet Gress, this is Ellen Troy of the Board of Space Control. You think you are about to die. I know why. But you won't die and you won't accomplish your mission."

The speakers gave back nothing but the hiss of the aether.

"Dr. Gress, you think your orbit is the same as Leyland's was, or close enough. But your capsule will not pass through the gap in the ringwall. You cannot make course corrections without our cooperation. You will not hit the antennas. You can save yourself, or you can die for nothing."

For several seconds the speakers were silent except for the sound of the cosmos. Then a sad, dry voice issued from them: "You're bluffing."

Sparta caught Van Kessel's eye. His face sagged. "Mr. Van Kessel," she said quietly, "just so you'll know what we're up against: according to my colleague, Mr. Redfield, Piet Gress is a representative of a fanatic sect that believes our solar system has been invaded by aliens in the distant past and is about to be invaded again. The wrinkle is, Gress and his friends are actually looking forward to the invasion. But they're eager to keep this all a deep, dark secret from the rest of the inhabited worlds. They are so eager, in fact, that some of them like Gress are willing to kill themselves and a lot of other people, just to keep us unwashed masses in the dark.''

Van Kessel's eyes were bulging in his florid face. ''That's the craziest thing I've ever heard.''

''I couldn't agree more,'' Sparta said fervently. ''But it's not the first time a gang of maniacs has sacrificed themselves and any number of innocent bystanders to their beliefs, and I doubt it will be the last.''

She turned back to the microphone. ''No, Gress, I'm not bluffing,'' she said to the invisible inhabitant of the capsule. ''I knew about your plans before you were launched''—*about two minutes before you were launched, thanks to Blake*—''and steps were taken to alter your trajectory''—*steps, leaps, desperate measures: I jumped from a speeding moon buggy and I read the acceleration of your capsule and read the phase reversal and my belly burned and I gushed a burst of telemetry at the trackside power-control receiver in the code I'd memorized and I did my best to override the signals your capsule was sending too, all before I hit ground again, and I pray that I succeeded but who knows?*—''and you will not hit Farside Base. You may hit the moon, but not where you want. You may sail on into space forever. But you will not destroy the antennas. Save yourself, Gress. Use your maneuvering rockets.''

Gress's voice scratched from the speakers. ''I say you are bluffing.''

Blake leaned close to her and touched the filament mike. He raised his eyebrows: *let me talk?*

She nodded.

Blake said, ''Piet, this is Guy. I bring you a message from the sanctuary of the Initiates.'' He paused. ''All will be well.''

''Who are you?'' Gress's angry demand came instantly.

Blake said, ''One of us. A friend of Katrina's. Of Catherine's''—he glanced at Sparta: *forgive me, but how wrong can I be?*—''but it's too late. They interfered with the launch. Whatever happens to you, you're not going to hit the antennas. And Gress, they know where to look now. They could find the home star with one thirty-meter dish on Earth." Blake let that sink in. On the speakers there was nothing but the hiss of empty space.

Gress's voice, suddenly louder, filled the room. "You are an impostor, a traitor." He could have been on the edge of tears.

Blake said, "Save yourself!"

There was no sound from the speakers, no image on the flatscreens, which sparkled only with noise.

Blake stood away from the mike. "Sorry. Guess he wants to die."

The watch went on. Piet Gress's capsule, like Leyland's, rose and at last began to fall slowly back toward Farside.

In the control room the shift changed, but Sparta and Blake and Van Kessel stayed. They sipped bitter coffee and talked in desultory tones about Istrati and Penney and Leyland and Gress and Balakian. Penney was in custody, exercising his right to keep quiet, and Istrati was in cold storage, but base security reported that other members of the smuggling ring they'd picked up on suspicion had begun talking freely.

Katrina had been taken into protective custody. Nobody had read her her rights. Nobody had explained anything to her.

Exactly what Gress—with Balakian's help?—had done to cause Leyland's near-death was a still-unsolved puzzle. Sparta ordered base security to reconstruct the movements of the two during the twenty-four hours before Leyland's capsule was launched. The security people reported back almost too quickly: it seemed that neither of them had ever left the radiotelescope operations area.

"If they didn't have access to the capsule, how

could they have interfered with the launch?" Van Kessel asked.

Sparta was silent, lost in thought. Dark circles had formed under her staring eyes. She was hunched over, clutching her belly.

"Maybe I can answer that," Blake said to Van Kessel. "Gress is a signal analyst; it was probably easy for him to decode your power control signals. All he needed was a transmitter loaded with a pre-set code, set to go off when Leyland's capsule reached the right point in its launch—a signal strong enough to override the capsule's onboard transmitter. He could just as easily have put the capsule's computers out of whack with a remote command, as soon as it left the track."

"A remote transmitter . . . ?" Van Kessel was skeptical.

"There's one aimed at the track right now," Sparta whispered. "The radiotelescopes. Every receiver can be used as a transmitter. Every transmitter can be a receiver." She knew now, although she said nothing about it, that the source of the disorienting, queasy sensation she felt when she stood on the launcher track was a burst of test telemetry from the antennas, still under repair.

"Once Security gets around to it," Blake said, "I'll bet they'll find Gress was feeding in a little extra programming. And that Katrina had a hand in the fine alignment of the telescopes. She had something to say about the target list, after all."

Van Kessel shrugged. "We'll see." He looked at Sparta. "Do you think she deliberately picked Leyland after all?"

"That was as much her bad luck as it was his," she said. "He just happened to be the next load down the track. He was in the right place at the wrong time."

Time crept by. As Doppler readings from radar stations around the moon poured into the control room, the estimates of Gress's trajectory became ever more refined.

Van Kessel was the first to put it in words. "Gress is not going to hit the moon."

Gress could not know that, of course, since he apparently refused to believe what they told him and had stopped responding on the link. Sparta watched the bright lines on the graphic screens, the lines that diagrammed Gress's rush toward the moon, and she tried to imagine what he must be thinking, what he must be feeling, as the bright backlit mountains of Farside rushed toward him. The man wanted to die, wanted the face of the moon to rush up and crush him . . .

Van Kessel was watching Sparta. She had shown no surprise, no emotion at all, at the news that Gress would miss the moon.

"You *were* bluffing—weren't you?" Van Kessel asked.

"We must have been lucky," she whispered.

"But if Gress could program Leyland's capsule so precisely with a remote transmission," Van Kessel demanded, "why couldn't he program his own? He's *riding* in the thing!"

Sparta looked at Blake's round, handsome face and saw that eyebrow lift again. Why, indeed? Blake was wondering—and what exactly had Sparta been up to when she'd jumped out of the speeding moon buggy? It was not the sort of question Blake would ask her in public.

Coolly Sparta addressed Van Kessel. "Maybe with Leyland he had . . . beginner's luck."

Van Kessel grunted. "Are you saying there's something about this that the Space Board doesn't want known?"

"That's an excellent way of putting it, Mr. Van Kessel," she said.

"You should have said so in the first place," he grumbled. He kept his questions to himself after that. Whatever it was the Space Board wasn't telling him, he doubted he'd ever find out.

Once more the alarm went out to the base. This time the measure was strictly precautionary. A few people strolled to the deep shelters, but the bolder workers went out on the surface to watch as Gress's capsule soared over the crest of the Mare Moscoviense rimwall.

When the capsule streaked soundlessly overhead, brilliantly floodlit by the sun that was still low in the east, it had a kilometer of altitude to spare.

Seconds later Gress was arcing back into space.

Sparta, at the edge of exhaustion, called him again. "We've calculated your orbit with a little better precision, Dr. Gress. You'll go wider on each swing. Eventually you'll end up in the spider web at L-1. Your rations probably won't last that long."

There was nothing but the vacant hiss of the aether. It went on so long that everyone but Sparta and Blake had given up, when lights flickered on the consoles, and the weary controllers stirred. Flatscreens unscrambled. Shortly Gress's haggard voice came over the radiolink. "You have control of this capsule now," he said. "Do what you want."

"He's taken the capsule's maneuvering systems out of manual," said Van Kessel.

Before anyone else in the room could respond, Sparta had tapped coordinates into the launch director's console. "In a few seconds you will experience some acceleration, Dr. Gress. Please be sure you are secured." She had rewritten the capsule's program and locked it off before Van Kessel could confirm her calculations.

"We could have done that," Van Kessel grumbled.

"I didn't want to give him time to change his mind."

The consoles indicated that somewhere above the

moon the engines of Gress's capsule spurted
flame—

—and aimed him toward an early recovery at
L-1.

Sparta was bruised with fatigue.

"Do you need to be here any longer?" Blake
asked.

"No, Blake. I need to be with you."

There was one more stop to make before the long
day was over. Katrina Balakian was being held in
the tiny detention facility at Base Security under
the maintenance dome. Sparta and Blake looked at
Katrina's image on the guard's flatscreen. The astronomer sat quietly in an armchair in the locked
room, staring down at her clenched hands.

"Catherine?" Sparta asked Blake.

He nodded.

"We'll go in now," Sparta said to the guard.

The guard keyed the combination into the pad
on the wall, and the door swung open. Katrina did
not move or look at them. The smell that wafted
out of the room was oddly traditional, instantly
recognizable. It was the smell of bitter almonds.

Seconds later Sparta had confirmed that Katrina
Balakian had died of cyanide poisoning, self-
administered from that most ancient of cloak-and-
dagger devices, a hollow plastic tooth. Her features
were frozen with the wide-eyed blue shock of one
whose breath has suddenly, irrevocably been cut
off.

"She smiled at Gress the last time she saw him,"
Sparta said to Blake. "I thought it was because she
loved him. Maybe she did, but she also knew he
was marching out to die for the cause."

"She was braver than he was, then, in the end,"
Blake said.

Sparta shook her head. "I don't think so. I think
when they open that capsule at L-1, they'll find a
dead man in it."

"Why would he let us send him to L-1?" Blake asked.

"To spite us. To let us know he died on purpose."

"God, Ellen, I hope this time you're wrong."

She wasn't, but neither of them would know that until late the following day. . . .

That night they found a nondescript room in the visitor's quarters, with brocaded walls and a carpeted floor and ceiling. The furniture was square and modern, soulless, but they didn't look at it. They didn't even bother to turn on the light.

Her armor came off slowly. She did not make it easy for him, but neither did she resist. And when both of them were without protection, they held each other close a long time, hardly moving, not speaking. Her breathing became deeper, slower, and he helped her lie down on the bed. As he settled beside her, he realized she was already asleep.

He kissed the fine down at the back of her neck. Almost before he realized it, he was sleeping too.

18

A third of the distance sunward of Farside Base, and more, Port Hesperus swung above the clouds of Venus on its ceaseless round. A tall, sad-eyed man sat in a dark room, pondering a flatscreen full of strange symbols, symbols that were old friends to him. His contemplation was suddenly interrupted.

"Merck, I'm afraid I have very bad news for you," J. Q. R. Forster said, his voice sticky with glee. He was working at a similar screen at the opposite end of the big room, an empty gallery in the Hesperian Museum. Although the museum was valuable property, located on the busy thoroughfare that belted Port Hesperus's garden sphere, it was temporarily unused except by Forster and Merck.

"Bad news?" Albers Merck looked up from the glowing flatscreen, a vague smile on his face. He swiped at the lick of blond hair that fell into his eyes each time he moved his head.

"I've identified the terminal signs that puzzled us so much."

"Oh, have you really?"

"Yes, just this very moment. It was the sort of thing that should have been obvious."

"Mmm?"

"Had it not seemed impossible."

247

"Impossible?"

"We've assumed that the tablets are a billion years old." How silly of us, Forster implied by his tone—

—but Merck nodded solemnly. "The only reasonable assumption. So long has Venus been uninhabitable, as the dating of the cave strata confirms."

Forster abruptly stood and began to pace the length of the room, which itself resembled a cave. It was roofed with a gaudy stained-glass dome, though many of the panes were broken and it was covered with opaque black plastic. Once the gallery had been filled with rococo bricabrac of the sort favored by the museum's founder. The man was dead now, and the place had acquired a gloomy reputation. The museum's trustees, who were among the backers of the Venus expedition, had let the archaeologists use the empty structure to house their research.

"The *cave* is a billion years old, certainly," Forster said. "There are caves in the Grand Canyon of the Colorado River that old. It doesn't mean no one has visited them since they were formed." Forster raised his hand. "No, don't bother to say it—I will grant, for the sake of argument, that perhaps some of the artifacts in the cave could be a billion years old, although we have no means of dating what we had no time to sample. But late last night it occurred to me—why was it not obvious *sooner*?—that the beings of Culture X could have used this site over a very long period of time. . . ."

The long-suffering Merck expelled an exasperated sigh. "Really, Forster, you are surely the only archaeologist in the inhabited worlds who could believe such a possibility. A civilization lasting a billion years! Dropping in on us from time to time. My dear friend . . ."

Forster had stopped pacing. "The signs, Merck, the signs. In each section of writing, the signs to the left are the mirror image of the signs on the right. Perfect copies in every detail—*except* for the terminal signs in the last line of the left section. . . ."

"The last line in every left-hand section has a different terminal sign, occurring nowhere else," Merck finished for him. "Clearly these are rare honorifics."

"Yes!" said Forster eagerly. "And I venture that the mirror-writing itself is honorific—a way of copying texts deemed worthy of preservation. Surely it is not standard; the Mars plaque is not mirror-writing."

Merck smiled diffidently. "Forgive me for turning your argument against you, but in a billion years, or a hundred—or even ten—customs could change."

"Yes, yes," said Forster, nettled. Merck had a point, but now was not the time to admit it. "Merck, I'm saying we can *decipher* these texts. That we already *know* the terminal signs!"

Merck peered at Forster with an expression that hovered between amusement and apprehension. "Do we?"

"This one—from the third set of panels. This is an Egyptian hieroglyph, a sun disc, the sound *kh* . . . ."

"Forster, it's a plain circle," said Merck.

"And this one, from the fifth set. Sumerian cuneiform for heaven . . ."

"Which perfectly resembles an asterisk."

"From the second set, the Chinese ideogram for horse—you think that's universal? From the ninth set, the Minoan Linear A character for wine. Did they drink wine? From the second set, the Hebrew letter aleph, which stands for ox. From the seventh set, a sign in the form of a fish from the undeciphered script of Mohenjo-daro . . ."

"Please, my friend," Merck said gently, "this is too much for me to absorb. Are you really proposing that Culture X dropped in on Earth during the Bronze Age, then flew to Venus to leave a memo of their trip?''

''Your polite way of saying I'm crazy,'' said Forster, ''but I'm not. Merck, we have found the Rosetta Stone.''

''On *Venus*?''

''Perhaps we weren't meant to find it—not without aid. But it is the Rosetta Stone nonetheless.''

''Putting aside the question of *who* was to aid us,'' Merck said, ''there is not a scrap of language we can recognize—except, possibly, these few scattered signs.''

''Those signs are meant to say that they knew humans then, respected us enough to record our symbols—that someday they wanted us to understand them. The means is here in these tablets.''

'How wonderful if you were right,'' said Merck. ''But how can we possibly do that, with a single dubious correspondence in each block of . . . ?''

''It's an alphabet, Merck. There are forty-two signs, alphanumerics. . . .''

''I don't accept . . .''

''I don't care, just listen. We were able to recover thirty paired blocks of text, and each left-hand block ends with a sign from Earth's earliest written languages. Each terminal sign on the left corresponds to a Culture X sign in the right-hand text. Those are *sounds*. The Egyptian for *kh*. The Minoan for *we*. The Hebrew, voiceless but surely *ah*. Originally there must have been one of our signs for every one of theirs. Some from languages we no longer know. Many pieces lost. But we can put it together. We can extract the meaning, we can fill in the gaps.'' Forster paused in his restless pacing. ''When we do, we can read what they wrote.''

Faced with Forster's enthusiasm, Merck threw up his hands in disgust and turned back to his flatscreen.

Forster too returned to his computer. In an hour he had what he thought was a good approximation of the sounds of the Culture X alphabet. In another hour he had used it to derive the meanings of several blocks of text. He stared in excitement as the first translations unscrolled on his flatscreen.

A kind of terrible excitement overcame him. He did not wait for the computer to finish spewing out translations before confronting Merck. "Merck!" he shouted, rousting him from his gloomy meditation.

Merck peered at him, unfailing in his struggle to be polite, but the sense of sadness—of tragedy, even—that hung about him caused the ebullient Forster momentary pause.

"We'll go into the uncertainties later. . . ." He pressed on. "Here's an appropriate place to start: the text tagged with aleph. Steady, man . . . 'In the beginning, God created the heavens and the Earth. . . .' "

Merck, expressionless in the shadows, gazed at Forster, leaping and cavorting as he read from the slip of plastic.

"Another, the third text, tagged with the hieroglyphic sun disk. It begins, 'How beautiful art thou, upon the eastern horizon . . .' An Egyptian hymn to the sun. Another, from China: 'The way that is known is not the way . . .' "

"Please stop," said Merck, rising from his chair. "I cannot deal with this now."

"You'll have to deal with it soon, my friend," Forster exulted, almost cruelly. "I see no reason why we cannot make an announcement tomorrow."

"Tomorrow, then. Excuse me, Forster. I must go."

Forster watched the tall, sad archaeologist slouch out of the darkened gallery. He had not even bothered to turn off his flatscreen.

Forster went to Merck's flatscreen and reached for the SAVE key. His eye was caught by the graphic signs on Merck's display, Culture X signs with Merck's notation beside them. Merck persisted in treating the signs as ideographs, not alphabetic letters. He persisted in finding arcane meanings for the texts that to Forster had suddenly become transparent.

No wonder Merck didn't want to think about anything until tomorrow. His life's work had just been destroyed.

For Merck there was to be no shred of relief; worse news was already traveling through space at the speed of light.

All night Port Hesperus hummed with revelations of the latest launch disaster at Farside Base. Artificial morning arrived, and Forster put any thoughts of a press conference out of his mind— partly out of respect for his colleague, partly out of simple practicality. So spectacular were the grisly developments on the moon that no announcement of an archaeological breakthrough could possibly compete for the public's attention.

More than twenty-four hours passed. Forster was having dinner alone in his cabin when he heard the last bit of horrible news—Piet Gress's capsule had arrived at L-1 with his corpse inside. Forster left his dinner cooling and went back in search of his colleague. . . .

A bright and featureless flatscreen was the gallery's sole source of light. Albers Merck sat at the long table, staring not at the blank screen but through it.

"Albers . . ." J. Q. R. Forster's voice echoed through the dark gallery, uncharacteristically soft. "I've just heard. Were you close to the boy?"

"My sister's son," Merck whispered. "I've seen little of either of them since he was very small."

"Do you believe what they are saying? That he tried to destroy the Farside antennas?"

Merck turned slowly to look at Forster. The gingery little professor was standing at the door with his hands hanging limp at his sides, looking oddly helpless. He had come to comfort his old friend and rival, but he had little practice in such matters.

"Yes, certainly," Merck said simply.

"What could he have been thinking? Why would he try to destroy that magnificent instrument?"

"That must be very difficult for you to understand."

"For *me* to understand! He killed himself!" In his indignation, Forster almost forgot that he was here to console Merck. "He tried to kill that other man. He could have killed a great many people."

Merck's distracted, otherworldly expression was unchanged.

Forster coughed. "Please forgive me, I . . . Perhaps I should leave you alone."

"No, stay." Merck said sharply and slowly got to his feet. In his right hand he was carrying something black and shiny, barely bigger than his palm. "Really, Forster, Gress's fate is of no interest to me. He had his assignment. He failed. I pray that I have not already failed mine."

"*Your* assignment. What's that mean?"

Merck walked to the far end of the gallery, past rows of display cases. Some of the cases housed real fossils, scraps of natural sculpture collected by Venus-roving mining robots over the years. Others contained duplicates, recently completed, of the creatures Merck and Forster had seen preserved in the cave, painstakingly reconstructed from their recordings.

Merck bent over a case holding a replica of the tablets. He stared at the rows upon rows of signs, incised in a polished metallic surface that looked uncannily like the real thing, although it was only metallized plastic. The real thing was buried beneath the Venusian rock. It would wait there as long as it had waited already; its metal was as hard as diamond.

Merck murmured words that Forster could not

hear. He seemed to be talking directly to the tablets.

"Speak up, man," Forster said, moving closer. "I can't understand you."

"I said, our tradition did not prepare us for these events. The Pancreator was to speak to those of us who had accepted and preserved the Knowledge. Only to us. But these"—he stared at the tablets—"are accessible to any philologist."

"What are you talking about, Merck? Who or what is the *Pancreator?*"

Merck placed the thing in his hand on top of the display case. It was a flat plastic disk. He turned toward Forster then, raising himself to his full imposing height in the shadows. "I grew to like you, Forster, despite our differences. Despite how often you have frustrated my efforts."

"You need a rest, Merck," said Forster. "It's obvious you've taken all this very hard. I regret it was I who proved you wrong about the translations, but that was inevitable."

Merck went on, ignoring him. "Sometimes I have even been tempted to help you with the truth, even though it has been my lifelong mission to steer you—and everyone else—away from it."

"You're speaking nonsense," Forster said bluntly.

"Unhappily for you, you've come to the truth on your own. So I have had to destroy your work . . ."

"What?" Forster turned to the blank flatscreen on Merck's worktable. He lunged at the mounded keyboard and stroked the keys, but the flatscreen showed him empty files. "I can't . . . What does this mean? What have you *done,* Merck?"

"What I've done here is being done everywhere such records have been recorded and stored, Forster," Merck whispered. "On Earth, on Mars, in every library and museum and university. Everywhere. It only remains to destroy the two minds that could reveal the truth. *You* would do so willingly. I can't blame you for that. And of course I could be forced.''

Forster looked at the thing on the case beside Merck. ''What the devil is . . .''

He lunged for Merck. A flash of intense light and a wall of seared air blew him back. His last image of Merck was of a tall blond man sheathed in flame.

EPILOGUE

The commander was waiting for Sparta and Blake as they stepped off the shuttle at Newark. He was crisp in his blue uniform. They were dressed for a vacation.

Sparta's greeting lacked warmth. "Our appointment is at your office tomorrow."

"Something's come up," the commander said hoarsely. He turned his blue stare on Blake. "Hello, Redfield."

"Blake, it's time you knew who this man really is. This is my boss. Commander . . ."

"Sorry, still no time to get acquainted," he said to Blake, interrupting her, but he gave Blake's hand a quick, very hard squeeze. "We'll have to talk as we go," he said to Sparta.

Blake looked at Sparta. "Am I included in this?"

"I don't know," she said. "Don't let me out of your sight." They hurried to join the commander, pushing past other passengers on the high-speed people-mover to reach his side.

"Somebody bombed the Hesperian Museum," the commander said, his throat full of gravel. "Proboda pulled Forster from the wreckage. Bad burns over about seventy percent of his body—nothing the medics can't fix in a few days. Merck's dead—not enough left to reconstruct."

"What happened?"

"We're not sure. Forster's having a little trouble remembering the last minute or two before the bomb went off."

"Proboda saved him?"

"Got there in three minutes, waded in, got burned himself. Vik's no intellectual, but he's just earned himself another commendation." The commander touched Sparta's arm to indicate that she should take a right where the corridor branched toward the helipad.

"We rate a helicopter to headquarters?"

"We're not going to headquarters," said the commander. "They're holding a loaded shuttle for us. It's going back up as soon as you're on it."

She was silent a moment. "There goes the R & R you keep promising me," she said at last.

"We'll owe you," said the commander.

Sparta looked at Blake, and for a moment her eyes were moist. Blake had never seen her cry, and she didn't oblige him now. Instead, awkwardly, she took his hand. They looked at each other as the people-mover trundled along, but she would not move to him and he would not force himself on her.

The commander looked sternly away and kept quiet, until at last he cleared his throat loudly and said, "Watch your step. Change to the right coming up."

Blake and Sparta broke away from each other. Sparta said nothing; her throat was swollen with the effort to control her emotions.

"The bombing of the Hesperian looks like part of a pattern," the commander said. "Archaeological stuff. All over the place. Some stolen, some destroyed." His tone indicated he couldn't imagine why anyone would be interested in "archaeological stuff." "How about you, Redfield? Any ideas?"

"Well, sir . . ."

"What you told Troy you were doing in Paris,

for example?'' He glanced at her. ''You leave anything out of that report, Troy?''

''Nothing of importance, sir.'' Her whisper was defiant.

''Now that you've blown your cover with these weirdos, Redfield, we probably ought to recruit you, but it will have to wait.''

''Where are you sending me, sir?'' Sparta asked huskily.

''Thing causing the most stir is this Martian plaque.''

''The Martian plaque?''

''Disappeared yesterday from Labyrinth City. You're going to get it back.''

''Mars.'' She swallowed. ''Commander, I wonder if you would allow me a few minutes to talk to Blake before boarding.''

''Sorry, no time.''

''But sir,'' she said angrily, ''if you send me to Mars we won't see each other for months.''

''That's up to him,'' said the commander. ''We're holding two seats, but he's a civilian. He doesn't have to go with you if he doesn't want to.''

It took a moment for it to sink in. Then Blake shouted and Sparta grinned. They clutched each other. The commander never cracked a smile.

APPENDIX:
THE PLAYFAIR CIPHER

The Playfair cipher was devised by the scientist Charles Wheatstone in 1854. His friend the Baron Playfair lobbied so effectively to have the cipher adopted by the British government that it became known by Playfair's name instead of Wheatstone's. Playfair turns plaintext into ciphertext by first preparing the plaintext in a specific way, then transforming the plaintext according to certain rules, using an alphabet square. The layout of the alphabet square varies according to a keyword.

This was Blake's plaintext:

TO HELEN FROM PARIS IF YOU FIND THIS FIND ME IN THE FORTRESS SEEKING THE FIRST OF FIVE REVELATIONS YOU WILL NEED A GUYDE

The rules for preparing plaintext are:

1) The plaintext letters are divided into pairs; for example, TO HELEN becomes TO HE LE, etc.
2) Double letters, if they occur in a pair, must be divided by an X or a Z. For example, the double L's in WILL NEED become LX LN, etc. (But the three S's in FORTRESS SEEKING become

SX SZ SE, etc.; using X once and Z the next time avoids calling attention to a letter that has been enciphered twice in the same way. Such a hint could betray part of the layout of the alphabet square.)

3) J in the plaintext is treated as if it were I. (Blake's plaintext contained no J's.)

So Blake's first step was to write out the plaintext thus: TO HE LE NF RO MP AR IS IF YO UF IN DT HI SF IN DM EI NT HE FO RT RE SX SZ SE EK IN GT HE FI RS TO FX FI VE RE VE LA TI ON SY OU WI LX LN EX ED AG UY DE

The Playfair alphabet square is five letters wide by five letters high. First the keyword is written (but no letters are repeated), and then the remaining letters of the alphabet are written, with I and J treated as the same letter. Blake's keyword was SPARTA, thus his Playfair square was:

S	P	A	R	T
B	C	D	E	F
G	H	IJ	K	L
M	N	O	Q	U
V	W	X	Y	Z

The Playfair transformation is based on the fact that the letters of each pair in the plaintext can occur in only one of three states. The pair can be together in the same row, together in the same column, or—most commonly—together in neither.

1) Each letter in a pair of letters that falls in the same *row* is replaced by the letter to its right; for example, ED becomes *fe*. The letter to the "right" of the last letter in a row is the first letter in the same row.

2) Each letter in a pair of letters that falls in the same *column* is replaced by the letter below it; for example, RQ becomes *ey*. The letter "below" the last letter in the column is the top letter in the same column.

3) Each letter in a pair of letters that appears in neither the same row nor the same column is replaced by the letter occurring at the *intersection* of its own row and its partner's column. Pair order must be preserved: first determine the intersection of the first letter's row with the second letter's column, then the intersection of the second letter's row with the first letter's column. It helps to imagine that the two plaintext letters determine two corners of a square inside the alphabetical square; then the ciphertext letters lie at the opposite corners of this smaller square. For example TO becomes *au*.

.	.	A	R	T
.	.	D	E	F
.	.	IJ	K	L
.	.	O	Q	U
.	.	.	.	.

4) Since I and J are identical, a transformation to IJ may be written as either I or J, at the encipherer's whim.

Blake transformed the plaintext thus:
TO HE LE NF RO MP AR IS IF YO UF IN DT HI
au kc fk uc aq ns rt ga ld xq zl ho fa ik
SF IN DM EI NT HE FO RT
tb ho bo dk up kc du ts
RE SX SZ SE EK IN GT HE FI RS TO FX FI VE RE
ek av tv rb kq ho ls kc dl tp au dz dl yb ek
VE LA TI ON SY OU WI
yb jt al qo rv qm xh
LX LN EX ED AG UY DE
jz hu dy fe si qz ef

Sparta found the cipher in this form:
aukcfkucaqnsrtgaldxqzlhofaiktbhobodkupkcdutse
kavtvrbkqholskcdltpaudzdlybekybjtalqorvqmxhjzhudy
fesiqzef

Knowing that the system was Playfair, and surmising that the key was SPARTA, Sparta had only to divide the ciphertext into pairs, reconstruct the alphabet square, and, using the same rules, transform each cipher pair back into its plain equivalent:

au kc fk uc aq ns rt ga
TO HE LE NF RO MP AR IS . . .

MAELSTROM
AN AFTERWORD BY
ARTHUR C. CLARKE

There cannot be many science fiction novels that end with a 40-page appendix full of mathematical equations and electric-circuit diagrams. Don't worry—this isn't one of them; but just such a book inspired it, half a century ago. And with any luck, during the next half-century it will cease to be fiction.

It must have been in 1937 or '38, when I was Treasurer of the five-year-old British Interplanetary Society (annual budget to start the conquest of space, about $200), that the BIS was sent a book with a rather odd title, by an author with an even odder name. "Akkad Pseudoman's" *Zero to Eighty* (Princeton: Scientific Publishing Company, 1937) must now be quite a rarity: I am indebted to my old friend Frederick I. Ordway III (responsible for the technical designs in *2001: A Space Odyssey*) for the fine copy I possess.

The snappy subtitle says it all:

> Being my lifetime doings,
> reflections, and inventions

also
my journey round the Moon

Quite an "also"; I can hear the author's modest cough.

He was not, of course, really Mr. Pseudoman, as the preface made clear. This was signed "E. F. Northrup," and explained that the book had been written to show that the Moon may be reached by means of known technologies, without "invoking any *imaginary* physical features or laws of nature."

Dr. E. F. Northrup was a distinguished electrical engineer, and the inventor of the induction furnace which bears his name. His novel, which is obviously a wish-fulfillment fantasy, describes a journey to the Moon (and around it) in a vehicle fired from the earth by a giant gun, as in Jules Verne's classic *From the Earth to the Moon*. Northrup, however, tried to avoid the obvious flaws in Verne's *naive* proposal, which would have quickly converted Ardan *et al.* into small blobs of protoplasm inside a sphere of molten metal.

Northrup used an electric gun, *two hundred kilometers* long, most of it horizontal but with the final section curving up Mount Popocatepetl, so that the projectile would be at an altitude of more than five kilometers when it reached the required escape velocity of 11.2 kilometers per second. In this way, air-resistance losses would be minimized, but a small amount of rocket power would be available for any necessary corrections.

Well—it makes more sense than Verne's Moon-gun, but not by much. Even with 200 kilometers of launch track, the unfortunate passengers would have to withstand 30 gees for more than half a minute. And the cost of the magnets, power stations, transmission lines, etc. would run into billions; rockets would be cheaper, as well as far more practical.

I am sure that "Akkad Pseudoman" would have

been surprised—and delighted—to know that men first circled the Moon aboard Apollo 8 at Christmas 1969; the date he gave in his novel was June 28, 1961. Incidentally, he was not the first to propose this scheme: the Winter, 1930 *Science Wonder Quarterly* has a beautiful Frank R. Paul illustration of a line of giant electromagnets, shooting a spaceship up a mountainside. It could very well have served as the frontispiece of *Zero to Eighty*.

A few years after reading Dr. Northrup's book (which is still full of interesting ideas, including a remarkably sympathetic—especially for the time—treatment of Russian technology) it occurred to me that he had made one slight mistake. He had put his electric launcher on the wrong world; it made no sense on Earth—but was ideal for the Moon.

First: there's no atmosphere to heat up the vehicle or destroy its momentum, so the whole launching track can be laid out horizontally. Once it's given escape velocity, the payload will slowly rise up from the surface of the Moon and head out into space.

Second: lunar escape velocity is only one-fifth of Earth's, and can therefore be attained with a correspondingly shorter launch track—and a *twenty-fifth* of the energy. When the time comes to export goods from the Moon, this will be the way to do it. Although I was thinking of inanimate payloads, and launchers only a few kilometers long, suitably protected human passengers could be handled by larger systems, if there were ever enough traffic to justify them.

I wrote up this idea, with the necessary calculations, in a paper titled ''Electromagnetic Launching as a Major Contribution to Space-Flight,'' which was duly published in the *Journal of the British Interplanetary Society* (November, 1950); it may be more conveniently located in my *Ascent to Orbit: A Scientific Autobiography* (Wiley, 1984). And because a good idea should be exploited in every possible way, I used it in fiction on two occasions: in the chapter "The Shot from the Moon" (*Islands in the Sky*, 1952) and in the short story "Maelstrom II" (Playboy, April 1965, reprinted in *The Wind from the Sun*, 1972). This is the tale which Paul Preuss has ingeniously worked into *Venus Prime*, Volume 2.

Some twenty years after the publication of "Electromagnetic Launching" by the BIS, the concept was taken much further by Gerald O'Neill, who made it a key element of his "space colonization" projects (see *The High Frontier*, 1977; Gerry O'Neill is justifiably annoyed by the Star Warriors' preemption of his title.) He showed that the large space habitats he envisaged could be most economically constructed from materials mined and prefabricated on the Moon, and then shot into orbit by electromagnetic catapults to which he gave the name "mass drivers." (I've challenged him to produce *any* propulsion device that doesn't fit this description.)

The other scientific element in "Maelstrom II" has a much longer history; it's the branch of celestial mechanics known as "perturbation theory." I've been able to get considerable mileage out of it since my applied maths instructor, the cosmologist Dr. George C. McVittie, introduced me to the subject at Kings College, London, in the late '40s. However, I'd come across it—without realizing—in dear old *Wonder Stories* almost two decades earlier. Here's a challenge to you: spot the flaw in the following scenario. . . .

The first expedition has landed on Phobos, the inner moon of Mars. Gravity there is only about a thousandth of Earth's, so the astronauts have a great time seeing how high they can jump. One of them overdoes it, and exceeds the tiny satellite's escape velocity of about thirty kilometers an hour. He dwindles away into the sky, toward the mottled red Marscape; his companions realize that they'll have to take off and catch him before he crashes into the planet only six thousand kilometers below.

A dramatic situation, which opens Lawrence Manning's 1932 serial "The Wreck of the Asteroid." Manning, one of the most thoughtful science fiction writers of the '30s, was an early member of the American Rocket Society, and was very careful with his science. But this time, I'm afraid, he was talking nonsense: his high jumper would have been perfectly safe.

Look at his situation from the point of view of Mars. If he's simply standing on Phobos, he's orbiting the planet at almost eight thousand kilometers an hour (a Moon that close to its primary has to move pretty fast). As spacesuits are massive affairs, and not designed for athletic events, I doubt if the careless astronaut could achieve that critical thirty kilometers an hour. Even if he did, it would be less than a half-percent of the velocity he already has, relative to Mars. Whichever way he jumped, therefore, it will make virtually no difference to his existing situation; he'll still be traveling in almost the same orbit as before. He'd recede a few kilometers away from Phobos—and be right back where he started, just one revolution later! (Of course, he could run out of oxygen in the meantime—the trip round Mars will take seven-and-a-half hours. So maybe his friends should go after him—at their leisure.)

This is perhaps the simplest example of "perturbation theory," and I developed it a good deal further in "Jupiter V" (reprinted in *Reach for Tomorrow*, 1956). This story, incidentally, was based on what seemed a cute idea in the early '50s. A decade earlier, LIFE Magazine had published space-artist Chesley Bonestell's famous paintings of the outer planets. Wouldn't it be nice, I thought, if sometime in the 21st century LIFE sent one of its photographers out there to bring back the real thing, and compare it with Chesley's hundred-year-old visions?

Well, little did I imagine that, in 1976, the Voyager space-probe would do just this—and that, happily, Chesley would still be around to see the result. Many of his carefully researched paintings were right on target—though he couldn't have anticipated such stunning surprises as the volcanoes of Io, or the multiplex rings of Saturn.

Much more recently, Perturbation Theory plays a key role in *2061: Odyssey Three;* and I won't promise not to use it again one of these days. It gives all sorts of opportunities for springing surprises on the unsuspecting reader—

—Over to you, Paul Preuss!

Arthur C. Clarke
Colombo, Sri Lanka

INFOPAK
TECHNICAL
BLUEPRINTS

On the following pages are computer-generated diagrams representing some of the structures and engineering found in *Venus Prime*:

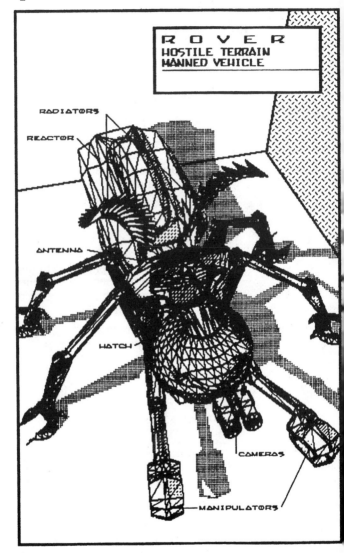

R O V E R
HOSTILE TERRAIN
MANNED VEHICLE

RADIATORS

REACTOR

ANTENNA

HATCH

CAMERAS

MANIPULATORS

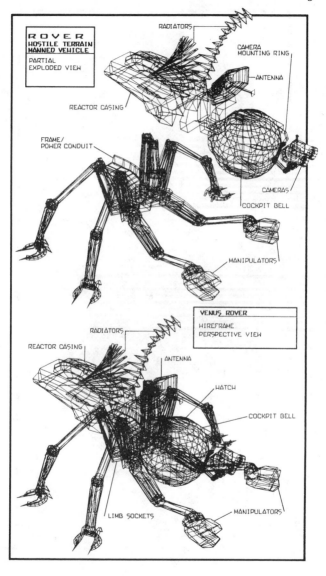

ROVER
HOSTILE TERRAIN
MANNED VEHICLE

PARTIAL
EXPLODED VIEW

RADIATORS

CAMERA
MOUNTING RING

ANTENNA

REACTOR CASING

FRAME/
POWER CONDUIT

CAMERAS

COCKPIT BELL

MANIPULATORS

VENUS ROVER

WIREFRAME
PERSPECTIVE VIEW

RADIATORS

REACTOR CASING

ANTENNA

HATCH

COCKPIT BELL

LIMB SOCKETS

MANIPULATORS

4

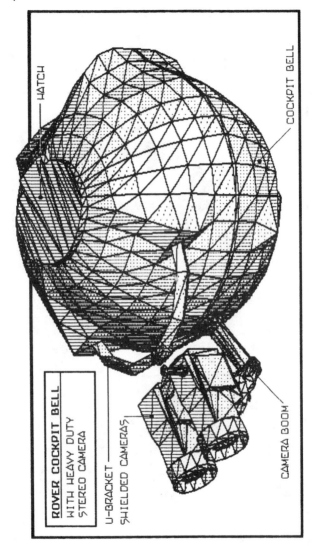

ROVER COCKPIT BELL
WITH HEAVY DUTY
STEREO CAMERA

HATCH

COCKPIT BELL

U-BRACKET
SHIELDED CAMERAS

CAMERA BOOM

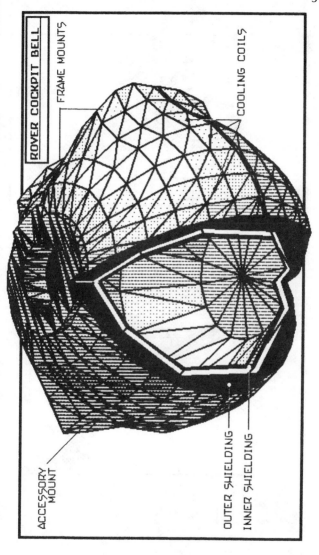

ROVER COCKPIT BELL

FRAME MOUNTS

COOLING COILS

ACCESSORY MOUNT

OUTER SHIELDING

INNER SHIELDING

6

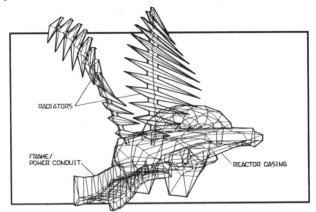

VENUS ROVER
REACTOR COMPONENTS

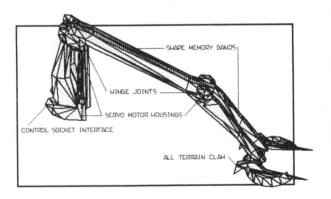

ROVER LIMB
SELF-CONTAINED
INTERCHANGEABLE UNIT

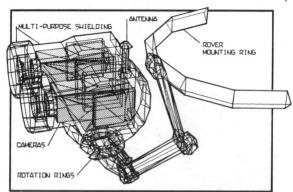

MULTI-PURPOSE SHIELDING

ANTENNA

ROVER MOUNTING RING

CAMERAS

ROTATION RINGS

STEREO CAMERA

REMOTE
BOOM
ASSEMBLY

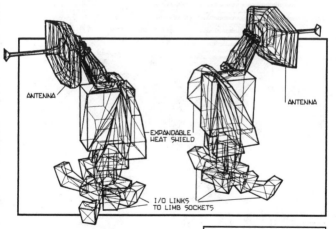

ANTENNA

ANTENNA

EXPANDABLE HEAT SHIELD

I/O LINKS TO LIMB SOCKETS

VENUS ROVER

CONTROL/COMMUNICATION NEXUS

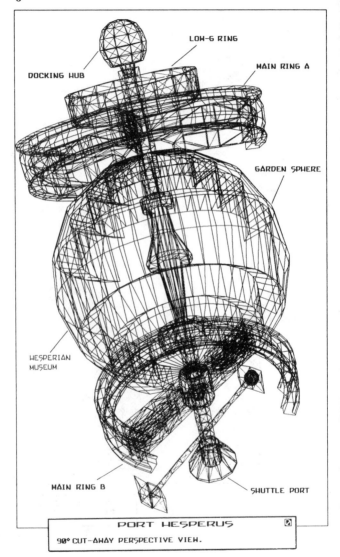

DOCKING HUB

LOW-G RING

MAIN RING A

GARDEN SPHERE

HESPERIAN MUSEUM

MAIN RING B

SHUTTLE PORT

PORT HESPERUS

90° CUT-AWAY PERSPECTIVE VIEW.

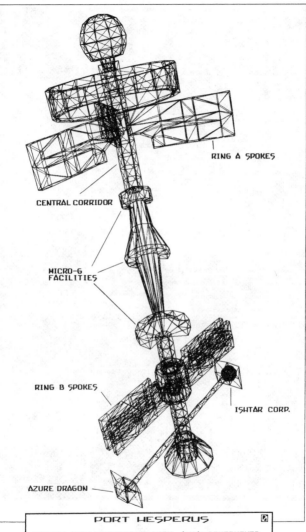

RING A SPOKES

CENTRAL CORRIDOR

MICRO-G FACILITIES

RING B SPOKES

ISHTAR CORP.

AZURE DRAGON

PORT HESPERUS

90° CUT-AWAY PERSPECTIVE VIEW. AXIAL COMPONENTS

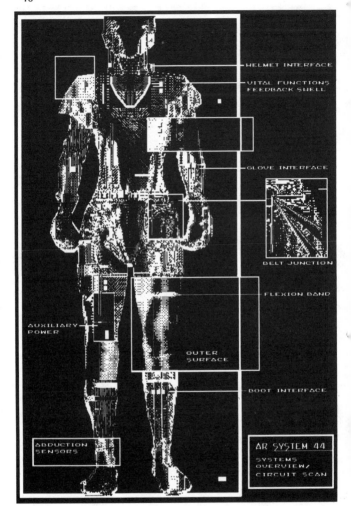

HELMET INTERFACE

VITAL FUNCTIONS
FEEDBACK SHELL

GLOVE INTERFACE

BELT JUNCTION

FLEXION BAND

AUXILIARY
POWER

OUTER
SURFACE

BOOT INTERFACE

ABDUCTION
SENSORS

AR SYSTEM 44

SYSTEMS
OVERVIEW/
CIRCUIT SCAN

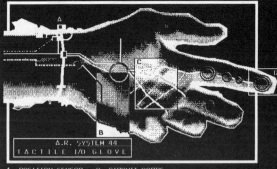

A. POSITION SENSOR   C. CIRCUIT CORDS
B. OUTER SURFACE   D. ULTRA DENSITY TACTILE SENSORS

A.R. SYSTEM 44
TACTILE I/O GLOVE

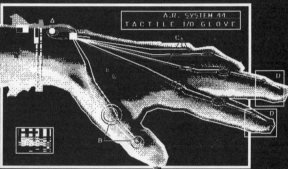

A. ABDUCTION NEXUS   C. CIRCUIT CORDS
B. ABDUCTION CABLES   D. SWITCH SIMULATORS

A.R. SYSTEM 44
TACTILE I/O GLOVE

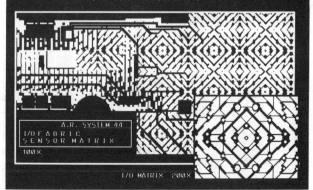

A.R. SYSTEM 44
I/O FABRIC
SENSOR MATRIX
100X

I/O MATRIX 200X

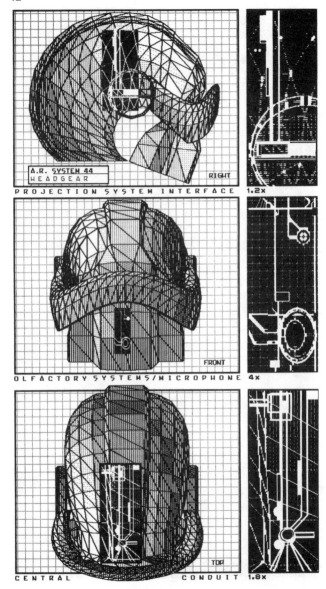

A.R. SYSTEM 44
HEADGEAR

RIGHT

PROJECTION SYSTEM INTERFACE 1.2x

FRONT

OLFACTORY SYSTEMS/MICROPHONE 4x

TOP

CENTRAL CONDUIT 1.8x

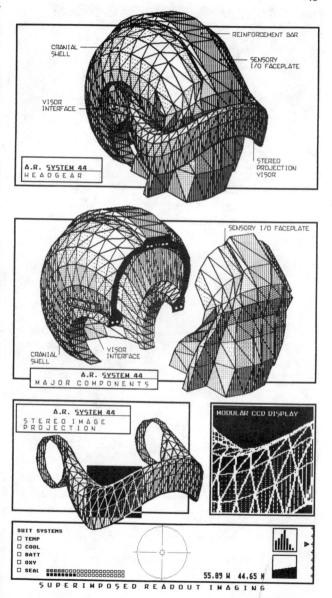

CRANIAL SHELL

REINFORCEMENT BAR

SENSORY I/O FACEPLATE

VISOR INTERFACE

STEREO PROJECTION VISOR

A.R. SYSTEM 44
HEADGEAR

SENSORY I/O FACEPLATE

CRANIAL SHELL

VISOR INTERFACE

A.R. SYSTEM 44
MAJOR COMPONENTS

A.R. SYSTEM 44
STEREO IMAGE PROJECTION

MODULAR CCD DISPLAY

SUIT SYSTEMS
☐ TEMP
☐ COOL
☐ BATT
☐ OXY
☐ SEAL

55.89 W 44.65 N

SUPERIMPOSED READOUT IMAGING

14

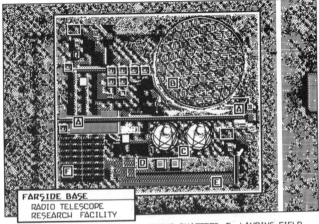

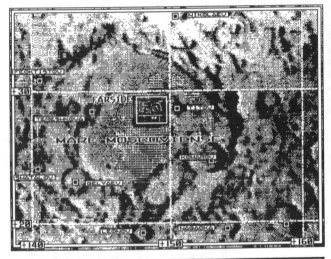

FARSIDE BASE
RADIO TELESCOPE
RESEARCH FACILITY

A. CATAPULT LAUNCH SYSTEM   C. LIVING QUARTERS   E. LANDING FIELD
B. RADIO TELESCOPE ARRAY   D. HYDROPONICS   F. SOLAR PANELS

MARE MOSCOVIENSE
TYPICAL ELEVATION SECTION

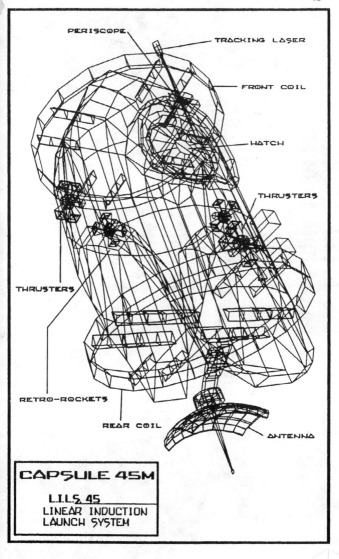

PERISCOPE

TRACKING LASER

FRONT COIL

HATCH

THRUSTERS

THRUSTERS

RETRO-ROCKETS

REAR COIL

ANTENNA

CAPSULE 45M

L.I.L.S. 45
LINEAR INDUCTION
LAUNCH SYSTEM

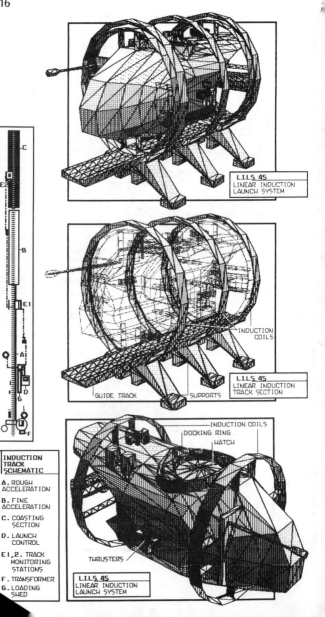

L.I.L.S. 45
LINEAR INDUCTION
LAUNCH SYSTEM

INDUCTION
COILS

L.I.L.S. 45
LINEAR INDUCTION
TRACK SECTION

GUIDE TRACK   SUPPORTS

INDUCTION COILS
DOCKING RING
HATCH

THRUSTERS

L.I.L.S. 45
LINEAR INDUCTION
LAUNCH SYSTEM

INDUCTION TRACK SCHEMATIC

A. ROUGH ACCELERATION

B. FINE ACCELERATION

C. COASTING SECTION

D. LAUNCH CONTROL

E1,2. TRACK MONITORING STATIONS

F. TRANSFORMER

G. LOADING SHED